Through the CRACK

Charrita D. Danley

Charrita D. Danley

This is a work of fiction. The characters, incidents, and dialogues are products of the author's imagination and are not to be construed as real. Any resemblance to actual events or persons, living or dead, is entirely coincidental. References to actual historic events are used in a fictitious manner, solely to add realism to the story.

THROUGH THE CRACK
Published by Chideria Publishing

© 2004 by Charrita D. Danley

International Standard Book Number: 0-9755574-0-8
Library of Congress Control Number: 2004095287
Cover Art by Ashley B. Hosey

Cover Design by
Nelson Brown & Christine Shirvington
omni business solutions

All Scripture quotations are from
The Holy Bible, King James Version

Contact:
Chideria Publishing
P.O. Box 960726
Riverdale, Georgia 30296
www.chideria-publishing.com

Printed in the United States by:
Morris Publishing
3212 East Highway 30
Kearney, NE 68847

In Reverence
to
God

whose divine plan for my life amazes me daily as I walk in His grace and favor.

In Respect
for
Ora Lee Wilson

whose long life testifies that He forsakes not the righteous.

In Memory
of
Annie Mae Wilson and **Willie Taylor**

artists whose creativity was confined within the borders of a small Southern town that had not the ability to recognize their gifts nor the capacity to nurture them.

In Honor
of
Thomas L. Danley and C. Dianne Danley

parents who believed that I could and encouraged me to be everything that I dreamed of becoming.

In Love
for
Charlotte D. Danley and Cassaundra D. Gray

sisters who have shared with me, as I with them, their joys, their pain, their dreams, their fears, their love and their lives.

I have been blessed to have many people in my life that I can truly call "friend." You have been with me for many years, through many seasons, in many situations, and you have endured the test of time. Each of you has a special place in my life.

My Friends,
who have waited many years to see this dream become a reality.

Diann Alexander, Denise Arrington, Felecia Bratton, Juanita Washington Britton, Tomeka L. Brown, Nina Cofield, Aunjanue Ellis, Nona Coleman Ferguson, Charmayne W. Fillmore, Renthesa Hardy, Ashley B. Hosey, Yolanda Rodgers Howsie, Durrell Knight, Machelle S. Kyles, Bridgette Jones, Robin Lumpkin, Massie McAdoo, Jacqueline Lidell McWilliams, Suzzanne O'Quinn, Debra Williams Polk, Debra Reynolds Richardson, Meta Rome, Josie Singletary, Jennifer Hunt Smith, Shelia Smith, Angalita Stephens, Nicole Verrett, Linda Washington, Sandra F. Washington, Tracy McKelphin Watkins, Tonya Watkins, Khalilah Watson, and Danny Williams.

All of My Loved Ones and Supporters,
who encouraged me along the way with a word or deed.

Harold & Nita Billingsley, Kidada Brown, Charlie & Renee Crawford, Jeffery Gray, Bernadette Greene, Corliss Bacon Goree, Keonda & Taylohr Grant, Vanessa Greene, Vickie Hall, Celis Hartley-Lewis, George Patrick Johnson, Samantha Lewis, Carol Griggs Mack, William & Ruby Meeks, Cynthia Morris, Henry & Kaye Myles, Madrica Nettles, Gail Anderson Patterson, Arthur & Geraldine Peyton, Sheryl Perkins, Michael Rome, Shontay Souter, Linda Swain, Sandra McCray Sweet, Gloria Rayford, Carrie Thomas, Cassandra Tennin, Sabrena Thurmond, Kris Turner, Faye Tiller, Patricia Trowles, Dr. Jerry W. Ward, Jr., Rostine P. Webb, Adair White-johnson, Jacqueline Wilson, Lise Wilson, Terry Wilson, and Vivian Wilson.

I could go on…There are many that space and time do not allow me to mention, but know that you are loved and appreciated!

This book is dedicated to those who have traveled the roads that lead to that distant place called "Unconditional Love."

To the one who served as my guide...

I appreciate the process, and I will forever cherish the journey!

Charrita

Chapter 1

It was the day of uncovering, the day that Truth would confront Lie.

Outside, the sun shone brightly exposing everything in sight, while inside it was dark and dreary, bearing no sign of the radiance that reigned beyond the door. A huge gray cloud engulfed the Morgan family home; it was the kind of cloud that fills the sky when a storm is near.

Vickie sat in the recliner in front of the television smoking Virginia Slims cigarettes back to back. The cloud hovered about her as she stared blankly watching the smoke rise from her cigarette and settle in its place. The cloud above her was so thick that she expected rain to come pouring down from it at any moment. The television was on, but it was watching her more than she was watching it. Her mind was on something else--her last conversation with her sister Vanessa.

Thoughts of Vanessa weighed heavily on Vickie's mind, and she always knew when Vanessa was mad, because unlike herself, Vanessa always made it crystal clear. The night before, Vanessa had made it clearer than ever, so now Vickie sat wondering just how long it would be before Vanessa stormed through the door. Vanessa never said that she was coming but something inside of Vickie knew that her sister would be there soon. The last thing Vickie wanted was a sermon, and she was sure her sister had already prepared her notes. Vickie didn't mind her sister being saved; they were raised in the church. It was the sanctified and filled with the Holy Ghost part that bothered her. She never knew what to expect.

Vickie felt ashamed. As a matter of fact, she was even ashamed to look at herself. She knew she looked as horrible as she felt, if not worse. Talk about a bad hair day, Vickie had had

6

a bad hair month. Her light brown hair was strewn all over her head, and it hadn't been combed in days. Her smooth olive skin had turned dark and ashy-- like burned coals. The faded jeans and T-shirt she wore were dingy from days of uninterrupted wear, and her clothes gave off a foul scent that revealed how she spent her time.

If Vanessa were to see Vickie in this condition she would hit the ceiling, or maybe even Vickie. It was a terrible situation, and Vickie knew it. Not wanting to add any more fuel to the fire, Vickie got up from beneath the cloud of smoke and went to clean herself up, and the cloud followed.

As she ran a tub of hot water, Vickie poured in some of her Victoria's Secret bubble bath, something she hadn't used in a long time. She lowered herself on her knee, placed her hand in the water, and flicked it back and forth. The warm water felt inviting as it swooshed against her hand. Not having had a bath in a while, Vickie had forgotten just how peaceful it could be. Her plans were to sit in the tub and soak until she got rid of the loud odor seeping from her pores.

Vickie also wanted to use the bath to relax and totally emerge from her body and mind. She knew that some down home blues would take her exactly where she wanted to go. There had been a point in her life when gospel music would have been her choice, but as of late, she took her problems to the world rather than to God.

Vickie walked over to the portable radio and turned on the power. The song, "Bag Lady" blared out of the speakers. Nervously, Vickie switched to WCDG, the station that played the blues all day long. She was carrying plenty of baggage, and was not interested in hearing nobody tell her about her issues. She already knew just how heavy those bags were she was hauling through life.

The slow mellow sound of the blues began to calm Vickie's nerves as she slowly lowered herself into the bathtub. The heat from the water quickly opened her pores. Instantly, her body felt relief. Vickie scrubbed up the soap and began to viciously scrub herself as the ash detached itself from her body and floated freely in the now dingy water. Feeling somewhat

7

refreshed, she slowly leaned back in the tub and exhaled a long sigh of relief!

That sad fact is that Vickie didn't realize that the inside of her body needed a cleaning ten times more thoroughly than the outside. She had only barely touched the surface of her seemingly insurmountable problems. There was so very much more lying below the surface—deeply within her soul! It had been buried beneath her desperate desire to be perfect, but now the time had come for her imperfections to be resurrected. Instead of exploring the source of her own problems, Vickie focused her attention on the radio and the troubles that the blues singers bellowed and crooned in their sad songs.

The radio station was really "jammin". The disc jockeys were playing all the songs that made her a blues fan: "Ain't No Sunshine When She's Gone" by Bobby Bland; "Steppin' Out Steppin' In" by Denise LaSalle; and "It Don't Hurt No Mo'" by Buddy Ace. Vickie wanted them to bring it on because she enjoyed the serenade of non-stop music. After twenty minutes of playing the great blues classics, the DJ played a song Vickie had never heard. That was unusual because she was an avid blues fan. The singer crooned, "You can run, but you can't hide." Vickie had lived in Mississippi, the birthplace of the blues, and she was convinced that the blues didn't lie. She believed that the blues was the kind of music that tells the truth (good or bad, right or wrong). It makes you see what you don't want to see and hear what you really don't want to hear. Searching for the message in the music, she listened ever so attentively to the song, and by the time the record finished, Vickie had come to realize that she had been trying to run away from her problems; however it hadn't worked. She was finally ready to admit to herself that she was, indeed an addict-- a crack addict.

Truth smiled.

On the phone the night before, Vanessa had asked Vickie if she was using drugs. Vickie wondered how her sister could even ask her something like that, and more importantly, why on earth had she admitted such a thing. After all, she didn't really think she had a drug problem. And even though Vickie was now ready to accept the reality of her addiction, she still was not ready for a face-to- face confrontation with her sister.

Just because I use drugs doesn't mean I am an addict, does it Vickie asked herself? When her conscience answered "no," she continued talking to herself. As a matter of fact, I don't have to have drugs. That's it! That's what I'll tell Vanessa. I'll just have to think of a way to take back my confession and make my new story believable.

Within minutes of deciding to face her problem, Vickie decided to deny it.

Lie smirked.

To help prove her point of not needing drugs, Vickie tried to remember the last day that she hadn't put drugs into her system. According to her recollection, it had been so long ago that merely searching for the date gave her a headache. Nevertheless, she was determined to remember the date so she could throw it in Vanessa's face. The more she thought, the more pain she endured. It felt as if someone was pounding her head with a hammer each time a thought crossed her mind. She had only experienced this type of pain once in her life, and that was when she was seven years old and had fallen from a high sliding board on the rocks below. At the moment, she wished her parents were present to comfort her like they had been then; unfortunately, they were both dead. Finally, Vickie realized that she had been getting high everyday since her daughter, Vonshay, graduated from Ferguson High and left for a summer program at Tougaloo College, the school she planned to attend in the fall.

Vickie was proud of her daughter. Vonshay had graduated from high school with a 3.8 average, and an academic scholarship to college. She was well-mannered, obedient, and had never caused her parents any problems. So many parents had wished, hoped, and prayed for a child like Vonshay, and Vickie had one. Wanting to celebrate her daughter's success and her own good fortune, Vickie could think of no better way of celebrating than getting high. So, that's what she had done... non-stop, as if there would be no tomorrow.

Oh well, that was just a few weeks ago, she thought as she tried to remember the current day's date. Once again, a sharp

9

pain went through her head. She decided that remembering was not worth the pain she was enduring. She stopped thinking about it and vowed to find out later. Right then, she just wanted to enjoy her bath. She dismissed everything else from her mind.

When Vickie emerged from the tub about thirty minutes later, she tuned back in to her surroundings. Putting on her robe, she heard the radio announcer speaking. He began, " A year ago today, July..." Vickie did not hear anything else he said. She dropped to her knees and began to scream. This couldn't be happening to her. "How could over a month pass without me knowing it?" she yelled aloud. "What about Vonshay's birthday? Did I give her something? Did she like it? How old is she?"

Hearing the last question roll off her lips, Vickie sprawled across the floor and began to moan as huge teardrops fell from her eyes. The pain in her head subdued; the pain in her heart took control. She rocked and she moaned. She shivered and she cried. Eventually, she drifted off into a deep sleep, knowing that she really did have a drug problem and wishing that she would never have to wake up and face her sister, her daughter, or herself.

Vickie slept for hours, not because she wanted to, but because her body forced her to. She hadn't slept in days. It was a much-needed rest. Lately, she had spent every hour of every day getting high or trying to find a way to get high. When she woke up, she felt a sense of peace. A burden seemed to have been lifted from her, but things are not always what they seem. She got up from the floor and began looking for something to wear.

Everything she tried on hung from her hips, which were at one time shapely. Almost all of her clothes were too big because of the tremendous amount of weight she had lost on her crack diet. She didn't want the missing pounds to be too obvious, so she looked for something that would camouflage her shape. Finally, she came across a brown sleeveless sundress. It was the closest thing to a fit that she could find. Vanessa had sent the dress to her the summer before. When she first got the dress, she had loved the way it fit her well-shaped body, but that day was different. Neither the dress nor any other piece of clothing that

10

she put on looked presentable. After taking almost everything that didn't look good on her out of the closet, Vickie began to tackle the drawers. She was jerking them so hard and slamming them so furiously that Vonshay appeared at the door.

"What's wrong, Mama. What are you looking for?" Vonshay asked, noticing the piles of clothes throughout the room. Her deep-set eyes showed concern. No matter how hard Vonshay tried, she could never keep her feelings a secret. Her eyes always told.

"Something nice to put on. We may be having company," Vickie responded, trying to hide her astonishment. She had forgotten that Vonshay was at home, but she wouldn't dare reveal that to her daughter. She could see the pain in her child's beautiful brown eyes, eyes that once danced with joy.

"Who?" Vonshay asked, though she already knew the answer.

"Don't worry," Vickie assured her. "You'll be glad to see 'em, and they can't wait to see you. Personally, I don't want anybody to see me looking like this. Everything I own is too damn big."

"Mama, that's not a problem. That's how people wear their clothes now. Nobody wants stuff stickin' to 'em all the time, especially as hot as it is. Put your little red Capri pants set on. It'll be cute. But to be honest Mama, what you're wearing ain't half as important as what you're going to do with your head. It's a mess!"

"I know, honey. Will you wash it for me?" Vickie asked her.

"Washing ain't gon' get it. You need the works. I've got some perm in my room. Slip something on and come down the hall to my *beauty salon*. I don't usually work on Monday's, but I'll make an exception because this is an emergency if I ever saw one!"

Vonshay smiled as she walked out of the room and went to get her utensils together. She was glad her Mama was letting her do her hair because it had been looking bad. Even though

11

Vickie had nice strong hair, it still could not survive neglect, which was about the only type of treatment it had gotten lately.

Vickie grabbed a pair of jeans and a big T-shirt and slipped them on. The jeans were so baggy she felt like a teenager in a rap video. Oh well, she thought, no one will see me.

Everything was already in place when Vickie arrived at the *shop,* which Vonshay had set up in the kitchen. The perm, a comb, shampoo, conditioner, a blow dryer, and curlers were laid out on the counter. Vonshay was standing behind a chair with her plastic gloves on, beckoning Vickie to take a seat. "I see you made it. You're a little late, but I guess I can work you in," she beamed, showing off her beautiful smile. She looked exactly like Vickie had when she was eighteen, tall and shapely with curves in all the right places. Vickie hoped that eighteen years from now her daughter's life would be in a much better state than hers.

Vonshay sat Vickie in the chair and began applying the perm to her mother's hair. Feeling a cool sensation from the chemicals, Vickie relaxed, closed her eyes, and let her mind wander. The first place it stopped was the clinic where she found out that she was pregnant with Vonshay...

Vickie had gone to the doctor because she hadn't been feeling well. She threw up almost everything that she ate, and she felt weak. Her friends told her that she should go and get a shot because a virus was going around. The doctor told her that he would need to run a few tests to determine what her problem was. She had no idea that one of the tests would be a pregnancy test. The thought of pregnancy had never crossed her mind. Vickie had only had sex once, and she was sure that that couldn't be enough to make a baby. So when the doctor told her that she was six weeks pregnant, Vickie was in a daze.

The fresh autumn air met Vickie at the door when she walked out of the clinic. It was October and the beautifully colored leaves fell gracefully from the trees. Vickie kicked the same leaves from her path over and over again as she paced back and forth in front of the clinic. After she passed the door the seventh time, she didn't turn around. Her feet would not let her. She followed their lead, not knowing her destination.

Since Vickie did not know where she was going, she attempted to figure out how she had gotten into such a mess. She had her whole life ahead of her and so many dreams to follow. One of the dreams was to have a baby, but it was at the bottom of her list, beneath finishing college, getting married, and starting a career. Now she would have to put it at the top. Abortion was not an option. If she hadn't learned anything else from her years of Sunday School, she knew for a fact that God is the source of all life. There was no way she would try and take something that she didn't have the power to give.

The thought of being a mother overwhelmed Vickie. The weight of her thoughts was so heavy that it forced her to rest. Her body settled on a bench in the park. There she hung her head and cried and cried and cried. Her tears fell to the dry earth, and it drank them as soon as they touched its lips. There were more than enough tears to quench the earth's thirst. Vickie's eyes were so full of water that she didn't see the message that the dying trees offered her. The trees were losing a part of themselves, but they did not fret because they understood that if they waited, a new season would come and bring with it an opportunity to embrace new life- - very good!!

When Vickie discovered she was pregnant, she was a seventeen- year-old freshman at Tougaloo College, a private Black college about two hours from Ferguson in Jackson, Mississippi. She had chosen Tougaloo because it was a very respectable institution, and the fact that her high school sweetheart was already enrolled there was merely a coincidence. At least that's what she had told her parents and tried to believe herself.

Vickie knew deep down that Andre' had been her main reason for choosing Tougaloo. She was so in love that she would have followed him anywhere. He was everything that she thought she wanted in a man and the only man that she would consider giving herself to. She couldn't wait to get to school and show him for the first time how much he really meant to her. Now that she had shown him, she wondered if it had been worth the price she had to pay-- motherhood.

13

Having gained some strength from her rest, Vickie raised her weakened body from the park bench and went back to campus where she crawled into her bed and cried. For three days, she would not leave her room or accept any calls from Andre'. After every other attempt he made to reach her failed, Andre' sneaked into the girls' dorm and up to her room.

"Baby, what's wrong?" he asked, seeing Vickie sitting on the bed staring into space as if she didn't know where or who she was.

The sight of Andre brought more tears to Vickie's eyes. She tried to tell him what was wrong, but only muffled sounds escaped her lips. Andre' wiped her tears away, but others replaced them immediately. After several failed attempts to understand what Vickie was trying to say to him, Andre finally realized that she had said, "I'm pregnant." Saying the words out loud for the first time made Vickie's situation more real to her. Before Andre' could respond to her announcement, she began to holler and cry out loudly.

Andre' tried to calm Vickie by reminding her of the consequences he would face if he was caught in the girl's dorm. Unable to control herself, she continued to wail. It wasn't until Andre told her not to worry because everything would be all right that she quieted down. Andre' sat and rocked her with his hand gently massaging her stomach until sleep overcame her. He leaned her back on her pillow and covered her up. Before he left, he gave her a tender kiss on her cheek. As he walked back to his room, the words "daddy" and "husband" played over and over in his mind. The smile on his face was broader than that of a child on Christmas morning.

After about twenty minutes, a tingle went through Vickie's scalp. It reminded her of her mother putting a hot comb to a section of over-greased hair in order to straighten it. She opened her eyes and saw Vonshay standing in front of her asking, "Are you ready?"

"Yeah," she replied. "This stuff is burning."

"I told you it was time, but you acted like you didn't hear

me, so I just left you alone. What world were you in?" Vonshay inquired as she washed the chemicals from her mama's hair.

"A world just before you came into the world. I was thinking about you and your daddy and how happy he was when he found out I was pregnant with you." Vickie's tone changed. "Too bad his happiness didn't last forever like he said, or he wouldn't have left us," she said maliciously.

"Mama, let's not go through this again," Vonshay said irritably. "Daddy left _you_, not me."

"I can't tell, Vonshay. It looks like you're right here with me, and he's not with either one of us," Vickie said.

"If I recall correctly Mama, you are the one who told him to leave," Vonshay reminded her. "Now you get mad 'cause he left," she said loudly, wringing her mama's hair, wrapping a towel around it.

"When was the last time you talked to your daddy?" Vickie asked ignoring Vonshay's last remark.

"Last night."

"Oh" was all Vickie could say. She never won when Andre's name came up because his daughter stood up for her daddy no matter how many promises he broke. She wondered if her daughter's love for her was as strong as it was for him. She didn't believe that it was, but she loved her little girl just the same. There's something special about that bond between daddies and their daughters. Daughters love their daddies for who they are, and daddies love their daughters because they are. This love never outgrows itself; it always leaves room for change. It is the simplest kind of love; yet, the hardest kind to obtain.

Vickie didn't know how to explain to Vonshay that her father was not a good husband. Vonshay only knew him as a father, and he was damn good at that; so his daughter believed that he handled everything as he did her. The picture Andre had painted of himself for his daughter was a masterpiece, but it was a fake. He was really a mean person, and in a subtle kind of way, he had trained Vonshay to be the same way. Fortunately, the child had also picked up some of her mama's kindheartedness. With the combination of the two traits, she was well prepared to

15

deal with the world. The only reason Vickie stayed with Andre' all of the fifteen years that she did was because the both of them wanted Vonshay to grow up with a father.

"What kind of new style are you going to give me?" Vickie questioned, breaking the silence.

"Don't worry. Anything'll be better than what you had," Vonshay said. She was laughing so loudly at her mental picture of her mama's hair before the perm that she could barely get the words out.

Vickie was relieved that the tension had subsided and she joined in. "Mama loves you baby," she said in between spurts of laughter.

"I love you, too, Mama. A bushel and a peck and a hug around the neck," Vonshay responded.

A smile broader than the one on her face spread across Vickie's heart. She had taught Vonshay that chant when she was just a toddler. The fact that she still remembered it led Vickie to think that maybe her child did love her as much as she loved her father. Just maybe. She still couldn't forget that there was something between Vonshay and Andre' that she couldn't compete with. Every time she tried, she failed. Vickie had lost so many battles trying to compete with Andre for their daughter's love that she knew she couldn't win the war. Explaining her drug addiction to her daughter would be a major defeat. She felt that the enemy was bound to win.

Vickie sat quietly, wondering what to say next. This seemed to have been a good time for Vickie to explain her problem to her daughter, but she didn't know how. It had been so long since the two of them had spent quality time together and shared a laugh that she did not want to ruin the moment. Their laughter continued as Vonshay bragged about the difference she would make in the appearance of her mother's hair. Though

Vickie continued to laugh, she was no longer amused, but simply afraid. She was afraid of speaking the truth about her life.

Chapter 2

The bus ride from Atlanta to Ferguson was long and tiring. Vanessa tried to make herself as comfortable as possible in the second row seat that she chose. The back of the bus was less congested, but there was no way she would even consider sitting in the back of a bus because she knew the struggles that her ancestors had gone through so she wouldn't have to. She had always been taught to learn from the past and respect those who had made the present possible. The world's state of affairs convinced her that the lesson was no longer being taught in her community, but every chance she got, she did her part to take a stand and teach her people respect for themselves and each other.

As the bus maneuvered its way on I-20W across Georgia and Alabama, Vanessa stared out of the window at all of the land and homes in the middle of nowhere and the small towns that didn't even have traffic lights. She wondered how it felt to live in such a small area. She couldn't imagine having to drive several miles just to pick up a forgotten item from the store or to sit down to a meal at a restaurant. Ferguson was by no means a great metropolis, but it did have the conveniences of grocery stores, restaurants, nightclubs, and riverboat casinos- - its latest attraction.

When the bus stopped in Anniston, Alabama, a lady boarded with two cute little girls dressed in denim jumpers with red T-shirts underneath. The girls chose to sit in the seats across the aisle from Vanessa. When they were seated, the lady gave them bags with food and drinks. She made them repeat to her the instructions she had given them on how to behave. Once the girls had done this, the lady said, "Mama loves you. Bye." She kissed them both on the cheeks and turned to Vanessa. "Could you keep an eye on them for me?" she asked with a pleasant smile. "Sure," Vanessa said as she nodded her head and smiled back.

"They're going to Tuscaloosa and my mama will meet them at the bus station."

"I'll make sure they get to her," Vanessa assured the lady before she left.

The girls looked as if they were about ten and thirteen years old. Ironically, the ten year old seemed to be the one in charge. She was in control of the toys, the food and the conversation. Her older sister simply followed her lead. According to the laws of nature, things should have been the other way around, but there are always exceptions to every rule.

The interaction between the two girls reminded Vanessa of herself and Vickie. Vanessa was four years younger than Vickie, but she had always been in charge of both of their affairs. Vanessa assumed the position of overseer because of her aggressive nature and Vickie's passive one. She never relinquished the position to her older sister because Vickie could not deal with the responsibilities that came with the job. All of her life, Vanessa carried both of their loads. Now, she was on her way back home to pick up a new one...

It was pleasant to watch the little girls fall asleep in each other's arms and it brought tears to Vanessa's eyes. They acted so much like she and Vickie had when they were around the same ages. She thought about her own childhood when the loads she had to carry were much lighter.

When Vanessa and Vickie were growing up they were very close, almost inseparable. At first, their parents forced the closeness between them. They had to share a room, toys, food, candy, friends, and clothes--those few pieces that were not identical. The sharing was not enforced because there was not

19

enough money to support two children, but it was enforced to promote a bond between the two sisters that would never be broken. This was the type of bond that their mama, Vera, always wished for, but she was an only child.

Having no siblings, Vera had an idealistic view of what sisterhood was all about. As a child, she had cried for someone to talk to, so she did not understand it when her daughters were angry and did not want to speak to each other. Though she made them talk in her presence, she knew that there were days that they never spoke when they were alone. Vera had dreamed of having someone to play with, so she found it disturbing when her daughters said that they were tired of playing with each other. She had longed for someone with whom to share, so she was burdened when her daughters fought over ownership and refused to share with each other. Vera had good intentions, but she didn't realize that *having* a sister is a lot different from *wanting* one. The minor conflicts between her daughters did not mean that they did not have a sisterly bond; they did. Her daughters' interactions were typical for sisters, but she didn't know that because she had never been a sister; she had only wanted one. Even though, she was privy to first-hand experiences, she only had second-hand information. She learned as much as she could from the lessons her daughters taught her.

Since Vickie was four years older than Vanessa, she started school first and began to have her new friends over to play. As a toddler, Vanessa was not concerned, but at the age of four, she became jealous because all of Vickie's play-time was being spent with everyone except her. One day she announced to their mama, Vera, that Vickie was no longer her sister.

"Why would you say a thing like that?" her mama had asked.

"Cause she don't play with me no more. She found a new sister to play with," whined Vanessa. In the middle of her statement, tears began to stream down her chubby little cheeks.

Vera reached out to comfort Vanessa, but she couldn't get her to be quiet. Vanessa cried until her cheeks were as red as a rose. Vera took Vanessa in her arms and rocked her from side to side. While she rocked her youngest daughter, she sang to her softly:

> *Jesus loves me, this I know. For the Bible tells me so.*
> *Little ones to him belong. They are weak but he is strong.*
> *Yes, Jesus loves me. Yes, Jesus loves me.*
> *Yes, Jesus loves me. For the Bible tells me so.*

Before Vera had finished the last words of her song, Vanessa fell asleep. Vera hoped that Vanessa understood that Jesus would always love her, and that He would be everything she needed Him to be. Nonetheless, she also wanted Vanessa to be able to depend on her sister's love as well. She lifted her daughter's limp body and put her in the bed.

After Vera calmed Vanessa, she was ready to deal with Vickie. She went to the door and called Vickie in from playing with the other children in the neighborhood. Vickie ran to the door. "Ma'am?" she asked with a puzzled look on her face.

"You and Mama need to have a big girl talk. Come to the table and sit down," Vera said. As she was about to begin her lecture, her husband, John, came in.

"Hi, Daddy," Vickie said as she jumped in his arms to kiss him.

"Hey, baby," he responded. "Where's your sister?" he asked as he leaned over and kissed his wife on her cheek.

"She's napping," Vera answered. "She cried so hard today that I couldn't get her to stop. She says that Vickie doesn't play with her anymore." She directed her last statement to her daughter. "Vickie, she thinks that you've put her down for a new sister and her little feelings hurt," she explained.

"I don't wanna new sister!" Vickie exclaimed with her feelings now hurt. "What does she mean?"

"When your friends come over, you push Vanessa to the side. You act like you don't know or want to know her."

"But she's little, Mama. She can't play big girl games."

21

"Did you ever try to teach her?" her father asked.

"No, but I didn't know she cared."

"Of course, she cares," said Vera. "You're the only sister she's got and the only friend she knows. You'll always have friends, but no one should take the place of your sister. You have each other now and you always will. You're the oldest so you have to look out for Vanessa. You understand?"

"Yes Ma'am," Vickie said with teardrops forming in her eyes. She slowly got up from her seat and dragged to her room to talk to Vanessa.

When she got to the room, Vanessa was sleeping, so Vickie decided to play games. She stared at Candyland and all the other games on the shelf. After choosing several games to play and realizing that it was no fun playing alone, she reached for some books. She read silently until she heard Vanessa stirring, then she leaned over and whispered in her ear, "I'm sorry I hurt your feelings. You're my best friend. You always will be."

Vera and John had come to get the girls up for dinner and were standing in the door watching. A big smile came across their faces. "It worked," John said. "She'll look after her little sister." Neither of them could have known that their last-born would end up taking care of their first- born. It wasn't the natural order of life, but even in nature, things sometime go awry.

From that day on, Vickie did not leave her little sister out. When her friends came over, they all played together. When she was invited somewhere, the host already knew that it was an invitation for two. People began to call them "those Morgan girls." A lot of people didn't even bother to learn their first names, since both of them answered when one was called.

Vanessa enjoyed having her sister back. She wanted to be around her all the time. She even put her twin bed next to Vickie's so they could talk late at night when they were supposed to be sleeping. To make sure they were as close as she thought they were, sometimes Vanessa would challenge Vickie's friends just to see whose side her sister would take. Vickie always sided with Vanessa. It made Vanessa feel good to know that now her sister really did put her before her friends.

Their closeness lasted for a while, but not forever. Puberty was much stronger than their relationship. The two grew up together almost as the same person, but inside two distinctly different personalities developed. Outside of their sisterly bond, being opposites would have been their only other attraction to each other, had there been an attraction at all. As each year of their lives passed, their differences became more and more apparent and their once close relationship suffered.

Vickie was a cautious and caring person who shared whatever she had with anyone. She always followed her parents' and her teachers' directions. All adults loved her because she was polite and respectful. Vanessa, on the other hand, was quite different. Her concern for others did not extend very far past her immediate family. Vanessa did respect her elders, but not because she thought they all deserved it; only because her parents insisted upon it.

Because both Vera and John worked, Vickie and Vanessa were at home alone after school. This time was usually wartime for the two. Since Vickie wanted everything perfect, she was ready to get started on chores as soon as she hit the door. Vanessa was not. She didn't think it mattered when they did them, as long as they were done when their parents got home. Because their parents had made the chores a team project and no one had specific duties, Vickie could not get away with doing her part and letting Vanessa get in trouble for not doing hers. If something didn't get done, they would both be held responsible.

One day when they came in from school, Vickie divided the chores between them, and Vanessa agreed with the division. Vickie was running around busy as a bee while Vanessa was on the couch watching reruns of *Good Times* on TV. Vickie was almost finished with her work, but Vanessa hadn't started. Vickie was furious. She began cursing Vanessa and demanding that she get up at that moment. Vanessa merely ignored her. Vickie continued to rant and rave. Vanessa suggested that Vickie do her part of the work for her since it was so important that it be done immediately. That was what Vickie normally did

23

because she was afraid of whippings and punishments, and Vanessa was not. However, that day was different. Vickie decided that she was not going to do Vanessa's work. She vowed to make her sister do it herself.

Some things are easier said than done. Vanessa knew that, mentally, Vickie wasn't strong enough to "make" her do anything. Physically, it would be an even battle. But the battle would only occur, if and only if, Vickie could convince herself to fight, and Vanessa seriously doubted that she could.

Vickie's anger rose steadily. Instead of screaming down the hall at Vanessa as she normally did, she decided to scream at her face to face. Vanessa was stunned when she heard her sister's footsteps. As Vickie's voice started up the hall and grew nearer, Vanessa began to prepare for the fight. She got off the couch and stood in the middle of the den, still watching *Good Times*. She was not going to let Vickie bully her. She decided that if Vickie tried, she would have to beat her down. She wished that Vickie would wait until *Good Times* went off before she started clowning. It was Vanessa's favorite show, and each time she watched it, she was glad she didn't live in a small house with a big family that was always fighting. The one day that even the Evans' were getting along, she was going to have to fight her own sister. Not today, Vanessa thought to herself.

When Vickie made it to the door, she stopped and was very quiet. Vanessa saw tears in her sister's eyes. She hadn't realized until that moment how pissed Vickie was. Being mad was one thing, but being mad enough to cry took things to a whole new level. They stared intently at each other. Finally, Vickie broke the silence.

"Go...do...your...part ...of...the...work. NOW, Vanessa!" she yelled slowly as if she were afraid to speak any faster.

"And what if I don't?" Vanessa asked curtly.

"You will, 'cause I'll make you!"

"Hmph. In case you didn't know, don't nobody make Vanessa do nothing. Especially not you."

"I will when I bust you in your face," Vickie screamed.

With her last words barely out of her mouth, Vickie leaped toward Vanessa and pushed her to the floor. The two girls wrestled on the floor hitting and pulling at each other until they heard a loud crash. Both of them jumped. When they looked around they saw their mama's beautiful hand-painted vase shattered. They scrambled to their feet to head for the super glue and ran dead into their parents. The sisters-turned-enemies knew what was in store for them: major whippings, punishments, and apologies...

Noticing a decrease in the speed of the bus, Vanessa put her thoughts on hold. When she looked out the window to see why they were slowing down, she discovered that they were turning into the bus station in Tuscaloosa. Vanessa woke the sleeping girls, who had sparked her journey down memory lane, and helped them get all of their things together. When the driver opened the door, she walked them into the station, released them to their waiting grandmother and said "bye."

Vanessa went to the counter to get a Coke. As she stood in line, she stared at the cigarettes on display. As the cashier entered the price of the Coke into the cash register, she softly told him to add a pack of Benson & Hedges Menthol Cigarettes. After smoking a cigarette, Vanessa returned to the bus and reclaimed her seat. In an effort to take her mind off her troubles, she took the latest issue of *Essence Magazine* out of her travel bag and read an excerpt from a new novel. She wanted desperately to enter into the world of the characters, but she couldn't because her own world was begging for her attention. It would not allow her to get involved in the fiction. It demanded that she deal with reality. Reality was, at that moment, her sister. She closed the magazine and thought about Vickie.

Examining the changes that her relationship with her sister had weathered over the years, Vanessa chuckled to herself. They had gone from sisters to enemies to friends. Slowly the laughter turned to tears. So many emotions rushed through Vanessa's body that no particular one could claim dominance. She was feeling love, pain, and anger all at the same time. Every emotion was directed toward her only sister. She loved Vickie, but was hurt by her deception and angered by her actions.

Lie whimpered, imitating the effects of the pain he had carried into Vanessa's life…

For the past few months, Vickie had been asking Vanessa for money on a regular basis. Vickie always scheduled a date for payback, but the days often went by without a word from her. She would usually use Vonshay as an excuse to get money because she knew that Vanessa would not deprive her niece of anything, and the fact that Vonshay was a high school senior made the stories more credible. Vickie talked about expenses such as class rings, trips, invitations, pictures, proms, and much more. Other times she used household bills as excuses. The funding for her position at a local non-profit organization had been cut, and Vanessa knew that a weekly unemployment check was not enough to support Vickie and Vonshay, both of whom were accustomed to a much larger income, so she would send the money.

Vanessa wasn't a rich woman, but she was comfortable, mainly because she was a good steward over that which God entrusted to her. She was a faithful tither and she always gave, not just to her church but to other ministries as well. She recognized that ministry costs, and she did her part to make sure that the gospel went forth. And just as He promised, God opened up the windows of heaven. All the help that she had been giving Vickie lately was depleting her funds. After all, she had to live too, and being a professor at a Historically Black University was not a very lucrative profession, but it was fulfilling.

Soon Vickie's calls for money began to come more frequently. They progressed from once a month to once a week to every other day. Vickie was running out of excuses and Vanessa wanted to know where her money was going. Something wasn't right. When she called the house, Vickie was never there. Vonshay began to tell her about the notices of the mortgage being past due and the items that were coming up missing from the house. Whenever Vanessa did talk to Vickie and question her, Vickie would say that she had taken care of the bills and that someone was just borrowing the other things.

26

Vanessa believed every one of the lies Vickie told her until the weekend before her trip, when *Truth* caught up with *Lie.*

That Friday evening, Vanessa was lounging around reading when the phone rang. She started not to answer it, but something told her she had better. When she picked up the receiver, she could hear crying before the phone reached her ear. "What's wrong Vickie?" she asked without even saying "hello."

"You gon' be mad, Vanessa. I don't even know how to tell you this, but I'm in big trouble. I don't know what to do."

"What happened?" Vanessa asked calmly. She was tired of hearing Vickie's long, drawn-out, made-up pleas for money.

"Well, you know I been doing bad. I wanted to make some money real fast so I could pay you back and have a little extra for myself. See, it's this man I know who sells drugs. He makes money fast, so I asked him to let me hold some. I wanted to make him and me some money."

"You did what?!" Vanessa exclaimed. "Have you lost your fufreakin' mind?" I'm sorry, Lord, Vanessa said internally. She hadn't said what she wanted to say, but she sure had thought it, and it almost came out.

"I guess I have. Anyway, he said okay and gave me the stuff. I gave it to this boy down the street to sell for me. He came back and said that he was robbed. Now the man is looking for me to get his money. Last night he put a gun to my head and swore that he would kill me if I didn't pay. He's been over here three times today with his boys just beatin' on the door. Me and Vonshay are hiding on the floor so he can't see us through the blinds. My baby's scared to death."

"Can you blame her? Put Vonshay on the phone," Vanessa said dryly.

When Vonshay picked up the phone, Vanessa could hear the fear in her voice. She asked her what was going on and the girl burst into a long series of tears, words, and hiccups. She could barely make out what her niece was saying, so she asked for Vickie, after assuring Vonshay that she would take care of everything.

Vickie was whispering when she got back to the phone.

"They're back. They'll hear me if I talk any louder." Suddenly, she stopped talking.

In the background, Vanessa heard, "BOOM!BAM!BANG!BOOM!BAM!" Her mind began to race when she heard the loud banging. She thought about all of the horrible things these men could do to her sister and niece. She began to shiver.

"You there?" Vickie whispered.

"Shut up and let me talk," Vanessa said. "Do you realize what you did? You put you and your child in danger. These people don't play. Did you think *New Jack City* and *In Too Deep* were jokes?! Baby that was art imitating reality. Dealers don't play 'bout their money or their goods. They will kill you!"

Reluctantly, she asked Vickie how much money she owed the man. When she told her five hundred dollars, Vanessa could feel her temper raging. She tried to remain calm for the sake of her niece. "Okay, I'll send it. Call me when you get it and take it straight to him. Then call me back."

"Thanks, sis," Vickie whispered.

Vanessa rushed out the house to Western Union. She had been there so much lately that all the tellers knew her name. She had even been give a Western Union discount card, credit card, phone card, and T-shirt. This makes no sense, she thought. How could Vickie be so stupid and waste so much money? This is my last time bailing her out, she promised herself as she filled out the form. She looked at the others standing in line and wondered what their situations were. Did they have family members on drugs, or were they just doing a favor for a friend, or were they quick collecting a payment to keep from losing their houses or cars? Why was it that everybody in line was Black? Didn't White folks have financial emergencies, too?

When she reached the counter to make her transaction, Vanessa handed the young lady her form, watching closely as she entered all of the required information. With this transaction, Vanessa had sent her sister more money than she cared to remember. "This is it," she mumbled to herself as she reached for the receipt confirming her transaction. "I promise to God, this…is… it!!"

On her way home, Vanessa stopped by the store to get some coffee for the next morning. She had asked God to deliver her from smoking, and He had, but with everything that was happening she needed something to calm her nerves. She struggled with the thought of making the purchase. As she walked out of the store, she ripped the plastic from the pack. The Spirit reminded her that she had been delivered. She wanted to just toss the cigarettes but she couldn't. Right then, she felt that she needed them more than she ever had before.

When she got home from Western Union, Vanessa called to say that she had sent the money. Vonshay told her that Vickie had gone to pick it up. Vanessa and Vonshay talked while they waited on her to come back home. Vickie had promised to pay the guy and come straight home, but it was taking too long. The two of them tried to keep each other company without mentioning what was going on. When Vanessa had the urge to mention it, she lit a cigarette and let words filter out of her mouth silently with the smoke. Every now and then, one would ask the other what time it was. Hours later when Vickie finally crept in, Vanessa was so disgusted that she didn't even want to talk to her. She was just glad to know she was home in one piece.

Vickie's lack of judgment had really begun to bother Vanessa. She thought about it on a daily basis. Her sister was so heavy on her mind that she dreamed about her almost every night for two weeks straight. Usually, Vanessa would not be able to remember the details of the dreams, but she knew that Vickie was the main character. The Saturday night after she sent Vickie the five hundred dollars, she had a dream that she did not forget.

In her dream, she and Vickie were standing on a steep cliff in the middle of nowhere. There were no signs of life- - no trees, no vegetation, nothing. Vickie was extremely close to the edge. She was trying to tell Vanessa something, but Vanessa couldn't hear her. She could see Vickie's lips and body move as if she was shouting, but there was no sound. The closer Vanessa moved to her sister, the closer her sister moved to the edge. Vanessa made it within an arm's length of her, almost close

29

enough to touch her. She reached out her hand to Vickie in an effort to lead her away from danger. However, when Vickie reached to grab it, she fell backwards over the cliff. Suddenly, Vanessa could hear her sister's voice screaming, "HELP ME! Help Me! Help me...."

The sound of her sister's fading voice awakened Vanessa. She jolted straight up in bed and found herself soaking wet from both sweat and tears. Her navy silk gown was stuck to her moist skin. She rushed to the bathroom to wash her face. Once there, she decided to take a shower. The long hot shower soothed her body, but her mind was still muddled. When she pulled back the shower curtains, she was looking directly in the mirror. She saw her sister's reflection in her own. They looked so much alike, yet they were so different. "Girl, I have got to find out what's going on in your life," Vanessa said as if she was actually talking to Vickie. She dried the water from her body and returned to her bedroom.

She glanced at the digital alarm clock on the nightstand next to her bed. It was almost time for her to get ready for church, so she decided against going back to bed. Instead, she put on her robe and went to the kitchen where she fixed herself a pot of freshly brewed coffee. She sat on a stool, placed her favorite mug on the bar, and lit a cigarette. The combination of caffeine and nicotine had helped her make it through many bad days; however, on that day she needed something that neither of those things could give her. She needed some peace and understanding, the kind that she could only get from the Lord.

Since she had some extra time, Vanessa decided to call and check on Vonshay. She and Vickie hadn't talked since the incident with the drug dealers. Vanessa was too angry; Vickie was too ashamed. Before Vanessa had a chance to pick up the phone to call, her phone rang.

"Hey, TeeTee," Vonshay said softly.

"You'll live a long time," Vanessa chuckled. "I was just about to call you."

When Vonshay didn't laugh like she normally did, it was at that moment that Vanessa noted that the two of them were on the same wavelength. "TeeTee, there's a lady here who wants to talk to you," she said seriously.

"Put her on, honey," Vanessa said wondering who it could be.

"Hi," a voice said. "You don't know me, but my name is Janice, and your sister owes me money."

"For what?" Vanessa asked curiously.

"Drugs. I told her she didn't need to be hittin' that pipe because she got a pretty daughter gettin' ready to go to college and stuff and she gonna be needin' a lot, bein' this her first year and all," Janice said cautiously. She didn't know Vanessa personally, but she had heard that she didn't play. Janice didn't want to rub Vanessa the wrong way because she wanted her to pay off Vickie's debt with her, every cent of the six hundred dollars.

"What kind of drugs did you sell her?"

"Crack."

"Well, if you didn't think she needed it, why did you give it to her, especially if she didn't have the money to pay for it?"

"I, uh, was trying to help her out. She was cravin' it. She kept telling me it was her last time because she had to do things for Vonshay and I believed her."

"I'm sorry that she owes you money, but I can't help you because she owes me, too. Put Vonshay on the phone, please." Vanessa heard her niece closing the door behind the stranger and rushing back to the phone.

"Vonshay, does your mama have a drug problem?" Vanessa asked.

"Yes, TeeTee," she responded with a sigh of relief and regret.

Truth felt relieved.

"Well, why didn't you tell me?" demanded Vanessa.

"I was going to tell you, but I thought you knew. Plus, I can't get the words to come out of my mouth. I tried. They're not there."

"It's O.k. baby. When your mama gets home, tell her to call me right away. Don't tell her that I talked to Janice. I'm going to church and I should be back around 2:30 or 3:00. Have her call me then. Bye baby and be strong. I love you."

Vanessa sat motionless after she hung up the phone. She felt like she couldn't move a muscle in her body. I knew it, she kept telling herself. Vanessa did know all along that her sister had a drug problem, but she didn't want to believe it. She pretended that Vickie was telling her the truth about why she needed so much money, but deep down inside, she knew they were all lies. Now, she had been told the flat out truth, and she was forced to do something about it. Vonshay needed her and so did Vickie. At that moment, she wanted to crawl back into the bed and never get out again, but she couldn't. Her love and commitment to her family wouldn't allow it. Thinking of the many things she now had to do ignited something inside of Vanessa and her muscles finally began to move. She got up to get ready for church.

Vanessa loved attending church in Atlanta. Well, she liked attending one church in particular, Mount Moriah Baptist Church. She had always believed in God and attended church, but at St. James, her home church in Mississippi, she didn't stay in services very long because she never seemed to get anything out of the messages. She would stay until after the choirs sang, hoping that she would receive a message through song. It was hard, though, to get one from the "every member wanna be a soprano choir," a name she and her best friend, Christi, gave the choir during their childhood years. After attending Mount Moriah, Vanessa looked forward to attending church on Sundays and staying until services dismissed, which was sometimes three or four hours later.

It was at Mount Moriah that Vanessa had her first encounter with the Holy Spirit. Of course, she had seen people shout in church before, but it had never happened to her. Being from Mississippi, she had been taught that Baptist churches did not believe in the laying on of hands, speaking in tongues, dancing, and shouting for the Lord. "All that," they said, "is for the sanctified folks." She was shocked to find all these things taking place at Mount Moriah, a Baptist church. It took Vanessa a little time to get used to, but after experiencing it, she couldn't doubt it.

Her first personal encounter with the Holy Spirit was at an evening service. Vanessa carefully watched as people went to the altar to receive the Lord's anointing. She heard the pastor tell them that they had to have faith. He also insisted that people know that he had no power. "The power is the Lord's," he said. "My hands are merely instruments that the Lord has chosen. Give Him the glory, not me."

Standing in her pew with her hands raised, Vanessa asked the Lord to open her heart and her mind to believe and accept what was happening around her. She heard the preacher say that there was power in the building. He prayed that everyone there be touched and he extended his hands toward the entire congregation. Vanessa heard people falling to the floor, but she continued to pray her personal prayer. Suddenly, her legs began to move, bending back and forth. She tried to stop the movement by forcing them still and could not. Realizing that the power of the Lord was upon her, Vanessa gave in to the demands of the Spirit and allowed Him to take over. Her entire body became a symbol of praise unto the Lord. She danced before Him like she had never danced before. Her movements were not contrived and cute like they were when she directed her own movements. Under the direction of the Spirit, her movements were choreographed so well that they would put the Dance Theatre of Harlem to shame. After regaining control of her body, Vanessa could not stop thanking the Lord for allowing her to receive His anointing and experience the power of the Holy Spirit.

The Sunday that the conversation with Vonshay and Janice occurred, Vanessa went to church with her dream and other morning events fresh on her mind. She hoped that something in a song or the sermon would give her some direction. As usual, Pastor (as members of the congregation reverently referred to their leader) had exactly the right words to say. It was as if he had written his sermon only for Vanessa.

The title of the message for that day was "Don't Get Caught Up." The pastor talked about spiders and their webs. He discussed the beauty of the web that was so inviting, yet, carrying with it the danger of entrapment. He talked about envy, gossip, and drugs being webs that often draw humans in. He expounded on drugs, explaining how people believe that being high can remove all obstacles, and how problems seem as if they don't exist.

" All of this is false pleasure," he preached, "because when you're not high, the problems are still there. You can't get out of the drug dealer's web. He makes it so pretty for you. You wanna go in and check it out, but once he gets you in there, ain't no gettin' out. And just like the spider, the dealer and his drugs will suck all of your blood from you and drain you dry. Sometimes you think you ought to kill yourself, take away the life that God gave you."

"How many of you out there have been caught up in a web?" he asked, inviting   participation from the congregation. Hands flew up all over the building. The organist began to play. "How many of you know that God can set you free from that web, right now? He can knock that web down and send the spider on its way."

"Hallelujah" and "Amen" resounded across the room.

"Go head, preacher! Tell it like it is," yelled one man.

Another man whistled as the preacher continued the message as if he was singing a song. The organist followed his lead. The melody flowed with the rise and fall of his voice. The organist imitated the sound of his voice and the words he spoke. "Take it to the Lord. He knows all about your webs. He knows about your friend's, your mama's, your daddy's, your sister's and your brother's webs. If they don't know they're in a web, hmph, God will help you show ' em. He'll use you to save 'em. Ain't God all right? Yes He is. My God is all right. Let me tell you. They may get mad at you, hmph, even curse you out, but God will, I said God will take that worry off you. He… will pull you through. Just take it to the Lord. He'll make it all right. Won't He make it all right? I'm a living witness that God will make it alright...alright...alright."

Next, Pastor began to minister through song. He sang the old hymn, *He Knows How Much You Can Bear*. Before Vanessa knew it, she was standing on her feet with her hands raised and

34

tears streaming from her eyes. Pastor called for anyone who was caught up in a web or had friends and family members caught up to come down to the altar. Vanessa knew she should go, but she was glued in place. Several people came down and the Pastor began to pray. When he finished he said, "There is a lady here who didn't come down. Your sister is caught up in a web of drugs. Sister, I want you know that the Lord is going to use you to pull her through. Come on down and let me pray for you."

Vanessa could not believe that he was speaking to her. She knew that she had to go to the altar. She slowly stepped out into the aisle. She made it to the front of the church and Pastor placed his hands on her head and began to pray,

Lord, she has come to accept the strength and comfort that you have promised her. Help her, Father, to tackle the web that has her loved one bound. Give her peace, Lord, and guide her steps. In Your Son Jesus' name, we pray, Amen.

When he moved his hands from her, Vanessa's body went limp. She fell back into the arms of a deacon, who obviously knew that she would not be able to stand on her own. They sat her down on the front pew until she regained her strength. Then she returned to her seat saying, "Thank You, Lord." Now she understood her dream and knew that God was calling on her to get her sister out of the web that entangled her. She just wished that He had told her how to do it.

Back home from church, Vanessa changed into her favorite lounging attire, a long flowing caftan with rich earth tone colors. She wasn't planning on going anywhere, and she wanted to be comfortable while talking to her sister. She watched a movie on the Lifetime network, then turned to TBN to watch the broadcasts of her favorite bishops: Bishop T.D. Jakes of Dallas; Bishop Clarence E. McClendon of Los Angeles; and Bishop Eddie L. Long of Atlanta. She was confident that each of them would have a revelatory word for her situation, and they did.

Waiting for Vickie to call, Vanessa rehearsed what she would say. She had gone over her lines a thousand times before

35

the phone ever rang. When Vickie finally called, none of the words Vanessa had rehearsed were spoken. Everything she said flowed directly from her heart. She told Vickie about her conversation with Janice. She then cited all the times that she had sent Vickie money for things that were never bought and bills that were never paid. She talked about all the times she stayed out in the wee hours of the morning and how she had been neglecting Vonshay. She talked about the effects of drugs and lastly, she told Vickie that if she did not acknowledge her problem and get help, she would take Vonshay and raise her herself.

"I don't have a drug problem!" Vickie exclaimed as if she were shocked that her sister would even think such a thing. "I've been gamblin' on that damn boat," she said in an effort to justify all of the things Vanessa mentioned.

"Vickie, I love you and I wanna believe you," Vanessa said. "But I don't. Because I love you, I'm going to take your word for now. I am giving you a chance to get help and you're denying that you need it. But after tonight, if I find out that you're involved with drugs, you will be own your own. I'm not going to have anything to do with you until you do something about it, and I'm going to let Vonshay come and live with me. Is that understood?" Vanessa asked.

"I understand, " Vickie said in soft voice.

A few moments of silence passed and even softer than before she said, "I need help."

"Then you'll get it," Vanessa said with relief. She wanted to interrogate Vickie about everything that had transpired over the past six months, but she decided against it. Her sister had taken a major step by admitting her addiction and Vanessa thought it best to show her love and support. "I love you," she said, "and thank you for telling the truth. Go get some rest and we'll talk about it more later." Click.

"Umph," Vanessa said aloud. "Out of all the times Vickie called me about little stuff, why didn't she call me about this, something that could cost her her life?"

Being in charge of her sister's life was a tremendous responsibility for Vanessa. It required a lot of time and energy.

Many times, she didn't have much of either, but she gave what she had to her sister. She felt that she had to look out for Vickie because people always took advantage of her kindness and used it as a weakness. Vickie never saw things that way, so Vanessa had to clear her vision.

Whenever Vickie had any type of problem, she called on Vanessa for advice. Vanessa felt that many of her dilemmas only required common sense, but she helped her to make logical decisions whenever she was asked to. She couldn't understand how Vickie could make decisions based on what other people thought or needed, paying little attention to her own thoughts and needs. Hoping to redirect Vickie's thinking, Vanessa would always tell her sister, "Self-preservation comes first." Vickie's behavior showed that this statement had not impacted her in the least.

Vanessa felt that Vickie was too old to need to ask her about the basic things in life. She wondered if she had crippled her sister more than she had helped her by always working things out for her. It was obvious that Vickie depended on her not only for emotional support, but for spiritual and financial support, as well. Vanessa didn't really mind looking after her sister. She had done it for so long that it was a part of who she was. She did wish, however, that her sister were a stronger person, someone who could take charge of her own life. If Vickie were not so gullible, Vanessa wouldn't have to move back home to take charge of her sister's life.

That night, Vanessa began packing and making arrangements to go home to Ferguson indefinitely. Her car was in the shop being serviced, and it would not be ready for several days. She didn't have time to wait. She needed to get home fast. It was probably best that she not drive because she had a lot on her mind. Keeping her attention focused on the road would be difficult, and an accident was the last thing she needed. The thought of flying crossed her mind, but no major airlines serviced Ferguson. She would have to fly into Memphis and take a commuter plane to her hometown. The plane was small and only held about ten passengers. The passengers on board always felt the slightest disturbance in the atmosphere. She had been a

37

passenger on one of those planes before, and it wasn't an experience she wanted to repeat. She decided to take Greyhound and leave the driving to them.

Before getting into bed, Vanessa got down on her knees and prayed. In her prayer she thanked the Lord for all that He had done for her and asked Him to watch over and to strengthen her, Vickie, and Vonshay, as they struggled with the web of drugs that entangled them.

Once again, the slow pace of the bus caught Vanessa's attention. When the driver opened the door, she knew instantaneously that she was in the Mississippi Delta. She could feel the hot and dry heat, carrying with it the putrid odor of raw catfish. The heat and smell engulfed her so suddenly that she began to cough. She definitely had not missed it. Vanessa wanted to go into the small store, which also served as the bus station, but she changed her mind. She had a weak stomach. Stepping off the bus into the smell would make her coughing increase and her stomach contents decrease. She decided to stay on board.

She stood up and stretched, then sat back in her seat. Looking through the tinted glass on the windows of the bus, she saw aspects of country living. The mothers wearing straw hats to block the sun, and the fathers wearing dust covered overalls hugged their sons and daughters goodbye, glad that they were getting a chance to see a new place. She watched little children reach down and pick up the coins they dropped because they ran so wildly to the store. She watched smiles that lightened up their faces when they exited the store and pulled the wrappers off their first pieces of nickel candy. (When she had grown up, it was penny candy.) She watched the old men sitting on benches in front of the store, drinking beer and telling stories. She watched her people as they went about their daily routines. They all waved when the bus driver cranked the engine. She wondered if they would ever leave. She knew most of them never would.

As the bus pulled back onto the highway, Vanessa continued to look out of the window. The land in the Mississippi Delta was so flat that you could see from one town to the next without any obstacles. From water tower to water tower, the scenery remained the same. The vast fields screamed, "freedom," but the crowded rows whispered, "liar." The many miles of cotton fields Vanessa passed led her thoughts to her unknown ancestors who had to pick and chop cotton in those very fields from sunup to sundown for free. She visualized them in the fields with sacks on their backs, sweat on their bodies, and babies at their heels, struggling in the scorching hot sun to do the right amount of work, in the right amount of time, in an effort to avoid the right hand of the overseer who held the whip.

Slavery had been abolished over a hundred years, yet some of her people were still doing the same work, in the same fields, for the same long hours. For all of the hard work they did, after emancipation, they did not bring home much more than the slaves had. Forty years ago, they were paid ten dollars a day. Twenty years ago, they were paid twenty dollars a day, and ten years ago, they were paid thirty dollars a day. Within the last five years, a law that forced landowners to pay field workers minimum wage was finally passed. Subsequently, the land owners cut the workday from sunup to sundown to 8 a.m. to 12 p.m., just enough time to make thirty dollars a day.

With closed eyes, Vanessa said a prayer of forgiveness for the landowners and all of the people who had in some way oppressed her people. When she opened her eyes, the beauty of the snow white clouds dancing around the setting sun mesmerized her. It was as if God Himself were saying to her, "Welcome home!" She whispered, "Thank You, Lord" as she admired the splendor of His creation.

The closer Vanessa got to Ferguson, the more anxious she became. Reality began to set in. She was moving back home, to the place she had left ten years earlier. It was the place that had no space for her to release the very things it had stored within her. In her absence, the conditions there had become worse, the space smaller. If there was no space for her then, surely there was no space for her now. She was not the same person who had left with knowledge and dreams, trying to understand the ways of the world; she was returning with wisdom and visions, desiring to walk in the will of God. She needed more space now than she did then.

"What about me, God," Vanessa asked softly as she thought of how her life would be in Ferguson. God answered her, as He often did, by reminding her of a passage of a scripture. Her answer was in Habbakuk 2:3…"For the vision is yet for an appointed time, but at the end it shall speak and not lie: though it tarry, wait for it; because it will surely come.

Chapter 3

Vanessa stared out of the taxi's window as she rode down the familiar streets to her family home. She shook her head in disgust as she passed the vandalized buildings and dilapidated homes. When she was growing up, Black people had respect for their homes and neighborhoods and took pride in keeping them safe and clean. Back in the seventies, her parents were the first Blacks to move on Ashland Avenue, and they went out of their way to make sure that no one would be able to truthfully accuse them of causing the neighborhood to go down. Needless to say, the accusations were still made. Not because of the way they attended to their property, but because of their presence in the neighborhood.

As the taxi turned onto Ashland Avenue, Vanessa was proud that 701was still the best looking house on the block. Unfortunately, it didn't have much competition. The Whites had begun moving out a few years after her family moved in. Slowly, the number of Blacks in the neighborhood increased. The new neighbors who moved into the neighborhood were not as concerned about their property as the Morgan's were. What were once well-manicured lawns were now becoming yards filled with empty beer bottles and cigarettes. Vanessa decided that one of the projects she would get involved in during her time in Ferguson would be a neighborhood clean up. Her parents had worked too hard to increase the value of their home and

41

community for it to be diminished because of people who had no respect for themselves or their possessions.

As Vonshay combed out the curls that she placed so meticulously in her mama's hair, the doorbell rang. She darted off to the door, and when she flung it open, her auntie was standing before her.

"Hey Vonshay. How's TeeTee's baby doing?" Vanessa beamed, as she looked her niece over. She wanted to make sure that the child showed no physical signs of neglect.

"Fine," Vonshay said as she reached out for her aunt. She hugged Vanessa as if she were holding on for life. "I'm glad you're here, TeeTee," she whispered, while looking over Vanessa's shoulder toward the driveway.

"I am too, baby. Everything'll be all right soon."

"How'd you get here?" Vonshay asked disappointedly, when she didn't see Vanessa's gold Acura RL in the driveway. Not many people in Ferguson owned Acuras and Vonshay always looked forward to cruising in Vanessa's whenever she was in town.

"I took the bus," Vanessa answered. "My car is in the shop, but I'll send for it as soon as it is ready. For now I'll use your mama's car, but you'll get your chance to style and profile," she chuckled. Vanessa headed for the kitchen while Vonshay brought her bags in. She called out to Vickie on her way.

When Vickie heard her baby sister's voice, a chill went over her. She had felt that Vanessa was coming, but she hadn't really expected her to show up that soon. She hadn't even gotten herself ready to face her, and now it was too late. Vanessa was there- - and knowing her, she would get straight to the point.

In her mind, Vickie could see Vanessa prancing into the house in a cool brown sleeveless dress with a tasteful split, showing just enough to make men wonder, but not enough to let them know what was hiding underneath. She could see her light brown hair closely cropped, showing off its natural curls and complementing the golden undertones of her skin. She could hear her babbling about how well Vonshay looked and how she couldn't believe that her little niece had grown into such a lovely

42

young lady. She could feel the warmth that Vanessa carried with her.

Vanessa was such a pleasant person to be around, and the fact that her beauty was not simply skin deep added to her appeal. She was a down to earth sister who had a genuine concern for the well being of her people. She was especially concerned about her family and friends, and she was always there when they needed her. Vickie usually felt good about her sister's presence, but that day it frightened her. The knowledge of why her sister was there would not allow Vickie to enjoy Vanessa's warmth. At that moment, Vickie felt that her sister was more of an enemy than a friend.

Vickie stood up when she heard Vanessa's footsteps approaching the door. I could at least pretend that I'm glad to see her, she thought. "Hey sis," she beamed, showing a lot more enthusiasm than she actually felt. She was shocked to see Vanessa dressed casually in faded jeans, a brown T-shirt and brown sandals.

"Hey, Vickie," Vanessa responded as she reached out to hug her big sister. "What's up?" When she put her arms around Vickie, Vanessa noticed how thin and frail her sister's body was. She wanted to comment, but she fought the urge.

"I'm fine, girl what about you? You sure got here quick."

"What do you mean? I didn't tell you I was coming. How'd you know?"

"'Cause I know you," Vickie said with a little sly smile. "What's up?"

"Well, you are. I called around this morning before I left and checked on some things so we can get you straight. Now, do you want to go into treatment here or somewhere else?" Vanessa asked.

"I don't know. What do you think?" Vickie asked puzzled. She knew that Vanessa always took care of business, but she didn't know she would have done so much so soon. She hadn't even given Vickie a chance to explain herself, not that she had actually come up with an explanation.

"I think you should go somewhere else. The program

43

here is not that thorough and there would be too many people in your business. Remember, this is Ferguson. There is a Charter Hospital in Jackson that has a really good program, and you could be close to Vonshay, since she'll be in school there. I'll be here with her, but she still needs to be close to her mama.

"Yeah," Vickie said slowly, knowing that she didn't really have a choice in the matter. "What can I tell Vonshay?"

"You tell her the truth. That child's no fool. She already knows what's been going on. She's a very smart young lady, and she can handle it, especially since you're doing something about it. Explain to her that you have an addiction, you've been using drugs, and you're ready to stop, but you need some help to do it. She'll understand."

"But I don't wanna lose her. I've disappointed her so many times already. There's only so much she can take."

"Honey, you have a lady in there, not a little girl. God is not going to make her load any heavier than she can stand."

"I guess you're right, and you'll be here to look after her, won't you?"

"Of course, I will. I wouldn't have it any other way." Vanessa smiled.

"Thanks. I really couldn't do this without you. I'm glad you finally caught up with me."

"Yeah, well, I couldn't help it. Your lies were gettin' weaker and weaker. You didn't give me much of a choice. Actually, you must have wanted me to catch you."

"Well, maybe I did." Vickie said solemnly. "So how's HOTLANTA? Have you found that certain man yet?"

"Naw, girl, but I'm still waiting. He needs to hurry up and show his face because I'm getting a little old. What've you got to eat around here? I'm starving," Vanessa said, quickly changing the subject. She was not in the mood to explain, for the umpteenth time, her choice to be celibate and wait on God to send her a husband. Most folks, even church folks, just did not understand that. Still, she believed it was best to wait on the right man than to marry the wrong man.

Vickie dropped her head and the word "nothin'" slowly rolled out in a dry whisper. She was so ashamed. She didn't have any food in her house and no money to buy any. She wondered how her child had been eating.

"Never mind. I don't feel like waiting on you to cook anyway. I know you're still slow. We'll go out and eat. Sound good?" Vanessa asked, seeing the sad look on Vickie's face. She knew that her sister couldn't afford to eat out and that she would have to pay for it, but she didn't mind because both Vickie and Vonshay looked like they could use a good meal.

"I guess. Let me slip on some clothes and get Vonshay to finish combing these curls out. We'll be ready before you know it."

Vanessa smiled as her sister hurried from the room. She was glad that she was able to hide her anger and rage. She was really mad enough to hurt Vickie. She knew that admitting to her problem was a big step for Vickie, and she didn't want to discourage her by showing anger. Her sister was very fragile, and too much of anything negative would probably send her straight to the crack house, so Vanessa held her peace. Knowing that the power of life and death is in the tongue, she thanked God for holding her tongue.

Vickie got Vonshay off the phone so she could put the finishing touches on her hair. She told Vonshay that they were all going out to eat and that she wanted her to choose what she would wear.

"The same Capri set I told you earlier, Mama," Vonshay said.

"But it's..." Vickie started.

"But it's what you're going to wear," Vonshay blurted out before Vickie could finish. She was talking in a stern tone as if she were talking to a little girl who didn't want to wear what her mama put out for school. When she noticed the pitiful look on her mama's face, Vonshay smiled apologetically. Lately, she talked to her mama as if their roles were reversed. She couldn't help it. Her mama acted like a child, so she started treating her like one.

"It looks O.k., I guess," Vickie said after putting it on.

"It looks good, Mama. Now come on."

Vanessa browsed through the house while her sister and niece were getting ready.

It wasn't that she expected to see anything she hadn't seen before; she just loved the feeling of being at home. Taking in the beauty of every room in the house was a ritual for her.

Her first stop was the bedrooms. As she entered each of them, she thought about all of the family members and friends who had rested in them. When she went to the kitchen, the sun was beaming through the open blinds. Visions of her mother and father sitting at the dinner table discussing the day's events with her and Vickie flashed through her mind. When she walked into living room, which was rarely visited by anyone, she went directly to the piano, where she had spent hours of dreaded practice time. Her fingers played a few notes of *I Have Decided to Follow Jesus*, the first hymn she had learned to play. Her last stop was the family room. The warm and cozy feeling she got each time she entered the room always made her miss home. She stood at the fireplace observing the family pictures on the mantle. Everyone looked so happy, even Vickie. She wondered what could have happened that was so devastating that it turned Vickie to drugs.

"You girls ready?" she asked, hearing Vickie and Vonshay enter the room.

"Ready as we'll ever be," Vonshay replied, pointing at her mama.

"I'm ready," Vickie announced with pride. "If you're finished with your tour of the house, we can go."

They decided to have dinner at Golden Dragon, their favorite Chinese restaurant. They all ordered their usual. Throughout the meal, they laughed and talked about everything they could think of from family and friends to news and entertainment. Vanessa and Vonshay carried the conversation and Vickie just commented now and then, hoping no one noticed that she was behind on current events. Vanessa was eager to know what was going on in Ferguson but she didn't want to cross that fine line into gossip, so she tried to keep her responses at a minimum. Finally, Vickie drew up enough nerve to say something about her problem when dessert was being served. She wanted to say something earlier, but she couldn't find the words.

"Vonshay, we're all going to Jackson tomorrow," Vickie said. Mama hasn't been herself lately. I've been using drugs heavily, and it's not good for me. I don't wanna use 'em anymore, so I'm going to get some help. The doctors in Jackson are a lot better than the ones here, and I want to make sure that I'm all right. Plus, I wanna be close to you. Do you understand what I'm saying, baby?"

"Yeah, Mama. You don't have to talk to me like I'm five years old. I've *been* knowing what's goin' on. How long is it gon' take?" Vonshay asked with attitude in her voice.

"I don't know. We'll find that out tomorrow."

"Why do I have to go?"

"I want you to see the place and listen to what the people are going to say so you'll understand what's goin' on."

"Oh" was the only response Vonshay gave.

"You really should go Vonshay. Your mama needs your support," Vanessa said in an understanding tone.

"Well, who's gonna support me while she's gone? Never mind. I just remembered that I'm old enough to support myself," she said sarcastically.

"What do you mean by that?" her mama asked.

"What do *I* mean by it?! That's what you told me. What *you* meant by it is the real question here."

"I don't remember saying that," Vickie responded with insult in her eyes.

"It figures. You haven't remembered too much of anything lately, including my birthday. I turned eighteen years old. You told me that it would be the best birthday I ever had, and you were nowhere to be found. Must not have been that important, huh?"

Vickie said nothing. Vanessa could see all of the hurt, shame and guilt in her eyes. She came to her sister's rescue. "Vonshay in all of your years this is the first time your mama ever forgot your birthday, right?"

"Yes."

47

"Well, doesn't that let you know that something is going wrong, and she doesn't have any control over it. You should be glad that she wants to get help. You're a big part of the reason she's seeking help. Try to be more understanding, O.k."

"Where was she when I needed understanding, in the streets somewhere? She don't know what I was goin' through being at home by myself all the time and worryin' about her."

"No, she doesn't know. That's why you need to talk about it and tell her how you feel, but it's a way to do everything and raising your voice at your mama is not the answer. I know that your feelings are hurt by all of this. Still, you don't ever talk to your mama like that again. I don't care how mad you are! Do you understand me?"

"Yes," Vonshay said. She was surprised to hear Vanessa talk to her that way.

Her TeeTee had not fussed or raised her voice at her since she was smaller, so she knew that this had to be serious and that she had crossed the line. She decided to apologize to her mama. "I'm sorry, Mama, if I upset you. I'll go with you tomorrow. You forgive me?"

"Yeah, baby, Mama forgives you, and I'm sorry too."

"For what?"

"For missing your birthday and anything else that I did to hurt you these last few months. Mama really didn't know what she was doing. Those drugs were in control more than I was."

Vickie expected Vonshay to respond, but she didn't. She ate her ice cream and said nothing else.

"Well, it'll be taken care of soon," Vanessa said, lighting her after dinner cigarette. It was amazing how easy it was for her to smoke again. She had been tempted often, but it was a struggle, even when she gave in to the craving. Since this thing with Vickie, she reached for a cigarette without giving it a second thought. The fact that her sister smoked didn't make it any easier for her to resist.

When she and Vickie finished smoking their cigarettes, they all left the restaurant, riding in silence all the way home. Upon entering the house, Vonshay immediately went to her

48

room. Vickie stopped in the kitchen to light a cigarette at the stove. When she turned and saw Vanessa reaching for the coffee, she sat down at the table.

"Vickie, you have to give the girl time to grasp everything," Vanessa said calmly, as she sat down across from her sister.

"I don't understand. I have the problem. I messed up. I'm goin' to rehab. What does she need to grasp? It has nothing at all to do with her. I did everything myself. She'll be right here with you gettin' whatever she wants while I'll be locked down in a hospital for crazy folks. What more does she want?"

"Her mama, maybe? Sure, she might think that staying here with me is fun, but she doesn't want me here full time. You're her mama, and she wants you. Is anything wrong with that?" Vanessa asked, struggling not to reach for a cigarette.

"I guess not if that's what's goin' on, but I think she's looking for a reason to run
off to Andre'. She tried it before you know."

"I know, Vickie, but that's the girl's daddy, and nothing is wrong with them bein' close. Most mamas wish that their children knew their daddies, let alone had a relationship with them. Here you are mad because your ex-husband loves his daughter and she loves him. Hmph. Girl, you need to let that go. You ain't got no *real* baby mama drama and you need to thank God for that.

"What is real baby mama drama?"

"Real baby mama drama is when your baby daddy say he ain't baby's daddy and won't help you with the baby so you put child support on him and he demands a DNA test and when the test comes back positive and he quits his job and you're right back where you started."

"Oooh! Now that's drama for real. O.k Vanessa, I get the point but take care of my baby while I'm gone."

"I will, Vickie. I will. I'm going unpack so I can go to sleep because that bus ride really wore me out. Good night," she said, thankful that she had made it through the conversation without any drama from her sister.

"Good night," Vickie said as she watched Vanessa leave the room. I don't believe it has come to this, she told herself. How could I let a little white rock control me? I guess it was bigger than I thought! I've lost my money, my job, and my only child. I know she hates me. I've been treating her so badly. I need some serious help. I'm going to that rehab place and get myself straight. I've got to make my child love me again. Lord, let my baby love me again.

Once Vanessa entered her room she did not have the energy to unpack. She said a short prayer, pulled a gown out of her suitcase, slipped it on, and stretched across the bed. Recapping her day's events, as she often did, she remembered that she had left her purse in the kitchen. In the past that would not have bothered her, but now she knew that her sister was an addict and that she might do anything to get a fix, including stealing from her. She jumped out of bed and hurried to the kitchen. She flicked on the light and saw her purse on the counter. Vickie was nowhere in sight, so she rambled through it to make sure there was nothing missing. She felt ashamed when she found everything in its place. She wondered how she could have ever believed her sister would steal from her.

As Vanessa walked back down the hall, she heard music coming from Vonshay's room. It was so loud that the walls were trembling. When she opened the door she heard Musiq Soulchild singing, *Love*. Tears were falling from Vonshay's eyes. Vanessa wondered how long it had been since Vickie had told her daughter she loved her. She walked over to Vonshay's bed, sat down and took her niece in her arms. Rocking gently, Vanessa stroked Vonshay's head and whispered in her ear. "Don't cry, baby," she pleaded. "Everything is going to be just fine. You know TeeTee has never lied to you, and I'm not about to start now. I love you and I'll do everything I can to straighten things out." Vanessa rocked Vonshay until no more tears fell from her eyes. Then she kissed her, told her she loved her, and tucked her in.

50

Chapter 4

Vonshay was tired, but her mind refused to give her body the rest that it desired. She tried crying herself to sleep as she had so many times before, but to no avail. She glanced around the room, searching for something to focus her attention on to keep her from thinking about her mother. Everywhere she looked she saw items associated with memories of Vickie. Eventually her eyes rested on the silver jewelry box on her dresser. It was a gift from her mother. She quickly glanced in the other direction and her eyes were drawn to the painting of a little girl praying which hung above her head. Her mother had insisted on buying it and hanging there to make sure Vonshay never forgot to say her prayers. Like clock work, the last thing Vonshay did before she went to sleep at night and the first thing she did when she awoke every morning was say her prayer. All of her life she had heard that "prayer changes things." Now she wondered if she had wasted her time. As much as she had prayed for her mama, things seemed to get even worse.

Confusion planted itself in the forefront of Vonshay's mind; no thought could enter nor exit. She could not understand how a thirty-five year old woman with a decent job and common sense could throw her life and her money away on drugs. It just didn't add up for her. She felt her mama should have known better. In her mind, women with drug problems were ghetto women who lived in the projects with more children than they could afford to take care of or rich women who lived in mansions and sent their children to boarding schools and had enough money to hide their habits. She had heard about the ghetto women selling food stamps and using money from welfare checks to buy drugs because they didn't have a chance at a better future, and the rich women spending all of their money and then checking into the Betty Ford Center because they couldn't get beyond their past. She didn't think, though, that women like her mama with bright futures and pleasant pasts would use drugs. Why should they? She thought that they would know better than that, but she was wrong. Her smart mama, with all of the finer things in life, had been dumb enough to believe the hype.

Vickie was so dumb that she tried to play Vonshay for a fool. Vonshay could not believe it. Her mama had always bragged about how intelligent and observant Vonshay had been since she was a toddler, and now she offered her lies that even a blind man could see. She used lies to explain the changes that were taking place in her life, changes that she didn't realize Vonshay had noticed, until her daughter confronted her about them. Vickie really knew better than to try and put anything over on Vonshay, but the drugs didn't.

In her heart, Vonshay had wanted to believe her mama's lies, but her head refused to allow her. She knew that accepting lies as truth would only break her heart into more pieces. She wanted to protect her heart, so she doubted the things that her mama told her. She didn't realize that doubt could be as painful as belief. Doubting her mama tore her apart. Her mama was supposed to be the person that she could believe in and trust when everyone else was lying. But, her mama was lying to her more than anyone ever had. She did not understand why.

Vickie had used various forms of drugs for as far back as Vonshay could remember, but she had never lied to her. Vonshay began to wonder if it was drugs that made her mama act that way or if her mama had been faking with her all those years. She was beginning to believe that her mama had simply gotten tired of faking. She tried to trace the path of the presence of drugs in her life, hoping to figure out what had gone wrong and when.

When Vonshay was a toddler, her parents and their friends smoked these little cigarettes that made them laugh. They called them "joints." As she got older, her parents sent her and their friends' daughter, Michelle, to her room while they were getting high. She and Michelle knew what went on in their absence because the smell of the funny cigarettes, combined with incense, would float through the house. They also knew that the best time to ask for permission to do something or go somewhere was when their parents were smoking. Their chances of getting a "yes" were much better then. As a matter of fact, they had a perfect record. They got what they asked for every time.

It wasn't until she was older and her friends started smoking the same cigarettes as her parents that Vonshay realized that smoking marijuana is illegal. She hadn't seen anything harmful happen as a result of it, so when her peers started pressuring her about trying it, she agreed. Everyone seemed to like it, and she figured that her parents wouldn't mind since they did it too.

She tried it after school one day at her friend Chanelle's house. She would rather have tried it with Michelle, but she had moved away. Chanelle took so long to roll the joint that Vonshay got nervous. She was about to change her mind. To expedite the process, she went to help Chanelle and ended up rolling the joint herself.

"I thought this was your first time," Chanelle had said, looking in disbelief at the perfectly rolled joint Vonshay presented her.

"It is," replied Vonshay. "I've just seen it done before." She hoped that Chanelle wouldn't ask her where. She couldn't very well tell her at home.

The two girls lit the joint and began smoking. Vonshay's first inhale made her choke. She coughed constantly, but she continued to smoke. After the second joint, they headed for the kitchen to get an after school snack. They ate like there was no tomorrow, then, fell asleep. When they woke up it was almost seven o'clock. Vonshay had told her parents she would be at Chanelle's, but she'd said that she would be home around six. She called her parents to tell them that she was still there and would be home soon. On her way home she kept thinking that her parents would know what she had been doing as soon as she walked in the house. When she got there, neither of them noticed the dizziness and fatigue that she thought were written all over her face. She was relieved, yet disappointed. Her body was so tired and drained from her day's activities that she vowed never to smoke another joint and she didn't.

About the same time that her friends discovered weed, her parents discovered a new drug, cocaine, and added it to their list of habits. Commercials on TV warned people of the dangers of drugs, and drug activities were major plots on prime time shows, so Vonshay definitely knew what cocaine was when she saw it in her home.

Her parents kept the drug in small brown bottles with black tops. When the top was unscrewed and removed, a small silver spoon dangled from it. The spoon was used to scoop the drug out of the bottle and sniff it into their noses. They didn't do this in front of Vonshay, nor did they think she knew anything about it, but she did. She watched them when they weren't watching her. She never bothered to ask them what it was they were doing, because she already knew.

One morning before going to school, Vonshay asked Vickie for lunch money.
Vickie told her to look in her purse and get it. She went in her mama's purse and grabbed a folded dollar and left. She unfolded the dollar while standing in the school's lunch line talking with her friends. As she opened the dollar, a sparkling white powder began to fall from it. Vonshay couldn't believe her eyes. It was cocaine! Her friends acted as if they weren't aware of what it was, so she pretended not to know either. At home, she told her mama about what happened. "I must have wasted a BC," Vickie said. "And I must be Suzy Sausagehead," Vonshay said to herself.

She knew drugs were illegal, but she didn't know why because the only effects she saw and experienced were laughter and hunger. She thought that those things were a part of life. It wasn't until after her parents' divorce that she began to see a totally different side of drug use.

Vonshay was fifteen when Andre' moved out. He moved to Memphis, which was about a three-hour drive from Ferguson. In the beginning, Vonshay felt lost without her daddy. She enjoyed spending time with him and doing daddy and daughter things together. He had always been a constant part of her life, and she didn't want that to change. She put forth extra effort to remain close to him. She visited Andre' frequently and he visited her as well. Through their phone conversations and visits, their relationship remained in tact.

After Andre' left, Vickie began to use drugs more frequently and less conspicuously. Vonshay would find the little brown bottles, papers, and all kinds of paraphernalia just laying around the house. Occasionally, she would pick something up and tell her mama that she found it. The first time Vonshay gave her mama a pack of Top papers, Vickie had an embarrassed look on her face. She apologized to her daughter constantly for leaving the papers out, but not for using drugs.

As time went on, Vickie's carelessness continued and her apologies ceased. She wasn't interested in whether Vonshay knew that she got high or not. Really, she wished that her daughter would stop telling her that she found stuff. It really wasn't lost. Vickie knew exactly where she had left it. She thought that Vonshay was being a little too grown and a little too nosy. She paid the bills at the house, so she felt she had the right to leave whatever she wanted around.

To get away from her daughter and her speculations, Vickie started spending more time away from home and less time with Vonshay. She started out being gone a lot on weekends and it gradually progressed until she was gone everyday. Sometimes she was gone for days at a time.

Vonshay liked Vickie being away because she could do whatever she wanted. Her mama wasn't there for her to ask permission, and she had stopped leaving notes and numbers as to her whereabouts. Vonshay was basically on her own. She enjoyed every minute of it. She could eat what she wanted when she wanted. She could have company whenever and how long she wanted. She was living the life, or so she thought.

One Friday night after a football game at her school, Vonshay had decided to go to the after-party in the school gym. She and her friend Chanelle waited until the party was bumpin' before they made their grand entrance. They were both pretty girls and they were smart, so all eyes turned when they entered. They walked around and mingled with familiar faces. One unfamiliar face caught Vonshay's eye. It was a boy from another school. The cutest boy she had seen in all her life. She kept watching him, and he kept watching her. Eventually he came over and introduced himself. They ended up talking and dancing the entire night. When the party was almost over, he walked her outside. He kissed her and she kissed him back. It was her first real kiss. Her heart beat faster than it ever had. She felt like she was in another world. She had never been that attracted to a boy before. She knew it must be love.

Vonshay couldn't wait to get home and tell her mama about the new feeling she had experienced. Vickie wasn't home. For three days, she waited for a chance to talk to Vickie. The chance never came. She thought about telling Vanessa, but she was so far away, and she would probably give her a lecture about kissing leading to sex and the fact that premarital six is not in God's will. But after the lecture, she would share in Vonshay's excitement as if she had just experienced her first kiss as well. That's what Vonshay loved about her aunt—she wasn't one of those "holier than thou" Christians who judge everything people do as if they have never done anything themselves. They seem to forget that *all* have sinned and fallen short.

Vonshay needed to explain her experience face to face. She decided to tell one of her teachers, Miss Lenear, who had been her junior English teacher the year before. She still went by her room to chat after school and she was sure that her favorite teacher wouldn't mind listening to her. Miss Lenear was excited for Vonshay. Vonshay liked Miss Lenear because she seemed to have it all together. When she walked into the classroom, she commanded attention without ever speaking a word. She related to her students on their level while challenging them to rise up to hers. Even after Vonshay moved on to her senior year, Miss Lenear didn't stop teaching her. In their conversations, she would ask Vonshay questions that made her think about things in ways she had never thought about them. Simple answers didn't satisfy Miss Lenear; she wanted answers that were well thought out. She freely shared her thoughts and wisdom about life, love, and relationships. She was living out the dreams that she had envisioned for her life, and she assured Vonshay that she could do the same if she put her mind to it and not allow the situations in her life to discourage her. She helped her plan for her future.

Miss Lenear was one of the few teachers left who recognized that teaching is not simply a job, but a calling to many jobs, including mother, father, sister, brother, friend, and counselor, to name a few. Whenever Vonshay stopped by her classroom, she made her feel so comfortable and showed so much interest in her life that Vonshay even discussed her parents with her. She told her how the divorce made her feel, how much she missed her daddy. She even told her that she thought her mama was using drugs and that it was getting out of hand. That was something she had never told anyone, not even her TeeTee.

Miss Lenear listened to Vonshay, consoled her, and counseled her, but she never once said anything negative about Vickie. She promised never to mention their conversations to anyone else and she didn't. She became Vonshay's 'play' Mama. She spent time with her, listened to her and talked to her about life and feelings. She did all of the things that her 'real' mama had stopped doing.

Living without any supervision and having a 'play' mama had become fun to Vonshay, but deep down inside she missed Vickie. Vickie would be in and out of the house but she never said much to her daughter anymore. Vonshay wanted her mama to cook for her, to tell her to clean up, to make her go to bed, or to say she couldn't go out. Actually, she just wanted her mama to be there for her. Not having her mama around was not as much fun as she had initially thought it to be.

Vonshay knew that her mama was getting high when she was away from home. She could hear her coming in the house giggling at nothing, knocking over things and looking for food. She always left something out for Vickie to eat, whether she cooked or ate out. She knew that her mama couldn't live off drugs alone and she doubted that she was eating right because of all the weight she was losing. Unfortunately, Vickie hardly ever ate what Vonshay left out. She would go to the refrigerator grab a Coke and go to her room.

It was hard for Vickie to sleep because she was so geeked up. Vonshay would wake up all through the night and hear the TV playing and her mama laughing. By the time morning came, Vickie was just winding down. She would be ready to go to sleep when it was time to go to work. A lot of mornings she did not leave home. Other mornings she would leave home and go get high. She would tell Vonshay that she had been to work. Vonshay knew better because she had started calling and checking to see if Vickie had been in. Most times she hadn't.

Even if Vonshay hadn't called to check, she would know when her mama hadn't been to work. She would be sitting around the house looking depressed when Vonshay came in from school. Immediately, Vickie would ask her for money. This usually meant that she had spent her money earlier that day getting high. The first few times Vickie asked for money, Vonshay gave it to her. After all, it was money that Vickie had given her. Soon, Vickie began to ask for money the same day she gave it to Vonshay. Money that once lasted two weeks wouldn't even last a day. Getting high had become very expensive for Vickie. She no longer just snorted cocaine; she smoked it. At first she smoked pure cocaine, but the high cost of it led her to a cheaper version, crack.

Vonshay ended up taking a job at a local Burger King. She had never worked before, but she needed money. Vickie no longer gave her an allowance. She wasn't even taking care of basic household needs. There was never any food, toiletries or other household supplies. She had to borrow lunch money from friends. She hated having to ask people for money. She wanted to tell her daddy, but she was afraid he would try to take her away. She decided to talk to her mama.

When she complained to Vickie about the way the house was being run, Vickie complained back. She said that her program at work had not been funded again and that all of her money was going to bills. Vonshay had a feeling that the program was still receiving funding, but her mama was not receiving her funding because she didn't show up for work. She also knew that all her money was not going to bills because delinquent notices were appearing every day. Vickie had a lie for everything Vonshay mentioned, so Vonshay stopped talking. She shook her head and tried to do what she could with the little she had.

The day Vonshay picked up her first paycheck, Vickie came to her job and asked her for money. Vonshay told her that she hadn't cashed her check.

"I'll cash it for you, get the twenty dollars, and bring the rest back," Vickie said.

"That's O.k. Mama. I'll do it when I get off," Vonshay responded.

"I need it now! I have to pay the gas bill by 5:30. Give me the money!"

"The gas bill is more than twenty dollars."

"I know. I already got the rest."

"Let me see it."

"It's in the car. You don't believe me or somethin'? Well forget it. When you come home and can't cook food or turn on the heater, don't say one word to me."

Vickie stormed out of the door and Vonshay went into the bathroom and cried. Vonshay left work early and went home. Vickie was there, but the TV in her room was gone. Vickie asked Vonshay for the twenty dollars again.

"You couldn't get that much when you pawned the TV?" Vonshay asked bitterly.

"I didn't pawn the TV, I let somebody use it. Now just give me the money."

"For what? The gas company is closed. Besides the gas isn't off."

"You asked me for what?! 'Cause I'm your mama and I said so. How the hell can you act like you don't wanna give me twenty dollars and I been takin' care of you all of your damn life. You get one little funky check and you think you all that! Well ain't this somethin'?" she yelled.

"Mama, I've got to have lunch money this week and we need some soap and tissue," Vonshay replied. She couldn't believe her mama was talking that way to her.

"I *been* buying you lunch and stuff for the house. When did it get to be your job all of a sudden?" Vickie asked adamantly.

"It's not!" Vonshay said sadly.

"I *know* it's not!" Vickie retorted as she reached for Vonshay's purse. She grabbed a twenty-dollar bill and stormed out of the house.

Tears came to Vonshay's eyes again. "I just don't understand mama anymore," she yelled to the deaf walls. "I'm tired of this and I don't have to live like this. Why should I try and take care of a house and I'm only seventeen years old? I've got a daddy and I can live with him in Memphis. He always wanted me with him anyway, but no, I had to be with my mama. Some choice I made. Well, there's no time like the present to do the right thing. I'm going to Daddy!"

Vonshay hated to leave, but she had to. She couldn't stand to see her mama killing herself, nor could she continue to deal with the stress that had become a normal part of her days. She called her daddy to come and get her. She didn't want to tell him everything that was happening, but she had to tell him enough to convince him that she needed to leave. She contemplated what she would say. Then, she called.

Vonshay told Andre' that Vickie was in a strain because her company was cutting back and had moved her from a salaried employee to a consultant. She explained that her mama was having trouble trying to pay the bills and that there wasn't enough money for things she needed for school and senior activities.

"Well, doesn't the money I send take care of that? " he asked.

"It's still not enough, Daddy," Vonshay answered. She hadn't seen a child support payment in months. Her mama had said that Andre' wasn't sending them.

"I don't see why not. What in the hell is she doing with my money?! It's to be spent on you and not on her. I can take better care of you than she's doing and she can send me the child support every month!"

"Daddy, will you just come and get me, please?"

"Get your things together. I'll be there in a few hours."

"O.k. Bye."

When Vonshay hung up the phone, she started packing. She didn't know how long she would be gone, so she took as much as her suitcases would hold. There was still a lot left. She waited and waited. It seemed as if time were standing still. She wanted to do something other than just sit and wait.

She decided to call and say good-bye to all of her friends. When they asked why she was leaving, she told them, "It's part of the child custody arrangements." She was too ashamed to tell the real reason to anyone other than Ms. Lenear. Talking on the phone made the time go faster, and before she knew it, Andre' was pulling up. She was glad that Vickie wasn't home because she didn't want to deal with her. She just wanted to leave. And she did just that.

When Vickie came home that night, Vonshay was gone. She didn't notice because she was too high. She stayed up all night, so she could talk to Vonshay while she got ready for school. She wanted to apologize for saying the things she had said and taking her daughter's money. She didn't hear Vonshay getting ready for school, so she went to her room. It was empty. Where is she? Vickie thought. Did she leave without me hearing her? She couldn't have because I was up all night, she remembered.

Vickie began to panic. She called all of Vonshay's friends to see if she had spent the night with any of them. None of them had seen Vonshay since school the day before, and none of them told her about her going to Andre's. They figured she should have known. She waited a while and then called the school. Vonshay had not come in that morning. Finally, she called Vanessa, her personal thinker.

Vickie told her what had happened. Well, actually she told her that Vonshay was missing. She didn't bother to mention the events that led up to the disappearance. While she was thinking of places her daughter might be, the thought of Andre' crossed her mind. He was the last person she wanted to talk to, so she asked Vanessa to call and see if he had heard from Vonshay.

"Hey Andre'. This Vanessa. I don't want to alarm you for no reason, but Vickie doesn't know where Vonshay is. We were wondering if you've heard from her."

"Oh she just realized the child is gone. I see Vonshay isn't very high on her list of concerns."

"So you have heard from her?" Vanessa asked with a sigh of relief.

"Yeah, She's sitting right here next to me," he said.

"What is she doing in Memphis?!" Vanessa exclaimed. Her shock was obvious.

"She needed a break. Your sister is puttin' a lot of pressure on her. Too much if you ask me. My baby needed a vacation, so I came and got her."

"In the middle of the year? Without her mama knowing?"

"Doesn't look like her Mama gives a damn, since she just realized she's not there."

"How long are you planning on keeping her?"

"'Till she's ready to leave. Tell Vickie not to bother to call us. When Vonshay's ready to talk to her, she'll call her. Thanks for callin' though. I see that you're still the one in charge."

"Well, you know how it is. What is Vonshay planning on doing about school?"

"She's going here."

"She's going to change schools her senior year? Does she really want to do that?"

"Not really, but it's either live here peacefully and graduate from White Haven or catch hell from Vickie and graduate from Ferguson. Right now, *here* is her choice."

"What is Vickie doing that's so bad? Is she mistreating her or something?"

I think you better ask her that."

"I will. Tell Vonshay I love her and I'll call her later. Bye."

"Bye."

Vickie was relieved when she first found out that Vonshay was with Andre'. Then she got mad. "How in the hell is he gon' come steal my child and not say one word to me? He must be losing his damn mind or somethin'," she yelled.

"Vickie, it seems like Vonshay wanted to go. She must've called him because I don't see him driving all the way down there unannounced for no reason."

"Why would my baby wanna leave me? She's got everything she wants right here."

"I don't know. That's what I wanted to ask you. Andre' said something about you putting pressure on her."

"What kinda pressure?" she asked.

"You tell me!" Vanessa demanded.

"Hell if I know. That's probably somethin' he told her to convince her to come up there and stay. Fillin' her head up with all that jive. He always did wanna take my baby. When he sees it ain't as easy as it looks, he'll be shipping her back."

"Well, maybe she's going through some changes. She'll be back," Vanessa said trying to comfort her sister's feeling of loss.

Vonshay loved living with Andre'. She hadn't realized until she got there how much she really missed him. He gave her everything she thought she wanted. He bought her clothes, shoes and jewelry. He gave her money to get her hair and nails done. He had long talks with her and he even cooked and cleaned for her. He did all of the things that her mama had stopped doing. He gave her all of the attention she had been craving, but she still

63

missed her mama. She thought that being with her daddy would fill her void, but the hole was even bigger and emptier than it was when she left.

A week after she left, Vonshay decided to call her mama. She didn't expect her to be home, and she wanted to just leave a message, but Vickie picked up the phone and a dry "hello" came out. Vonshay almost hung up because she didn't know what to say. She changed her mind and decided to talk.

"Hey, Mama," she said as cheerfully as she could.

"Hey baby," Vickie replied. "How are you doing? Everything O.k.?"

"Yeah. I just called to see what you were doing."

"Mama's not doing good. I'm not working much. I can't find a full time job and I'm all by myself. All my life, I just wanted to make you happy and give you what you wanted. Then when I don't have it like I used to, you leave me just like your daddy did. That hurts baby. I know I've taken you through a lot with the divorce and all and I'm sorry. I wish I could just die and you wouldn't have to worry about me."

"Mama, don't talk like that! I love you. I don't want you to die!"

"I know you love me, but you don't like me. I can't blame you 'cause I don't like my own self. If I just kill myself everybody'll be O.k. You wouldn't have to be worrying about me. I tried to put an end to it last night. I turned on the stove last night and put the flames out. I left the gas running and went to bed. I wanted to never wake up again, but I did. I kept coughin'. Finally, I made it in there and turned everything off. If I hadn't got hot and started coughin', I probably would've been dead."

Vonshay begged her Mama not to talk that way and not to hurt herself. Vickie agreed, but Vonshay wasn't convinced. After several similar conversations and daily thoughts of friends, Vonshay decided to go back home. Her mama needed her. She thought that if she went back, her mama would stop using drugs and stop trying to commit suicide. Faster than she had packed up to leave home, she packed up to return. Andre' didn't understand why Vonshay wanted to return, but he let her go. He understood that daughters needed their mamas and mamas, especially ones like Vickie, needed their daughters.

Vickie did not like being alone. From the time that she was a child, she had always wanted someone around her at all times. She managed to keep people around, so she never felt lonely. She lived with her parents all of her single life and the first years of her married life. When she gave birth to Vonshay, she was sure that she would never have to be alone again. When her parents died, she clung closer and closer to her child. Like most parents, Vickie didn't think about the fact that one day her little girl would be a grown woman and have a life of her own. Slowly, but surely, she began to realize this. Vickie was glad that Vonshay was independent, but sad that her role as caregiver had been diminished.

The day Vonshay returned home from her daddy's, Vickie welcomed her like she was a soldier returning from a foreign war. The house was spotless, and she had cooked a big dinner of fried chicken, rice and gravy, and green beans. It was the first *real* meal Vickie had eaten in a long while. Vonshay felt that her mama had found the strength to change from just knowing that she was coming back home. Later on, she began to notice some things that did not support her initial feeling. Her mama's clothes were dangling from her body, and dark sacks supported her eyes, giving them a worn appearance. She noticed a mark on Vickie's forearm that looked like a recent cut. Curious about the mark, she asked Vickie what had happened.

"I was cutting some fish, and I turned to get the grease out. When I turned back around I put my arm down on the knife and it cut my arm." Vickie explained over dinner.

"Oh," Vonshay retorted in disbelief. No knife she had ever seen stood with the blade facing upward on its own. She knew that her mama had intentionally tried to cut herself, hoping to bleed to death. Vonshay was furious at her mama's apparent ignorance. Vickie watched enough crime dramas to know that to be successful she should have cut her wrist and not her forearm. The woman didn't want to die. She wanted sympathy, and Vonshay had no sympathy for ignorance. In Vonshay's opinion, not knowing something was forgivable, but not trying to find out was a cardinal sin. Vonshay had little else to say during dinner. Afterwards, she went to her room to unpack. As she returned her belongings to their rightful places, she wondered if she had made the right decision.

A little later, Vickie came to Vonshay's room. "I lied to you about something," she said softly.

"I know. You lied about how you hurt your arm. I already know."

Vickie did not respond. She knew that her daughter knew. Sometimes she wondered if God punished her for her sins by revealing her secrets to Vonshay. She walked out and went back to her room and cried. She didn't like hurting Vonshay, but she couldn't seem to help it.

Lie dropped his head in defeat.

The first few weeks after Vonshay returned, everything went O.k. Vickie tried hard to be a good mama, but eventually, she went back to her old ways. She stayed away from home most of the time. She hardly ever worked and she lost more and more weight. Vonshay wouldn't give her any money, so she started begging Vanessa or whoever else she could think of. When that failed, she searched for other ways to get money. She acted as if she were desperate.

Vickie found a part-time job and worked off and on. On one of the few days that she chose to work, a payday, Vickie called Vonshay at home. She sounded really excited about something. She went on to explain to Vonshay that she had all of the company's payroll checks in her possession. She was planning on going out and cashing them. She wanted Vonshay to tell her the best way to do it. She trusted her daughter's judgment, and she knew that she always thought things through. She was not impulsive like her mama.

Vonshay hit the ceiling. She could not believe that her mama was actually thinking of trying something so stupid. On top of thinking about it, she had the nerve to ask her to help. "Mama, you will go straight to jail!" Vonshay yelled into the receiver.

"Not if I take them to those little check cashing places," Vickie responded. She wanted Vonshay to know that she had actually thought about what she was doing.

"Don't you know that they have cameras and they ask for I.D. Besides, everyone in town knows you. If something goes wrong, they'll be pointing at you. It's not even worth it 'cause you can't get away with it.

"But it seems so easy. They sittin' right here on my desk."

"Mama, it ain't as easy as it looks. Please don't do it."

"You don't think I should?"

"No, Mama. Don't do it."

"All right, bye, " Vickie said with an attitude as she hung up. She was actually mad at Vonshay for telling her not to do it, but she had sense enough to trust her judgment.

Vonshay didn't see her mama for almost a week after their confrontation on the phone. Everyday she waited in vain for her mama to return home. Based on the way Vickie sounded when she talked about the checks, Vonshay was sure her mama wasn't thinking rationally. She was afraid that she would do or say the wrong thing and end up dead or in jail. Vickie had not been back to work since the day she called Vonshay. None of her friends had seen nor heard from her. She didn't associate much with them anymore because they didn't indulge in the same activities as she did.

Everyday someone was calling threatening to disconnect some type of services. Vonshay stalled them as best she could, but she had no way of paying them on the days she promised. She knew that Vickie had probably spent all of her money on drugs. She expected her to come home when the money ran out. On the fifth day, Vickie called.

"Hey baby," she said with sorrow in her voice.

"Mama where are you?" Vonshay yelled. "I've been worried sick."

"I'm at the hospital. They found me sittin' on the side of the levee by the river. I was gon' jump in so you wouldn't have to worry about me no more."

"What hospital are you at, Mama?"

"I'm at Ferguson General. They got me in this room with a bunch of other people. I got to go now cause ain't but one phone.

Vonshay was trying to stop Vickie from hanging up when she heard someone pick up another receiver and call her mama's name. Vonshay knew that voice. It was a lady named Janice. Everybody knew that Janice sold drugs. Vonshay was so mad that she threw the phone across the room. Her mama was gone almost a week, and then she had the nerve to call and lie about being in the hospital so Vonshay would feel sorry for her. "How low can you go?!" Vonshay yelled as she placed the telephone on the receiver.

When Vickie came home that night, Vonshay was already asleep, so she went to her room and did not come out for days. Vonshay checked on her periodically to make sure she was still alive. Each time she opened the door to her mother's room, she found her Vickie sitting and staring, sometimes with tears in her eyes. If she could have, Vickie would have stayed in her room forever. However, that was not possible. On the third day of her seclusion, she was forced out of her room by the loud banging of a persistent drug dealer she owed money. She had to warn Vonshay not to let him in because she didn't have money to pay them, and she didn't want the bill paid at her daughter's expense, which was the threat the dealer had made.

Two days after the debt with the dealer had been settled, Janice came by looking for Vickie. She wanted to settle her debt, as well.

"Is your mama home," Janice asked Vonshay.

"I thought she was at your house," Vonshay said sarcastically, holding the door to her home half closed.

"She was, but she left," said Janice.

"Well, she ain't been here," Vonshay lied. She had dealt with an angry drug dealer on Friday night, and she didn't feel like dealing with one on a Sunday morning. You need to be in church somewhere, she thought to herself.

"You know her sister Vanessa's number?"

"Yeah, why?"

"I need to talk to her about your mama. Will you call?"

"I'll call her, but she's probably not there. You know, most *decent* people go to church on Sunday, she said with a hint of sarcasm in her voice, as she smiled to herself. She went anxiously to get the cordless phone. She dialed her auntie's number and let Janice talk to her. She waited patiently for the outcome of the conversation.

Vonshay wanted Vanessa to know about her mama's drug problem, but she didn't want to be the one to tell her. She was glad that Janice did it for her. She knew that once Vanessa found out, she would take care of the situation. Her auntie had always had a way of keeping things in order. Vonshay was ecstatic when her auntie confronted her mama and even happier when she arrived at the door...

Even after re-evaluating her memories, Vonshay still could not pinpoint exactly what had gone wrong. Settling on the thought that it had been a combination of things, she said a prayer and eventually dozed off into a peaceful sleep. She had not slept so comfortably in months. Her mind was at rest knowing that her Mama's problem would be taken care of.

The next morning, the aroma of hickory-smoked bacon drifted through the air. The smell tingled Vonshay's nose and woke her from her deep sleep. Instinctively, she looked at her watch. It was eleven o'clock. "I wonder why they didn't wake me up?" she asked herself. "Well, I didn't wanna to go anyway," she said, as she changed sleeping positions.

The smell of the bacon would not let Vonshay rest in peace. It smelled like her favorite kind--slab bacon. Her aunt always bought plenty of it when she came home because she could not find any in Atlanta that was comparable in taste. Thinking she was home alone, she decided to get up and fix her own breakfast, since no one had bothered to awaken her. She eased out of bed and went in the bathroom to wash her face and brush her teeth. She put on a robe and some slippers and followed the hickory-smoked smell down the hall and into the kitchen. She was stunned when she walked in the kitchen and saw her mama and auntie sitting at the table and the bacon in the skillet.

"Good morning," she said interrupting the conversation.

"Good morning," they responded in unison.

"How'd you sleep last night?" Vanessa asked.

"All right I guess," she replied. "I thought y'all had left me. Weren't we supposed to leave at nine?"

"Yeah," Vickie said, "but since we don't have a definite time to be there, we decided to let you sleep. You want some breakfast? I know slab bacon is your favorite."

"That's what woke me up. What you got to go with it?"

"Whatever you want," Vickie said. She was thrilled to be cooking for her child again.

"I want some pancakes with Mrs. Butterworth's syrup, some scrambled eggs and some grits!" she exclaimed. It had been so long since her mama had cooked her breakfast that she asked for all of her favorites. She didn't know when she'd get the chance again.

They finished eating breakfast and cleaned up the kitchen. Vickie washed and Vanessa dried, just as they did when they were growing up. Vonshay took care of cleaning the table, the counter, and the stove. When everything was spic and span, they all went to get dressed.

Vanessa was the first to finish. She stopped by Vonshay's room to see if she needed anything. She didn't, so she went to Vickie's room next.

"You need any help packing?" she asked.

"Packing?" Vickie asked with a puzzled look on her face." I thought we were just going to check the place out."

"We decided that Charter would be the one, so we may as well make one trip do. You can just stay today."

"Today?! I'm not ready today! I have to take care of some things first."

"Stop making excuses. I'll take care of whatever it is. If I can't do it, it doesn't need to be done. Get your luggage out. I'll help you pack."

Vickie begged Vanessa to give her one more day. She refused. Vickie tried to come up with all kinds of excuses, but Vanessa wouldn't fall for any of them. Finally, Vickie took out her garment bag and put it on the bed. Vanessa began going through the closet and drawers. Vickie just sat on the side of the bed staring at her sister and crying softly.

Vonshay heard the sobbing. She hated to hear her mama cry. Whenever Vickie cried, she cried. It had been that way since she was an infant. Even though she was madder than she had ever been in her life, she still couldn't stand hearing her mama cry. She knew that going to get treatment was the best thing for her mama right now, but she didn't want to be away from her. She felt lonely already. She decided to call her daddy.

Vonshay hadn't told Andre' about what had been going on because she knew that he would want her to come back and live with him. She wanted to be there for Vickie. Sometimes she felt that she was the only reason her mama hadn't taken her own life. She didn't want her to be alone. Now that her mama was safe and was going to get help, she felt that she could confide in her daddy. She picked up the phone and dialed him at work. The switchboard operator gave her a hard time.

"Office of Human Services, how may I direct your call?" asked the lady with the tape recorder voice.

"Andre' Stevenson, please," Vonshay said in her most professional voice.

"May I have your case number?" she asked.

"I don't have one. Tell him this is Vonshay."

"Well, he only talks to people with assigned numbers," she smirked. "Would you like to leave a message?"

"Yes, will you tell him that his daughter called and to please leave my case number with you, so I can talk to him the next time I call."

"Oh, you're his daughter. Hold on," she said, sounding a little ashamed.

Andre' picked up the phone in seconds. "Hey baby, how's it going? I'm sorry about the mix-up. I told these people that when my child calls to come and get me. I was going to call you

71

this evening. I thought you would still be getting your beauty rest about now."

"Well, I'm getting ready to go to Jackson with Mama and TeeTee."

"Goin' shopping' for school clothes?"

"Unh-unh. We're going to take Mama to the hospital.

"What hospital? For what?" he asked.

"Charter. She's got a drug problem and she's going to get help."

"A drug problem! Your *mama*? How'd that happen?"

"When you left Daddy, she started using 'em more than when ya'll were together. She started usin' them everyday. Now, she can't stop."

"How long has this been going on? Is this why you wanted to stay with me?"

"Yeah. It's been goin' on for a while."

"Why didn't you tell me? Betta still, why did you go back?"

"I knew you would've been mad and gone off on Mama. Plus, she didn't need to be here by herself."

"I understand. Are you O.k.?

"Yeah."

"Well it's good that you're there for your mama. She really needs a lot of love and support right about now. How long will she be there? Are you coming back here?"

"I don't know how long it'll be, but TeeTee's gonna stay with me. I gotta go, Daddy. I just wanted to tell you what's goin' on."

"O.k. baby, take care. Call me when you get back and tell me how it goes. I love you. And tell your mama to hang in there and I love her too."

"Do you really, Daddy?" Vonshay asked excitedly.

"Yes."

"Well we love you, too. Bye."

"Bye."

Vonshay went to her mama's room when she finished talking to Andre'. Vickie was still crying. She walked over to her mama and hugged her. Don't cry Mama," she told her. "Everything'll be fine. I promise."

Vickie heard the unconditional love in her child's voice. She looked up and saw the tears in Vonshay's eyes. She immediately began to wipe them away. She did not want her daughter to feel any more hurt than she already had. She knew that she had to be strong for her child's sake, if not her own.

"Mama's O.k., baby," Vickie said, as she tried to make her face smile.

"Mama, I love you and Daddy says that he loves you too," Vonshay said.

"What?!" Vickie asked startled. "You told your daddy what's goin' on?"

"Yeah, Mama. I just talked to him. He's not mad. He says he understands and he wants you to be strong. Why didn't you want him to know?"

"It's not that. It's just that I wanted to tell him myself."

"Like you were really going to call him before we left."

"Contrary to what you think, me and your daddy are still friends. We talk about a lot of things, especially things that concern you."

"I already know that you tell him all my business, Mama, but that's O.k."

"I know it's O.k. now, since you tellin' him my business."

The two of them smiled at each other and burst into laughter.

Vanessa joined in as she put the last piece of clothing in Vickie's bag. Well, that about does it," she announced, after she pulled the zipper closed. "Are you girls about ready?"

"I guess so, "Vickie responded with a look of happiness overshadowed by pain.

"Well, what's the hold up? Let's go!" Vonshay laughed.

"Not before we pray," said Vanessa, reaching for their hands. After a brief moment of silence, she began to petition God...

"Father God, I ask that You will watch over us as we travel on the highway today. Protect us from hurt, harm and danger as You direct our path. Encamp Your angels around us that we may arrive safely and we give You the glory, the praise and the honor, in Your Son Jesus' name, Amen."

"That was quick," Vonshay mused, as they loosed one another's hands.

"Well, when you talk to Him all the time, You don't have to pray a long prayer," Vanessa informed her niece. "I'm just adding to the conversation we had earlier."

"If that's the way it works, I guess I need to talk to Him a little more often," Vickie sighed a she reached for her bags.

"Whenever you feel like talking He's there," Vanessa said.

Vonshay burst into song... "Jesus is on the main line...tell Him what you want...Oh..."

"Call Him up and tell Him what you want," they all chimed in as they headed out the door.

Chapter 5

The two-hour drive felt like two days. The closer they came to Jackson, the more nervous Vickie became. She tried not to be obvious, but by the time they reached the Jackson city limits, she was a nervous wreck. She could not sit still. Before she finished with one cigarette, she lit another one with trembling hands. Vanessa prayed that she would never be as dependent upon cigarettes as she was at that moment.

"I don't wanna go, Vanessa," Vickie said in a childish tone.

"Vickie, we've been through this before. You know that you need to go. It's the only way you can get better."

"I can get better all by myself. I don't need no white man in a white coat with a white attitude telling me how not to use drugs. All I've got to do is just stop."

Lie became excited by the thought of winning this battle.

"Well, if that's all it is to it, why haven't you done it yourself?"

Vickie was quiet because she knew she couldn't do it herself. She had tried too many times before. If she could do it, it never would have gone so far. She sat quietly with her head lowered. She hoped that Vanessa would get lost and not be able to find Charter Hospital. Unfortunately for her, this was not the case.

"This is it," Vanessa said as she pulled into the hospital's parking lot.

"It's cute. Now, let's go," Vickie retorted.

"Come on, Mama. Don't act like that," Vonshay said softly. "It can't be that bad."

Vickie slowly turned her head towards the window and looked out. The place looked more like a high school than a hospital. There were several buildings joined together by outdoor walkways. The facility sat perfectly centered on the beautifully landscaped property. A wide array of red and yellow flowers and shrubbery was planted everywhere, even around the full-grown magnolia trees that offered shade. There was even a tennis court and a jogging path. It looked much better than Vickie had ever imagined. Still, she didn't want to stay there. "I said it was cute, but that does not mean I want to make it my home," Vickie said in a flip tone of voice.

"Let's just go in and check it out," suggested Vanessa.

When Vanessa and Vonshay opened their car doors and stepped out, Vickie just sat there. Vonshay went and opened her mama's car door.

"And the children shall lead them," Vanessa whispered.

"Let's go in, Mama," she pleaded. "If it doesn't feel right to you and the program isn't set up good, I'll tell TeeTee to find somewhere else. All right?"

"All right," Vickie said reluctantly. She took her daughter's outreached hand and stepped out of the car.

The three of them walked into the building and stopped at the receptionist's desk. Vanessa asked for Leigh, the young lady she had spoken with on the phone. They were offered a seat and asked to wait. Fifteen minutes passed before a young white lady about thirty years old appeared and introduced herself to them. Both Vonshay and Vanessa looked at each other with a sigh of relief. They were glad to see her because Vickie had threatened to leave the hospital twenty-five times while they were waiting.

Leigh opened the door to her office and invited them in. Hand painted pictures of flowers and sunsets filled the walls. To create a comfortable setting for patients and their families, the front portion of the office was a sitting area with a couch and chairs. It also contained a coffee table and end tables that matched the large cherry wood desk at the rear of the office.

Leigh offered them a seat in the sitting area. Vanessa and Vonshay took the ends of the couch and Vickie sat in the middle. Leigh offered them coffee, but Vickie was the only one to accept the offer. She hoped that it would give her a chance to get away from others, but Leigh fixed the coffee for her. She sat trapped between her sister and daughter. She wanted to make a run for it, but she didn't have the energy. She probably wouldn't have made it past the door.

Leigh began to explain the chemical dependency program at Charter. All patients who entered the program were required to matriculate at the hospital for a minimum of thirty days. When those days were completed, staff doctors evaluated the patients and made recommendations about discharge, based on each patient's progress and participation in the program. Some patients were prepared to leave at that time; others were not. Some needed to slowly enter back into society. In these cases, they were placed in a group home with other recovering patients.

All of the patients were assigned personal doctors. Most of them were psychiatrists, but many were also practicing medical doctors. There were nurses on duty at the hospital twenty-four hours a day, and they were all registered nurses. The entire staff was aware of and experienced with chemically dependent patients. Some of them were recovering addicts themselves.

After giving the brief overview, Leigh asked if there were any questions. Concerned and afraid, Vonshay had several questions that she wanted answered. "What will she do all day?" she asked.

To answer the question, Leigh handed each of them a daily schedule for patients and went over it with them. The schedule was very structured. It included specific times and places for each entry. Among the entries were meals, doctor's visits, group meetings, free time, activity time, and bedtime. There were still questions that the schedule didn't answer for Vonshay.

"Can she have visitors?" she asked.

"Yes, there are several visiting days. There are also special days set aside for family only, which include activity sessions, counseling, and a gourmet meal. All of our patients look forward to Family Day. They really enjoy it.

"From this schedule, that doesn't look like much free time," Vanessa said.

"It's more than it appears to be," Leigh assured her. "What about you, Vickie?" she continued. "Do you have any questions about anything?"

Vickie hesitated before she spoke. "I'd like to know about the living arrangements," she said.

"Oh, we have beautiful rooms," Leigh said proudly. "We call them suites. Let me take you to see one. As a matter of fact, we'll just look around at everything."

They all stood and followed Leigh out the door. On the way to the residential area, they passed through the lobby where patients visit with family, friends, and each other. The area was huge with several couches, chairs, and tables. There were games, cards, pens, paper, books, and other activities on a corner table.

"Look Mama, they have Scattergories and Guesstures," Vonshay said, knowing her mama liked those games and trying to make her feel comfortable.

"I see," Vickie said, dryly. She had a lot more than games on her mind.

There was a patio area with lawn furniture and more games outside of the lobby doors. It could be seen through a large picture window, which also offered a full view of the garden, tennis courts, and miniature golf course. Next to the lobby was the eating area, a large dining room with cafeteria-style service. The patients had a variety of foods to choose from and the blended aroma of the food floated through the air.

"That food sure smells good," Vanessa said hoping for a response from Vickie. Her sister never replied.

Before they reached the rooms, Leigh showed them the meeting area. It was a long hallway full of doors and partitions. They stopped to look in one of the rooms. It was a large brightly colored open space filled with rows of chairs. Leigh explained that each of the rooms was set up according to the type of activities to take place in them. Some rooms were set up for lectures, some for group therapy, and other for family therapy. They walked down a few more halls and finally, Leigh stopped at a door to one of the suites.

Vickie was anxious to get inside. Everything she had seen so far had looked adequate, but the room would tell the story. She tried to hide her anxiety by making conversation. "This place sure is big," she commented. "It seemed like it took us forever to get here."

"Sure did," Vanessa and Vonshay said together. They were glad that she finally said something.

"It is kinda big," Leigh said. "We have a lot of things going on here." As she finished speaking, the lock clicked open and they went inside.

The room was a cross between a college dorm room and a hotel room and there were two full-sized beds with matching comforters. A nightstand with a small lamp and an alarm clock stood beside each. There were lamps and clocks on each stand. The dresser with a larger mirror stretched between two mid-sized closets. At the back of the room leading to the bathroom were double vanities. The room was decorated with natural colors and abstract paintings were used to accentuate the color scheme.

The room appealed to Vickie. It was nice and clean with a lot of space. She hated to be cooped up. The only thing that she disliked was the fact that the room was set up to accommodate two people. "From the way things are set up, I won't be having my own room, will I?" she asked Leigh.

"I'm afraid not. We prefer that patients share rooms. When you're going through drug rehabilitation you often get lonely and depressed. We think its best to always have someone around that can share your experiences."

"Well, who will be my roommate?" Vickie asked. When she saw the smiles on Vanessa and Vonshay's faces, she realized that she had just committed herself to staying. "That is, if I decide to stay," she added for clarification. She could see the smiles quickly disappear.

"Her name is Carol," Leigh said, as if she knew that Vickie would stay. "I'll introduce the two of you after we talk a little more. Let's go back to my office."

This time Leigh directed them to the area of the office that contained her desk and some chairs. "So, what do you think, Vickie?" she asked.

"It's O.k." Vickie replied.

"Would you like to be a part of our program here?"

Before answering, Vickie looked at Vonshay and Vanessa. Both of them had pleading in their eyes. She turned back to Leigh and said, "It seems like you have a good program here." There was short pause. " I'd like to be a part of it."

Vonshay and Vanessa could feel tremendous weights being lifted off of their hearts and replaced with joy, the kind of joy that they could not hide. It shone brightly through their smiles of relief and approval. Vickie even smiled herself, although tears were forming in her eyes.

"That's great!" Leigh said, clapping her hands. "We're glad to have you. We need to fill out a few papers and then we can get you started."

Vanessa had already handled the financial portion of the arrangements before she left Atlanta, so filling out the papers did not take long. With Vonshay jogging her memory, Vickie responded honestly to the questions she was asked. She was embarrassed to answer a few questions in front of her child and her sister because they pertained to her drug habits. Seeing her discomfort, Leigh decided to skip the questions and ask them at another time. After all of the paperwork was completed, they went to the car to get Vickie's things.

While gathering her belongings, Vickie realized the seriousness of what she was about to do. It frightened her and she doubted and questioned her decision to stay. "I don't want y'all to leave. I don't wanna stay here," she said to her child and her sister.

"I know, baby, but you need to," Vanessa responded with tears forming in her eyes. She didn't want to leave her sister, but she knew that it was best.

"What I need is to be with my baby," she said.

"Mama," Vonshay said softly, "I need you with me healthy. You're sick right now. If you came home with me, it wouldn't really be you. It would be that sick person. Stay here Mama, so I can have the *real* you back," Vonshay begged, trying to hold back her tears.

"O.k. baby," Vickie said, seeing the sincerity in her daughter's eyes. "I know I need to be here and Mama's sorry she hurt you. Vanessa, I'm sorry I disappointed you. I'm the oldest and you set a better example than me."

She reached out to both of them. As they all hugged, tears flowed freely from every eye. After several minutes of crying, they began to laugh at and with one another. They were laughing at the fact that they had been crybabies when they were little and had never out-grown it. They were still crying at the drop of a hat.

Truth shed tears of joy as Lie turned and walked away.

Leigh waited on them at the hospital's entrance while they went to get everything out of the car. She was touched by what she saw. Many of the new patients and their families could not get past their anger about an addiction to show their love for one another. Unconditional love made the healing process so much easier for all parties involved, the people with the problem and their loved ones. Most people didn't realize that an addiction is not just the addict's problem, but becomes the problem of everybody who's around that person as well. It was obvious to Leigh that these ladies realized this. She was glad because the relationship they shared would enhance Vickie's recovery.

Back inside, they went to the room that Vickie was assigned. Leigh knocked and was invited in. Vickie's new roommate, Carol, was sitting on the bed when they entered. The first thing Vickie noticed was that Carol was white. Ugh, she thought, a white roommate, too! Leigh made the introductions and they all exchanged pleasantries.

"I hope you like it here," Carol said. "I'm sure we'll get along fine. I'm going down to the recreation room so you guys can have some privacy. When your family leaves, you can come and join me. I'll show you around and give you an update on what's going on in here."

"I'll do that," Vickie said pleasantly as Carol left. She really doubted that she would join her. She didn't have anything against white people; she just stayed out of their way. She claimed that she didn't like hanging out with them because they acted so silly. The truth be told, she was really afraid of their power. It had been used against her so many times. She hoped that Carol wouldn't take it personally.

After Carol excused herself, Leigh suggested that Vickie unpack and get her things settled in. Vonshay volunteered to do it for her. As she removed the toiletries, Leigh noticed a razor and glass bottles that contained perfume and facial care products. She informed them that patients could not have razors because they were dangerous. She also told them that everything needed to be in plastic containers and not glass ones. She said that the policy helped to prevent the patients from having unnecessary accidents.

Vanessa saw the disappointment in her sister's eyes. "Honey, I'll run down to the mall and replace everything," she told her.

"Thanks, Vanessa, but some things just don't come in anything but glass bottles, like my perfume."

"Girl, please. The perfume may not be in anything but bottles, but all of the shower gels, lotions, soaps and powders are not in glass. By the time you use all of them, you won't even need the perfume," she said jokingly, trying to cheer Vickie up.

"I know, but I don't want you goin' out and spendin' all your money on me. You've already done more than enough," she said in a pitiful voice.

"Don't worry about that. I can count my money better than you. That's what sisters are for," she said with a broad smile. She wanted nothing more than to make her sister feel happy. She was proud that she had made the choice to get some help and she wanted her to know that she supported her one hundred percent.

"Your first meeting is in a little while," Leigh informed Vickie. The meeting wasn't really mandatory, but Leigh knew that the longer the family was around, the harder it was for the new patient to adjust.

"Oh really?" Vickie asked. "I have to go to a meeting already? I just got here."

"I know," Leigh explained. "We want to get things rolling. You know the sooner you start the sooner you'll finish. And by the way, we also have special group sessions for family members and loved ones," she said, directing her attention to Vanessa and Vonshay. "You're welcome to attend, if you'd like. We really encourage it because it's helpful to everyone."

"That's good," Vanessa said. "Vonshay and I will try to make a few sessions."

"I'm going to go check on some things and I'll be back," said Leigh.

"O.k." Vanessa replied, glad that Leigh was leaving. "Vickie, I'm going to run up to the mall and replace this stuff. Is there anything else you need from there? Got your toothbrush?" Vanessa asked her. She knew that Vickie had a toothbrush with her. It was just something she said to make Vickie smile. When they were younger, Vickie would always leave her toothbrush at home when they stayed overnight somewhere. Vickie remembered and cracked a smile. It wasn't as big as Vanessa expected, so she decided to change the subject. "Vonshay are you going with me?" she asked.

"No, I'll stay here with Mama," she answered.

"No baby. You go with your auntie. Mama'll be all right. I'm going to get myself ready for the meeting.'

"O.k." Vonshay said. Although she wanted to spend some more time with her mama, she didn't argue. She left with Vanessa.

As soon as they walked out of the room Vickie began to cry. Everyone had left her. The only reason she told Vonshay to go was because she didn't want her to feel that she had to be with her. She really wanted her to stay, so she could hug her and

83

kiss her and assure her that everything would be all right. They each wanted to spend that time together, but neither wanted to impose on the other, so both of them missed out on what was sure to have been a beautiful Kodak moment.

Vanessa and Vonshay drove to a nearby Wal Mart. They excitedly replaced everything Vickie needed and bought other things she didn't need. They knew that the hospital would never feel like home, but they wanted to make her stay as comfortable as possible. They rushed back to the hospital to give her the care package. They never discussed their shared excitement, but they both knew that their feelings were mutual.

As soon as they walked into the waiting room, they ran into Leigh. She smiled when she saw the big purple gift bag that Vonshay was carrying. "Looks like you did more than replace a few things," she told them.

"Well, we saw some other things she might need, too," Vanessa said.

"If you give me the bag, I'll get everything to her. I think it'll be best if she doesn't see you before you leave," Leigh suggested.

"Why?" Vonshay asked with anger and confusion in her voice.

"When you all left, I went to check on your mother. I found her sitting on the bed crying. You had only gone to the store and she was grieving as if she were never going to see you again. I know it'll be worse if she sees you before you go back home. I don't want her to go through that again so soon. It's not good for her."

"But we can't just leave without telling her 'bye'! Then she'll think that we don't care, that we just dumped her here," Vonshay responded.

Leigh looked to Vanessa for help, but didn't get any. Vanessa felt the same way Vonshay did. She knew that as an adult, she was supposed to understand and to calm Vonshay down, but she didn't. She let her continue, amazed by her spunk.

"Where is she?" Vonshay demanded.

"She's talking to Carol right now. She's helping her to calm down."

"All she needs to calm down is to see us," Vonshay insisted.

"That will calm her for a while, but once you're gone she'll be worse."

"Well, that's when you can do your job. Right now I want to see my mama."

"Please, Vonshay. I know about these things and I'm only trying to do what's best for your mother. Let me give her the things and you go on home," Leigh pleaded.

Vanessa finally broke her silence. She gave up her emotional feelings and was guided by thoughts of her sister's well being. "Vonshay, Leigh is right," she said. "I want to see your mama too, but we would all be upset. Remember what happened at the car when we went to get her bags? You know it'll be worse, don't you?"

"Yes," Vonshay said. "But I want to see her."

"Honey, we have to think about what your mama needs," Vanessa interjected. "Feeling sorry for herself and crying all night is not it. We both know that that's what she'll do if we go in to say 'bye'. Why don't we give her the cards we bought and put a special note in each one? That way she'll know that we care about her a lot."

Vonshay was quiet for a few minutes. She took time to think about what her aunt and Leigh had said. She wanted to do what was best for her mama, but doing the right thing isn't easy when it hurts. She began fumbling around in the shopping bag and came out with two greeting cards. Vanessa smiled as Vonshay handed her a card to sign. She knew that her niece was going to do things her way and she was glad.

After they personalized their cards, they gave them and the shopping bag to Leigh. Vanessa also gave her twenty-five dollars for Vickie, which was the maximum amount of money patients could have.

"Put the money in your card and I guarantee that I'll give her everything right away," Leigh assured them, seeing that

Vonshay still wasn't totally convinced that she was doing the right thing.

Vanessa reached for Leigh's hand. Giving it a firm shake, she said, "Thank you."

"You're welcome. Drive carefully and call me about any questions or concerns," Leigh said, releasing Vanessa's hand and reaching for Vonshay's.

" Don't worry about your mother; she'll be fine," she promised Vonshay as she gently dropped her hand.

Vanessa and Vonshay smiled slightly and then turned and walked slowly to the car. They sat in silence a few moments, each of them saying a personal silent prayer. When Vanessa felt the peace of God resting upon her, she cranked the car and headed to the highway. They both felt as if they were leaving a piece of their hearts behind.

Chapter 6

"It sure is taking them a long time," Vickie said to Carol. She was tired of talking to her, even though Carol was doing most of the talking. She just wanted to see her sister and her daughter again before they went back to Ferguson. She knew that Leigh probably wouldn't call her out of the meeting to see them, so she was hoping that they would hurry on back.

When there was a knock at the door, Vickie said, "come in." She was sure that it was Vanessa and Vonshay. To her surprise, Leigh appeared wearing a big smile. Vickie waited a few seconds to give her family a chance to come in. When they didn't, she peeped out of the door. "Where are they?" Vickie wanted to know.

"Who?" Leigh asked, as if she didn't know.

"My daughter and my sister, who else?" she demanded, sensing that she was not going to like what she was about to hear.

"They're gone but they left something for you," Leigh said with a big smile. "Look at the size of this bag."

"Why didn't they bring it to me themselves? Were they that glad to get rid of me? I should have known that little crying was a front anyway."

"No, it wasn't anything like that. Believe me, they wanted to give it to you themselves."

"Well, why didn't they?"

" I didn't think it would be a good idea."

"You didn't think it would be a good idea. Who died and left you in charge of my life?" Not giving Leigh a chance to answer, Vickie continued. "How can *you* tell my family they can't see me. Is this some kind of prison or somethin'? I don't believe this!!"

Leigh had no idea that Vickie would respond this way. "Just let me explain, Vickie," she pleaded.

"Ain't nothin' to explain," Vickie screamed.

"Yes it is. I want you to know why I thought it would be better."

"Yeah. I would like to know how you came up with some bull like that," Vickie said with an expression of disbelief.

"Well, you know how upset you were when they left going to the mall. I didn't want you to get that upset again."

"Oh, so you did this for me. You thought it would keep me from being upset. So what do you call this?" she yelled loudly. "Do I look calm to you?"

Leigh's face saddened as she watched Vickie pace the floor. Her intentions had been positive, but the results had turned out to be negative.

"No, I'm not calm," yelled Vickie. "I'm pissed. That's past upset. As a matter of fact, I'm pissed off to the highest level of pissocity. So you see, your little plan not to upset me didn't work. It might work for these other fools 'round here, but not me. You can't control me!"

"But crack can!" Leigh retorted, tired of being treated like the bad guy. Her face cringed when she realized what her statement had provoked.

The slap came unexpectedly. Leigh stood motionless, as she felt the blood that rushed to her face when Vickie slapped her, trying to find its way back to its rightful place. She knew that Vickie was mad, but the situation had gotten out of control. There was only so much that she was going to take. She had every intention of helping Vickie, and she was not going to let her lay a guilt trip on her for doing her job. She never lifted a hand to strike back at Vickie. She knew that the woman was sick. It wasn't the first time a patient raised a hand to her, although it was the first time she was actually hit. "Did that make you feel any better?" she asked calmly.

Vickie screamed, "Does it look like it?" She shook her hand to try and stop the stinging she felt from the impact of it meeting the left side of Leigh's face. She didn't care that the woman's face was now flushed. She knew for herself that she had a problem, and she didn't need some holier than thou white woman throwing it up in her face.

"Well, now that you feel better, why don't you put all of your nice new things away so you can go to your meeting," Leigh said calmly.

Vickie just stared at Leigh, with eyes full of rage.

Carol, who had been quiet during the entire incident, finally spoke. "You can go on Leigh. Vickie and I will be down in a few." She looked at Leigh with eyes that said, "Get out!"

"O.k., I'll see you shortly," Leigh sighed, acknowledging that she had gotten the message. She left Carol and Vickie's room and went to her office.

"Girl, you really told her something," Carol said excitedly. She did the same thing to me my first day here, but I didn't have the nerve to hit her, even though I really wanted to. You just did what a lot of us around here wanted to do. How does it feel?"

Vickie was putting her new things away. She couldn't believe that Vanessa had gotten so much stuff. A lot of it she didn't even need. She wanted to enjoy this times, but Carol wouldn't give her a moment's peace. She finally answered, "It felt good at the time, but now I feel stupid. I didn't have any business hittin' that woman 'cause I didn't like what she said. Whether I want to admit it or not, she was telling the truth."

"Yeah, the truth does hurt sometimes. We just have to learn to deal with it. The bad part is we have to deal with it forever."

"Forever? Honey, once I get out of here, this will all be behind me," Vickie boasted.

"I hate to tell you, but it's not that simple. You're going to have this problem the rest of your life. You've just got to learn how to control it. If you use drugs once, you'll use them again.

You'll understand a little better once you get into the program. Let's go on down to this meeting before Miss Leigh comes looking for us."

"O.k." Vickie said, and they left.

When they walked into the meeting, it was already in progress and there was a man standing at the podium speaking. Vickie was glad that no one turned around to stare when they entered in. She hated for people to do that, but she had been guilty of it herself. She and Carol took a seat at the back and listened to the white male speaker describe his experiences with alcohol. Vickie didn't understand why an alcoholics meeting was important for her to attend when she wasn't an alcoholic. She didn't find out until after the meeting that the recovery programs for alcohol and drug addictions were very similar.

She took her attention away from the speaker and scanned the room. It's more Whites than Blacks here, she told herself. Out of the twenty-five people, only five are Black, including me. I wonder why there are no Black hospitals like Charter. I know for a fact that White people are not the only ones who need help with drug and alcohol addictions. By myself, I can name enough Black people in Ferguson with drug problems to fill up a place like this. If I add those with drinking problems to the list, Ferguson would need two hospitals. One wouldn't be enough to get the job done.

Ferguson had a chemical dependency program, but Whites managed it. It was assigned the smallest section in the local hospital from which to operate. The hospital board didn't give the program much funding, so the patients (the majority of whom were Black) were given very little attention and support. Most of the patients were people who were given ultimatums. They had to either get some help for their problems or lose their children and/or their jobs. Because they were forced into treatment, many went in with negative attitudes, stayed the required amount of time, and went back to doing the same things they did before they checked in.

When Vickie heard the applause, she joined in. The man had finished talking and a Black man was walked towards the front of the room. When he stood facing the patients, Vickie saw

90

that he was an average looking man. He looked to be about forty years old. He was not what a woman would call gorgeous, nor was he what she might call ugly. If Vickie had seen him in the grocery store, she would have noticed him, but she would not have stopped to do a double take.

He was not tall and fine, but he was of an average height with a medium built body. He was neither too big nor too small. She noticed how well he dressed and how perfectly his clothes fit. They fit as if his body were made for the clothes, instead of the clothes being made for his body. He wore a pair of navy slacks with a long sleeved striped oxford shirt and a burgundy tie. Somehow he made an average combination look exotic.

When the man began to talk, his voice captured Vickie ears. It was neither light nor heavy, but it had a soothing sound to it. She wanted him to keep talking. "Let's join hands and recite our creed," he said. Vickie joined hands with Carol and another man and listened as everyone spoke in unison. When they finished, he said, "Keep it simple."

The sound of the words he spoke captivated Vickie with their rhythmic flow. She stood waiting for more. Carol nudged her and told her that it was time for dinner. She slowly came out of the trance, and they headed for the cafeteria.

As they were leaving, Carol stopped to talk with a friend. She introduced Vickie, but Vickie did not partake in the conversation. She watched the average man with the not so average voice. She had never seen a man who looked so average, sound so unique. She pondered this so deeply that she didn't realize that the man stood right in front of her.

"I don't believe we've met," he said cheerfully.

A few seconds passed before Vickie was conscious of his presence and deciphered what he had said. "I don't believe we have," she responded. "My name is Victoria." She hated that name. "Please call me Vickie," she added quickly.

"Well hello, Vickie. I'm Dr. Winters," he announced.

He's a doctor, she thought.

"I'll be your doctor while you're here at Charter. I want to sit and talk to you as soon as possible. Also, I need to run a few tests. How about after dinner?" he suggested.

"That'll be fine," Vickie managed to say.

"Well, I'll see you in a few. My office is Room 244. Come as soon as you can," he said as he walked away.

"I will," she said. "I will."

When Carol finished talking, she came over and snapped her fingers in front of Vickie's face. The popping sound brought her out of her daze. They continued for the cafeteria. By talking after the meeting, they had missed the crowd. They were able to move quickly through the line, and they found a good table with a view of the garden.

"What's the hurry?" Carol asked Vickie. Her roommate ate so fast that she almost choked on her food. "The food is good, but not *that* good."

"I have an appointment with my doctor after dinner," she told her.

"Who'd they give you?"

"Dr. Winters."

"I hear he's one of the best ones here. He's a psychiatrist and a medical doctor."

"Oh really?" Well I hope he's as good as his resume'. I'm going to check him out now. See you back at the room."

"O.k. Bye."

"Bye," Vickie said, almost running out of the door. She stopped by her room to brush her teeth and fluff her hair. Then she headed for 244. She was apprehensive because she did not know what to expect, but she was thrilled because her doctor was Black.

She knocked on the door, and the doctor invited her in and offered her a seat. "I'll be with you in just a minute," he told her. "I have to finish signing these papers."

"No problem," she said as she looked around the room. She was stunned by what she saw. His office was large and impressive. Several medical licenses and awards hung neatly on the walls behind his oak desk. The plush burgundy leather chair that he sat in matched the two chairs in front of his desk and the couch and the chaise lounge in the sitting area, where paintings by Black artists hung. For the room's splendor, the only word she could come up with to describe the office was average. Just like the man it belonged to, the office was average, but unique.

"Finished," he gasped, as he looked up from the paper and directly at Vickie. "Now young lady, what are you doing in a place like this?"

"I'm still trying to figure that out," she said seriously. "I was hoping that maybe you could tell me. Isn't that what you get paid for?"

Both of them laughed lightly.

"I don't know either, but maybe between the two of us, we can figure something out." He totally ignored her last remark.

"Sounds good to me," she replied. She was so glad that they had given her a Black doctor, especially one who didn't treat her like she was less than him. She knew a lot of Black doctors who had forgotten that they were Black when they got M.D. behind their names. This man had two medical degrees, and he was still down to earth. She could appreciate that.

Dr. Winters asked Vickie some of the same questions that she did not feel comfortable answering in front of Vanessa and Vonshay. She figured that Leigh had told him to ask her, since she was probably mad with her now and could care less about her answers. For some reason, she still did not want to answer the questions. Nobody was there except her and Dr. Winters, but she didn't want to discuss her business with him. Noticing how uncomfortable she was, he told her that they would continue the conversation later and that the only thing he needed her to do before she left was to give him a urine sample. Reluctantly, she took the small plastic cup and went to the bathroom.

I don't understand why they give you such small cups, she thought. If this were the only space people needed to use the bathroom, then the toilet wouldn't be so big. I'll turn on the faucet so some water can run. Maybe the sound will help me because I don't really have to use the bathroom now. Well, it worked. Now all I have to do is get it in the cup. That might be hard, since I'm not equipped to aim it where I want it to go.

Well, half a cup should be enough for him to do what he has to. That's all I can give him right now.

Vickie came out of the bathroom and gave the urine sample to the doctor. Then, she went up to her room. She had put the rest of her things away when she noticed the two envelopes at the bottom of the bag. She reached in and pulled them out. Both of them were addressed to her. She could tell by the handwriting that one was from her daughter and the other was from her sister. She wasn't sure which one to open first. She decided to open Vanessa's and to save Vonshay's for last.

Vanessa's card was in a beige envelope. Its cover was a copy of a painting entitled *Sisters* by V. Hall, a new Black artist. The picture included two Black women, one standing behind the other. The sister standing behind had her arms on the other's shoulder in a comforting manner. A person looking closely could see the small tear drops on both of their cheeks.

This is just like Vanessa, she thought. She probably went all over town to find this one card. She always buys cards with Black figures or no figures at all. A card can say everything she wants it to say, but she won't buy it if anything on it symbolizes Whiteness. That girl knows she can make buying a card a chore, but that's my sister. She's always liked giving out cards for special occasions and sometimes just for no reason at all. She made cards a family tradition.

Vickie kicked off her shoes and made herself comfortable on the soft well-made bed. When she opened the card the money fell out. She smiled and proceeded to read the print.

> *Sister I am here for you. To give you whatever you need.*
> *It doesn't matter whether times are happy or sad,*
> *Whether you need loud laughter or silent tears,*
> *Whether you need space around you or a shadow over you,*
> *Whether you need an ear to listen to you or a mouth to speak for you.*

94

Whatever you need, I will give you.
With love in my heart and joy in my soul.

The card was signed, "Need I say more? Love, Vanessa".

Naturally, Vickie was crying by the time she finished reading the card. She knew that she would cry when she read Vonshay's card, knowing what she had put her only child through, but she didn't expect Vanessa's card to make her cry. Her sister's cards usually had a touch of humor. They were so seriously funny that they made you laugh to keep from crying. This one was totally different. It caught Vickie off guard and forced her to see the seriousness of her situation.

She figured that she might as well read Vonshay's card then, too, since she was already crying. She took the card out of its pink envelope. The cover displayed a beautifully colored rainbow background. Just looking at the cover, Vickie knew that she would be a basket case by the time she finished reading. Everything her child gave her was special to her. She was happy to be a mama and thrilled to know that her child cared enough to give her gifts. Every time she got anything from Vonshay, she cried. Getting something from her after all that she had done was even more heart warming. She cried before she even read the words.

Anxious to find out how her daughter was feeling about the current situation, she started to read.

Mama, I love you because. . .
You cared for me when I was a baby,
And I could not care for myself.
You played with me when I was a toddler,
And I had no friends of my own.
You took me to school for knowledge,
And I longed for you as you did for me.
You gave me responsibility when I was a teen,
And I can now take care of myself.
Though in each stage of my life
You gave me a special gift,

95

The most precious gift you gave throughout,
Was the gift of a Mama's love.

By the time Vickie finished reading the cover of the card, her eyes were overflowing with tears. She didn't think she could take reading the inside, but she had to. She opened the card to read and could not see the words clearly. Her vision was blurred from tears. She picked up a Kleenex, dried her eyes, and continued to read.

A mama's love is special.
It's like no other love you'll find.
It's there when you achieve.
It's there when you stumble.
It's always there.
I know that I am blessed,
To have a mama like you.
This card is to show and tell you,
That I appreciate all that you do!

Vonshay had written a note that read, "Mama be strong and get better. I miss you already! I love you a bushel and a peck and a hug around the neck. Love, Vonshay".

Vickie's tears overflowed. This time she didn't bother to wipe them away. She continued to cry as she thought about her life. She dwelled more on the bad times than the good because the bad times were what caused her to end up at Charter. She stretched her frail slender body across the bed and rocked from side. The pillow soaked up the tears that she shed like a sponge taking in water.

Carol walked into the room and saw Vickie crying with the two cards next to her. She walked over to the bed, which was now ragged from Vickie's movement, and tried to comfort Vickie by patting her back. She told her not to worry and to be thankful that she had someone who cared about her. Carol didn't. She knew what being alone was like. Both her parents were dead and she had no siblings, no husband, no children. That was alone.

Vickie saw the loneliness in Carol's eyes. Her mama had often told her, "There is always someone else out there who is a lot worse off than you. Be thankful for what you have." Hearing Carol describe how it felt to be alone caused Vickie to appreciate that she had a daughter, a sister, and even an ex-husband. She ended up comforting Carol, although Carol had intended to comfort her.

Vickie did not go to the recreation room that night. Her eyes were so puffy and red from crying that she did not want to be seen. She took a shower, put her nightgown on, and read a book that Vanessa placed in her bag. She couldn't remember the last time she had actually sat down to read. She enjoyed reading contemporary novels by Black women writers. Sisters had some serious stories to tell, and she couldn't wait to see what this sister had to say. After about an hour and a half of reading, Vickie went to sleep.

The next morning, she woke up around seven o'clock. Carol was already up and getting dressed. "Why so early?" Vickie asked.

"Breakfast is from seven to eight. You better get ready yourself," Carol told her.

"All right, " Vickie said, watching her closely. She was very stunned by the outfit Carol wore. It was a pair of tan linen pants with a white tank top and an oversized white linen shirt. Pretty good for a white girl, she thought.

Vickie got up and dressed. She couldn't let this white woman out dress her. It was her first full day, and she wanted to look cute. While in the shower, she went over her wardrobe in her mind and decided on the orange linen dress that Vonshay had packed for her because it enhanced her complexion. She slipped on brown leather sandals with a slight wedged heel that her daughter insisted she wear with the dress. Then she put on make-up, something she hadn't taken the time to do in a while. She fluffed her hair and looked herself over in the mirror. She hadn't looked that good in ages. She smiled and winked at herself in the full-length mirror that hung on the back of the door. When she finished admiring herself, they left for breakfast.

97

Vickie was finished eating and sipping on a cup of steaming hot coffee when she noticed the average, but unique, Dr. Winters enter the dining area. He stopped at several tables to greet both patients and staff. To Vickie's surprise, he stopped at her table and said that he wanted to see her when she was finished.

"I'm finished now," she said.

"Then come along," he said cheerfully. He led the way to his office and Vickie followed. Upon entering the office, he asked his assistant to hold all of his calls.

Uh-oh, Vickie thought. He wants some answers this morning. I wonder if I should I tell him what he wants to know?

"Don't tell!" *Lie* whispered. "Don't tell!"

Vickie found out that she didn't have to tell him anything. Her urine test had done all of the talking. "Vickie," Dr. Winters began after they were seated, "based on the amount of drugs in your body, you could be high into the next week without even taking another hit. I want to talk to the *real* Vickie and not the Vickie that the drugs have created. In order for me to do that, I'm going to admit you to the detoxification unit to cleanse your system of drugs. He paused to give Vickie a chance to respond. When she said nothing, he continued. "Now the hospital's detoxification unit is not a fun place to be. I can promise you that you won't like it, but you don't have a choice in the matter. I've already made the decision—you're going to the unit!"

Chapter 7

"You want something to eat?" Vanessa asked Vonshay when they entered Ferguson city limits in silence. Her niece had not spoken two words the entire trip home. She did not want to force a conversation, so she didn't pressure her. She wanted to give her time to think.

"No, I'm not hungry," Vonshay answered.

"Girl, you need to eat. Pops and potato chips won't get it. I'll make us a couple of sandwiches when we get home. Just something to put in your stomach so you won't die of malnutrition on me."

"O.k.," Vonshay chuckled, " but we'll have to stop at the store 'cause we don't have anything at the house."

"No problem," Vanessa said, swerving the car into the Super Foods parking lot.

Super Foods was the main grocery store in town. You could never go in without running into somebody you knew. It was totally impossible. Since Vanessa hadn't had a chance to see anybody, she figured it was as good a time as any to let everybody know that she was in town. All she had to do was see one person she knew, and the word would spread like wildfire via the local rumor mill.

Everybody in town knew everybody else's business, and when they didn't know it, they gave them some. By the time

Vanessa closed her eyes that night, five different stories about why she was there, when she got there, and how long she would be there would be circulating. If some of the stories told in Ferguson were ever put in print, lawyers would have a field day filing suits for libel and slander.

Vanessa decided to stock up on groceries instead of just picking up a few items. Vonshay pushed the basket as they strolled down each and every aisle like they were touring a museum. Actually, Vanessa preferred walking down each aisle and leaving the basket on the end aisle while she picked up what she wanted. Vonshay, on the other hand, wanted to examine every product the store had to offer and compare prices, so Vanessa let her do it her way.

The child acted as if she had never been grocery shopping before. Vanessa could tell it was something that she missed so she let her put everything she wanted in the basket, plus items she had never even tried.

Vonshay was so into shopping that she paid little attention to everything else, not even the basket that she hit. The crash of the two metal carts startled Vanessa. When she turned towards the sound, she focused her attention on the man who stood next to the basket. He turned from the shelf to investigate, and when his eyes landed on Vanessa, he scanned her body from head to toe to head. He didn't even notice Vonshay.

"Talk about running into somebody! Vanessa Morgan. Or have you gotten married on me and changed your name?" the man asked jokingly, yet seriously.

"Nope, it's still Morgan. And what about you Mr. Derrick Davis? I know somebody around here has snatched you up," she said, admiring the firmness of his body and noticing that he always dressed well whenever she ran into him.

"Girl please, I'm still waiting on you. Give me a hug!"

"Yeah right," Vanessa said with a big smile as she wrapped her arms around him. Derrick had been telling her that same story for years. She knew that he liked her, and she liked him but the timing never seemed right. When she was available, he was involved and vice versa. Still, in the last few years just seeing him affected her in a way she couldn't explain. He had charisma. He never put forth any effort to be noticed; people noticed him automatically. His walk, his talk, and his appeal came as naturally to him as smiles came to her, whenever she saw him.

"I'm serious. You know that I've always been in love with you. Are you still kicking it with..." he began.

"No," Vanessa interrupted before he could finish. She did not want any thoughts of him to enter her mind. It had taken her too long to clear them out. Some serious fasting and praying was required to get out of that relationship. She thanked God for her deliverance because she didn't have the strength to do it on her own. That man had given her the true blues.

Vanessa loved the blues, but for entertainment purposes only. She did not want them to be a part of her personal life. Before the break-up with her ex, she could not truly relate to the song "You've Got to Hurt Before You Heal" by Bobby Bland. During the break-up it became her personal anthem. She learned all too well what the singer meant when he crooned,

> *When you lose the one you love, your heart goes through changes.*
> *Especially, when the sweet memories, still hold their thrill.*
> *You never know, how long the wound will take to heal,*
> *It might take months, could take years.*
> *But that's the way love works; you've got to hurt, before you heal.*
>
> *Just when you think, the pain is all gone.*
> *Don't fool yourself, 'cause here's the deal,*
> *That's the way love works, you've got to hurt, before you heal.*
>
> *You're gonna cry, oh, you're gonna cry*
> *And when the tears, they may stop falling down your face,*
> *But they still fall down your heart.*

You never know, how long the wound will take to heal,
Might take months, could take years,
But that's the way love works; you've got to hurt before
you heal.

She had learned her lesson the hard way. She had hurt and she had healed, but she did not want to be reminded of the pain that the process had entailed. She had promised God that if He gave her the strength to a walk way, she would never step out of His will again.

"I never thought I'd see the day," Derrick said showing all of his straight white teeth. "But I'm glad I did. How long will you be in town? Maybe we can get together before you leave."

"I'll be here for quite some time. At least a few months."

"Oh girl, my heart can't take it. Why don't we go out this weekend and have a few drinks. We can hang out like we did back in the day."

"O.k. Let's do that," she said, blushing inside and out. Vanessa didn't go out and drink like she did back in the day because the more time she spent getting to know God, the less desirable drinking, smoking, and partying were to her. Nevertheless, she didn't believe that being saved meant being stiff-necked and boring. She saw nothing wrong with hanging out with an old friend.

"Same place, same number, right?"

"Right."

"I'll give you a call. It was a good, I mean, really good seeing you. Take care."

"You take care, too," Vonshay said giggling.

Derrick looked in her direction. "Vonshay? Girl, I didn't even see you. I'm sorry. How are you?"

"I'm fine," she said.

"I'll see you later," Vanessa said as he walked away. She watched his tall slender body disappear down the aisle.

Well, well, well. He still likes me, she thought. This might be interesting. I'm not dating anybody right now, and he's probably one of the few people around here that's worth any of my time. And, I already know him and I really like him. Hanging out with him will be something to do in this boring place, and it just might turn out to be more than that. He could be my husband and the father of my child. Naaaa. I think that's pushing a little too far too fast. I'll just see what happens.

"Oooooo, TeeTee!" Vonshay exclaimed. "I knew he liked you. He wasn't just comin' by the house to visit everybody like he always said he was. Now that I think about it, he didn't come 'til you were at home. Do you like him?"

"I don't know, girl. He's a good friend of mine."

"But he wants to be more," Vonshay giggled. She was tickled to death to see a man trying to holla (as her generation put it) at her auntie.

"You got everything you want?" Vanessa asked, trying to change the subject.

"Yeah, I got everything I want, but Derrick doesn't have everything he wants yet. He won't have that until he has you." She burst into a loud laughter. She could not stop laughing. She laughed so hard, she cried.

Vonshay teased Vanessa from the time Derrick walked away until the two of them arrived at home and put the groceries away. Then, Vanessa fixed them submarine sandwiches, and they ate them with Lay's potato chips and Coke while watching old episodes of Law & Order. Both of them were tired by the time the news came on, so they decided to turn in for the night.

"I'm going to try and take care of all of your mama's bills tomorrow," Vanessa said to Vonshay, as she lifted herself from the couch. "I want you to tell me what needs to be done, and show me what bills you have. We'll get all of it together in the morning."

"O.k. Good night," Vonshay said.

"Good night, baby," Vanessa responded. They both went to their respective rooms and closed the doors. After changing into her night-gown, Vanessa kneeled down and began to pray.

Lord, watch over my sister and give her the strength to overcome her addiction. Take care of her child in her absence and help her to understand what is happening with her mama. Remove all of her negative thoughts and feelings and show her that the love between a mama and child is unconditional. Then Lord, help me to hold everything together and to be a good guardian to my niece, to give her what she needs and understand what she must be going through. Remove from me, Lord, any hard feelings I have for my sister and heal all of our wounds. Lord, You sent me here and I pray that You watch over me and protect me as I try to do your will. Lord, thank You for all that you have done for me. Without You Lord, I could not have made it this far. Thank You Lord, thank You. In Jesus' name I pray. Amen.

Prayer always made her feel peaceful because she knew that God understood what she was going through, even when she didn't. She didn't just pray at night; she prayed throughout the day. Waking up in the morning, she thanked the Lord for watching over her through the night and asked Him for direction and guidance throughout the day, so that she would glorify Him with her words and actions. Whenever she faced a trying situation, received a blessing, did a good deed, or noticed God's hand at work, she stopped to tell Him thank You. This feeling of peace carried her through many days, and it didn't fail to carry her peacefully through her sister's first night in rehab.

Vanessa usually slept late when she wasn't working, but she was up the next morning by eight. She had never been able to sleep late when she had something on her mind that she needed to do. She got up, took a shower, and dressed. To her surprise, she heard music coming from Vonshay's room. When she opened the door to leave her room, she saw Vonshay admiring herself at the full- length mirror in the hall.

"Where are you goin' so early?" Vanessa asked her.

"With you, so we can take care of our business," she replied. Her expression implied that Vanessa should have already known the answer to the question.

"Oh," Vanessa said. Vonshay reminded her so much of herself. They both projected images of sistahs who mean business and don't take NO mess. This assessment of their personalities was true, but it was not complete. They were also

104

very kind-hearted. They kept that hidden from most people, so they would not be taken advantage of.

"I got all the bills together and the checks," Vonshay continued.

"Checks? What checks?"

"The ones Mama's been writing all over town and didn't have the money in the bank to cover."

"What?!" Vanessa exclaimed. "Lord, have mercy." This really frazzled her nerves. Why would Vickie do somethin' crazy like that, she wondered, rubbing her forehead. If she didn't have the money to cover the checks, she sure wouldn't have it to pick the checks up and pay fees. The bank charges thirty dollars a whop and these little stores in Ferguson charge up to fifty dollars for a bad check, plus the original amount of the check. It's not even worth the trouble. "How many checks has she written?" she asked Vonshay, sensing the desire for cigarettes.

"It's about ten that I know of. The people call here everyday wakin' me up. Some of 'em say they're going to turn it over to the police because they've been trying to work with Mama, and she keeps on lying about when she'll pay 'em."

Lie nodded his head.

"Do you know where they are?" Vanessa slowly dragged out, as if she were in a daze. She tasted nicotine in her mouth, so reached in her purse for a cigarette. There was only one. She knew she would need at least two before she left home.

"Most of 'em. I'll get the list together and call to see how much they are and how much of a fee they charge."

"Thank you. That'll be a big help to TeeTee. While you're doing that, I'll go through the bills and the mail." Vanessa lit her only cigarette and reached for the envelopes.

Vonshay handed Vanessa a huge stack of bills and cut off notices from the telephone, light, gas, and furniture companies. She told Vanessa which ones she had paid or at least paid a portion of to keep the services from being discontinued.

My sister, my sister, my sister, Vanessa thought, flipping through the envelopes. "Lord this is much more than I anticipated. I'll be flat broke if I try to straighten all this out, and I have declared that I will never be broke another day in my life.

105

She laid the stack of bills down because her head was beginning to hurt. When she glanced down at the stack, her eyes focused on an envelope from Ferguson Federal Bank. She slammed the pen in her hand down hard on the table. "I know not!" blurted Vanessa. As she picked up the envelope to open it, she placed the cigarette in the ashtray.

The envelope contained a notice of foreclosure on the house. The notice said that the mortgage had not been paid in months. If this had just been Vickie's house, Vanessa would have been mad, but it belonged to both of them, so she was furious.

Both of their parents had been killed in a car accident the summer after Vanessa graduated from high school. Since the house was left to them both and Vanessa was going off to school at Tougaloo, it was understood that Vickie and her family would live there until Vanessa finished school, and they made other arrangements. They were both over eighteen, so they did not want anyone trying to tell them what to do -- especially relatives that they had never seen or met. This included almost all of their relatives because the majority of people in both of the their parents families had left Mississippi and moved North during the Great Migration era.

When their parents died, the house was paid for. The girls were having hard times, so a few years later, the two of them decided to take a mortgage out on the house for extra money. Although Vanessa had gotten a full scholarship to Tougaloo, it only covered tuition costs. She had no money for books, room and board, or clothes. Vickie had only been married a few years and she and Andre' were still struggling. That was the reason they had lived with her parents in the first place. They felt that a little extra money would surely benefit them all.

They agreed that Vickie would pay the notes the first four years, since Vanessa was in school and Vanessa would pay them the following four years. Then they would alternate each year. This year was Vickie's year and it was obvious that she was not holding up her end of the bargain. Vanessa couldn't just watch what her parents had worked so hard for go to waste, but she was tempted to do it, just to prove a point to Vickie. After thinking about it, she knew that she wouldn't be able to forgive herself if she did. Her parents were proud of their house, and the fact that they were the first Blacks to move into the all-white neighborhood.

Vanessa closed her eyes, dropped her head in the palm of her hands, and began humming. She wasn't exactly sure if she was humming a particular song or just making a noise. She couldn't even think of the words she wanted to speak. She remembered the time she had seen her mama doing the same thing that she was now doing. She had asked her mama why she behaved that way and her mama told her this: "Chile, just live a little longer and you'll understand. Sometimes, all you can do is moan. You can't fix your mouth to say what you want it to all the time. Good thing is, God knows what's in your heart, even when you can't get it out your mouth." That was so many years before, but Vanessa didn't understand what her mama meant until that very moment.

Thankful for the revelation, she whispered, "Only You can do this, God…only You can give me peace in the middle of this storm…not the cigarettes, but You. Without inhaling another puff of smoke, she extinguished the burning cigarette.

Vonshay came back into the room with the information she had set out to retrieve, and it didn't make Vanessa feel any better. She really felt worse when she found out that Vickie had written over a thousand dollars worth of bad checks in just a few weeks. Vanessa decided that it didn't make sense for her to get all worked up over what Vickie had done. She couldn't change it, and she had to be strong, so she could look after Vonshay. Having her mama and her auntie in an institution at the same time would be more than the poor child could handle.

Vanessa and Vonshay took their lists and their bills and headed out. Vanessa didn't even know what she was going to say to the people at the bank, but she went anyway. As she drove downtown, she said a silent prayer asking the Lord to guide her tongue and to touch the heart of the banker that she would talk to about her situation.

The downtown area of Ferguson extended about three-fourths of a mile. It included two major streets, Main Street and

Mississippi Street, as well as several cross streets. Main Street was a one-way street that was lined on either side with well-manicured magnolia trees. The trees gave shade to pedestrians on the sidewalks while casting shadows which gave a false appearance of beauty to the aging one and two level connecting buildings that housed local businesses. Mississippi Street, where the post office, library, city hall, and several other government offices were located, was a straight four-lane street with very few trees. Both of the streets lead to the Ferguson Levee, which was the home of the local casinos.

The levee was built in the 1920's after the turbulent waters of the Mississippi River rushed into Lake Ferguson. The peaceful lake was not capable of handling such a large amount of tumultuous waters, so it spewed the waters into the city of Ferguson and left it helpless for several weeks. Immediately after the water evaporated, the citizens built the levee to protect their city from similar occurrences.

Vanessa noticed the many vacant buildings on Main Street as she sat at the seemingly never changing traffic lights at each intersection. Most of the closed businesses were previously run by local whites, but were no longer functioning because their goods had been over-priced. Once, people were forced to shop in these stores because they had nowhere else to go, but in the last few years, there had been an influx of Asians who were opening businesses everywhere and competing with the established businesses. They didn't understand much of what the customer said, but they knew how to figure out what they wanted, convince them to buy it *and* other items, and sell it at much lower prices than the other stores in town. The White-owned businesses began to compete by lowering their prices, and the Asians lowered theirs even more. Eventually, the White businesses were forced to close their doors.

All the buildings downtown that weren't stores or government offices were banks. The town had more banks than its citizens had money to put in them. Many of the older people still kept their money at their homes in secret hiding places. The problem was that there were no secrets in Ferguson. The whole town knew where the old people's money was kept, but

108

fortunately, no one would dare steal from them. They did other things that were more horrifying, but not making victims of the old and helpless was their way of showing respect for their elders. When crack entered the picture, it was an entirely different story. Addicts began stealing from everyone, including their parents and grandparents, aunts and uncles, neighbors and friends. They took anything anybody had that they thought they could use to get a hit.

Vanessa pulled into the parking lot of Ferguson Federal Bank where there were several matters of business she need to handle. Vickie had been dumb enough to write checks on the same bank that carried the mortgage. Vanessa had planned to go in alone, but she decided to let Vonshay accompany her. Inside the bank, Vanessa glanced around to see if she could spot a Black face sitting behind a desk. When she noticed a clean-cut Black man sitting behind a desk, they walked towards him.

As she approached the customer service area, Vanessa admired the confidence with which the man perused the papers on his desk. In her mind she asked God if this was the person whose heart He had touched. She stood in front of the huge oak desk unacknowledged for about three minutes, waiting to see how long she would be ignored. She knew that the treatment she received was not of God, and when she was finally fed up and about to speak, the man looked up from his papers and said, "Take a seat."

Whatever happened to good morning and may I help you? Vanessa wondered as she and Vonshay took a seat and explained the situation.

The man listened inattentively to Vanessa's speech and when she finished he said, "We can't help you."

Obviously, this isn't the man who owns the heart that God touched, Vanessa thought to herself. She knew that God didn't always drop blessings in His people's laps. Sometimes, they had to seek them out. She did not plan to be like those people who gave up on God's promises and refused to go any further, only to find out later that their blessings had been one step in front of them.

Vanessa stood up from her seat poised. You would have thought that the man had given her everything she asked for. She was disenchanted about the lack of respect she had been shown, but she refused to let her feelings be seen on her face. "I see that you can't help me," she said calmly, "but I'm sure someone else can. May I please speak to *your* manager, Mr. Meyers?" He didn't have sense enough to introduce himself, so Vanessa called him by the name on his employee I.D. badge. He didn't know like everyone else knew; Vanessa was not one to let mistreatment go by without letting it be known that she was aware of it and would not tolerate it.

The bank manager, an older white man who looked about sixty, came to talk with her. During the conversation, Vanessa explained her present situation, just as she had to the Black man, and expressed her disgust for the way she was treated by Mr. Meyers. The manager was very understanding and told Vanessa something could definitely be worked out. He offered to retract the foreclosure with the acceptance of two payments, so she wrote him a check for the agreed amount. He also volunteered to close Vickie's account and accept monthly payments on the negative balance without adding any additional fees. *He* was the one whose heart had been touched by God!

"Thank you so much for working with me," Vanessa told him as they rose to leave.

"No problem, Miss Morgan. I know exactly what you're going through," he said in a deep Southern drawl as he stood and walked them to the door. "My son is a recovering drug addict himself. I know what you're going through. Just hold on and keep the faith," he advised as he held the door open. He shook their hands firmly as they passed through the door and into the waiting area.

"I will and God bless you, sir!" Vanessa responded earnestly.

"May God bless you ladies, too!" he responded with a bright smile.

When the door closed, Vanessa paused and said "Thank-You Jesus"! She looked over at Mr. Meyers sitting with erect shoulders in his finely tailored suit and shook her head as she passed his desk. Sitting there like he's all that, she thought. "It's a sad day when White people treat you better than your own," she told Vonshay. "Blacks get these positions and big desks and don't want to be decent to other Blacks. They clown more over the white man's goods and money than he does. They act like *they* own it! I'm glad God is color blind because if the only people He could use were us Black folks—we'd be in a world of trouble."

"But you fixed him, TeeTee," Vonshay said with a smile. She was impressed with the way her aunt handled the situation and received everything she wanted.

"Vengeance is the Lord's, baby," she told her niece. "I'm just walking in His promises, and Honey, there is no walk like a walk with God. You best believe that! Now come on and tell God, 'Thank You.'"

"Thank you," Vonshay chimed, then added "Thank you Jesus!" for emphasis.

Vonshay had done a good job of trying to keep up the utilities in the house, so Vanessa only had to pay the balances on them. After doing that, she went to the local collection agency where most of Vickie's bad checks had been sent. She talked with a Black lady who was very courteous, and she made lenient payment arrangements with Vanessa. God had His people stationed at every post.

"At least some Blacks knew that they were still Black and cared about other Blacks," she told Vonshay, glad that the lady had restored some of her faith in her people. "It's becoming a rarity, you know."

"I know," Vonshay responded with appeasement. "Some of these folks in Mississippi *still* don't know they're free!" Vonshay said, reciting one of her aunt's favorite responses to race relations in her native city and state.

Once all of the immediate business was taken care of, Vanessa and Vonshay went home. Later on Vanessa decided to call her friend Christi. She had only talked to her briefly since she'd been there. Now that she was a little settled in, they would have a chance to catch each other up on the latest happenings in each of their own lives and everybody else's.

Vanessa and Christi had been best friends since kindergarten. As they grew, their friendship grew. After high school, their lives took different paths. Christi got pregnant and stayed in Ferguson to raise her child. Vanessa went to college and then moved to Atlanta. Even though they were separated by distance, they stayed in contact. They shared their experiences and each one learned from the other.

Christi always provided Vanessa with insight on how to deal with certain situations and not once did she bite her tongue. Whether Christi thought Vanessa was being silly, sensitive, sanctimonious, or just a down right mean, she let her know, and it was not a problem because Vanessa did the same. They loved their open and honest relationship, and they didn't fall out with one another over criticism, like most so-called friends. Regardless of the circumstances, they told each other what they thought, not what they thought the other wanted to hear.

"Hey girl," Christi said after hearing Vanessa's voice. "How'd everything go? Is Vickie O.k.?"

"She's all right. I called down there to check on her today. Her doctor said he put her in detox 'cause she was so high. He wants us to wait a few weeks before we visit. I didn't tell Vonshay though. I just told her that her mama was doing fine."

"Naw, you didn't need to tell her that. Did you get a chance to look for a job today? I just read in the paper that the school system needs some teachers. Nobody around here stays long because the children are out of control, and nobody wants to deal with them. Kids these days ain't nothing like we were in school, and ain't nobody to blame but their parents. I know you can handle their butts, though," she laughed. "Seriously, you should go talk to somebody over there."

"I'll do that. Mr. Lucas and I are cool. He'll probably hire me, but I want to check at the junior college, too. That will give me more free time, and it's a lot less restricted than the high school. But you know how White folks are about Black people teaching history at their schools. The White man wants

112

everybody to know *his* story and not the *real* story. But you know me, though. I'm going to tell it like it happened, whether they like it or not."

"That's what you're supposed to do. Why don't we get together soon and go out to have a drink or somethin'? You know they say I don't come out the house 'til you're in town."

"Let's go Friday. I saw Derrick in Super Foods and he wants me to meet him at *The Club*. You know I don't wanna go by myself."

"Girl you still scared of men. You talk plenty noise and ain't gon' bust a grape if somebody puts it under your foot. Don't be usin' me to try and block. I'll tell him to take it 'cause you need some. That's why you get so uptight. You need to relieve some of that tension, and you'll be all right," she laughed.

"You probably would tell him somethin' like that, but I hope he's got sense enough not to let you get him killed. He knows from experience that when I say 'no' I mean absolutely positively 'no'. No ifs, ands, or buts about it."

"Your mind and mouth say 'no'. Your body's hollerin', 'please take me'. It ain't got sense enough to tell you, but I will.

They both laughed for a few minutes with a few "Girl you crazy." and "Chile you need to stop." pauses in between. They stayed on the phone for about two hours, tripping on everything from local gossip to national news. Finally, they ended the conversation and Vanessa went to bed.

The next day Vanessa went out to look for a job. She talked with the dean at the college and the principal at the high school. Both of them offered her a job. All she had to do was decide which one to accept. She knew that the job at the college would require less of her time and effort, but she also knew that the students at the high school needed her more. She was not going to teach White kids who thought they knew everything when there was an opportunity for her to teach Black kids who needed to know everything. She owed it to herself, the children, and God to use the talent he had given her in the way that would glorify Him the most. After praying about it, she felt that He would get more out of her at the high school, where she would genuinely care about her work than at the college, where she

113

would just draw a check. She wanted to be good steward over everything God gave her, including her job, so the decision to teach at Ferguson High School was simple.

Vanessa was scheduled to report to work at the high school the third week in August. This meant that she didn't have a lot of time to get herself together. Because she left Atlanta so quickly, she still had business to take care of there. She handled what she could over the phone, and her friend Lynnsey handled everything else for her. Although Vanessa realized that it would be difficult supporting two households, she felt that she had to do it, and she knew that the Lord would make a way—He always did!

Friday morning, Vanessa went to the beauty salon to see if her old stylist, LaShun, could work her in, because she didn't have an appointment. She had always kept her hair looking nice. Before she moved to Atlanta, she had her hair done every week, but the cost of perms and cuts there were twice, sometimes three times as much as they were in Ferguson. Vanessa decided to do what she had always wanted to do with her hair-- go natural. So for her twenty-fifth birthday, she went to the barbershop and had her hair cut down to about one inch in length, and she had worn her natural hair in varying lengths ever since.

Although she wore it natural now and mostly took care of it herself, it was always good to go the salon. It gave her a special feeling to be pampered and have someone else style her hair. She could imagine the talk that would go on if she went to *The Club* without her hair having that freshly done glow. They would say things like, "Girl she doin' so bad, she don't even keep her hair up no more. She did that when she didn't do nothin' else. You think she on them drugs, too? You know her sister started looking rough by the head when she got on that stuff. She might be dippin' and dabbin' herself. That stuff can be hereditary, you know." They'll never get that chance, she thought.

LaShun had moved into her own shop since Vanessa's last visit. The shop had an urban flair to it that Vanessa found quite impressive for Ferguson. A circular maple receptionist's desk sat in the middle of the waiting area, which was filled with various styles of black leather chairs-some close together, others

114

far apart, for customers who preferred privacy. The limited seating implied that appointments times were set so that they would not become backed up and that the waiting period would not be very long. There were several glass and chrome tables filled with hairstyle and fashion magazines and others that held decorative arrangements. Painted portraits of women with varying hairstyles adorned the walls. The stylist stations in the back were maple with maple-trimmed mirrors shaped like Africa. The atmosphere gave Vanessa the feeling that she was somewhere other than Ferguson, Mississippi.

While waiting to be called from the lounge to the back, Vanessa listened to all of the women's conversations about who was doing what to who, when, how, where, and why. They even discussed who wasn't worth discussing. All of these conversations revolved around male/female relationships. The ladies went down the list giving the pros and cons on almost every man in town-- available or unavailable, young or old, with money or without money.

Since Vanessa hadn't been in the local "catch a man if you can contest" in a while, she listened very attentively to this part of the conversation. She had no intention of joining the competition because she was waiting to be found by her divine mate. Watching and listening to the women was a reminder to her of where God had brought her from and where He had taken her on her journey with Him. There was a time when she would have been in the middle of everything, so she took the time right then and there to thank God again for her salvation.

She couldn't believe that the women were having that discussion in a beauty salon full of a lot of women they didn't even know. They could have been discussing somebody's brother, father, boyfriend, or even worse, someone's husband. But they didn't seem to care, so she listened. She was glad to get the 411. She didn't recognize many of the names, so she figured the men must have been young like most of the ladies who were chatting.

It was sad that most of them were not over twenty-five and probably had not been out of Ferguson their entire lives. They thought that they had it together because they didn't have

115

jobs and could come to the beauty salon every week to get their hair done with drug money that their boyfriends had given them and a few of the other women there, as well. Vanessa shook her head as she watched and listened. Don't they realize that there's more to life than this, she questioned. She wished she could tell them all how crazy they were and knock some sense in their heads.

Lie smiled proudly as he listened to the evidence of his deception flowing from the women's mouths.

Finally, the women approached the subject of older men, and the first name out of their mouths was Derrick Davis. This was proof to Vanessa that they weren't women, but girls because Derrick was only thirty-five, so if that was an older man to them, then they were still babies. The entire time she was there, Vanessa pretended to balance her checkbook so she wouldn't look too interested in what they said, but when she heard Derrick's name, she quickly flipped over to a blank sheet in the 'notes' section of her wallet and began to jot down every piece of valuable information she could get. She convinced herself that she wasn't being nosy. After all, he was attempting to get involved with her, and she was considering having a relationship with this man. She had a right to know what the word on the street on him was, didn't she? Besides, she wasn't looking for gossip; it found her.

"Now that's one good lookin' man," said a lady in her mid' twenties.

"Yeah, baby," said another woman around Vanessa's age. Problem is, you too young to know what to do with a man like that. He needs a woman he doesn't have to teach."

"Age ain't nothin' but a number," the young girl said, flashing her gold tooth.

"Hmph. It's a number all right and that number carries a lot of weight with it. The higher the number, the heavier the load," the receptionist interjected from behind the counter.

116

The lady continued. "Derrick needs somebody 'bout his age. Somebody that likes the same things he likes. See, that girl he got at home ain't the one."

Girl at home, Vanessa thought. Oh, he's got some nerve! She cut her thoughts short because she didn't want to miss anything.

"She show ain't," the younger lady continued. She don't never wanna go nowhere or do nothin'. She just sits in that house with that baby while he be runnin' the streets all day and night. I know 'cause I stay over by 'em and sometimes he don't even come home. She don't say nothin' cause she scared of him."

"Hmph, if that was me, while he was steppin' out, somebody else would definitely be steppin' in. You know what I mean?" a newcomer contributed. They all laughed.

A baby? Vanessa thought. I'm trying to get over the fact that he lives with somebody, now I hear that he's got a baby! Well, there goes that idea. He's got too much baggage for me.

"But Derrick is good to a woman if he likes her," someone added. "He'll give up them dollars. You don't even have to ask him. You know some of these brothas just want you to beg em' for they money, but not Derrick. He knows he got to pay to play. And from what I hear he always pays his bills ahead of time."

"I'm ready for you, Vanessa," LaShun interrupted from the doorway.

She slowly got up, still startled from the conversation she had overheard. When Vanessa sat in the soft black leather stylist's chair she complemented LaShun on the overall vibe of her shop. The two of them chatted while LaShun washed Vanessa's hair and prepared her for the drier. Vanessa's mind was still on the ladies out front. When LaShun asked her how she wanted her hair, she told her it didn't matter. Being able to say that fearlessly was one of the main reasons she went to LaShun. The girl could do some hair! Vanessa could get a different style every week from the same haircut, and it always looked good on her. With so much on her mind, it was good to have a stylist she could trust.

"Don't put me under here too long," Vanessa warned LaShun as she led her to the drier. She hated sitting under the drier and LaShun knew it.

"Girl you act like a little child. If you sit still and don't bother your hair, it won't take that long to dry," LaShun insisted, although she knew that Vanessa would do exactly the opposite.

Surprisingly, Vanessa's drier time went by fast. She didn't realize it because she was thinking about what she heard about Derrick. She didn't know if she should even give him the time of day. He had two strikes against him; a woman and a child. She decided to consult Christi before she made a decision.

"Your hair looks good, TeeTee," Vonshay commented when Vanessa walked in the house. She ran her fingers through her auntie's hair. "It's so soft, too. Did you go to LaShun?"

"Yeah, I'm glad you like it. Anybody call?"

"Christi called. She wants to know what's up for tonight. Said you two had plans and she wanted to make sure you hadn't chickened out.

"O.k. I'll call her now," she said, heading for the phone. She waited for Vonshay to leave the room before she dialed the number. This was not going to be a public conversation.

"Girl, why didn't you tell me Derrick was livin' with somebody and had a baby?" Vanessa asked, after Christi picked up the phone. "I know you knew it."

"Why?" Christi repeated. "Because I didn't think you needed to know. That'll be just one more, well two more, excuses you'll use for not hooking up with him. You make enough excuses on your own, so I wasn't going to add any to the list. You need to stop trying to figure out why you shouldn't get none and go get some. Please yourself, girl. Don't worry about nobody else. If he's not worrying about the woman and the baby, why should you? Just get yours. Selfish as you are, I don't see why it's such a big problem."

"I don't believe you held out on me like that. Am I that pathetic that you hid vital information from me, just so I'll get some? It's not just gettin' some that's the problem. What if I do get it? Then what happens?"

"Well that's up to you, dear. Just see what happens tonight. We both know that you're not givin' it up too fast any way. Get some drinks, talk to him, and see where he's coming from. We don't like the conversation, we'll move on."

"Oh, it's *we* now?" Vanessa teased. "You a trip! I think it'll probably be best if I go with Bobby Bland on this one. He says, 'If I don't get involved, I sure can't get hurt.' I'd better do like the song suggests and 'stay in the safety zone.'"

Before Christi had a chance to respond to yet another of her friend's references to her favorite blues singer and his songs, Vanessa's phone beeped. She had a strange feeling that it was Derrick.

"Hello, Beautiful," he responded to her greeting. "Are we still on for tonight?"

She assuredly told him "yes."

"Why don't we meet at *The Club* around ten o'clock," he suggested.

"Let's make it nine," she said. "I don't want to be out too late."

"Sounds good," Derrick responded. "I'll see you then."

Vanessa clicked back over and told Christi to be ready at eight. She knew that if she told her eight, she wouldn't be ready until around nine. This would be good timing because she didn't want to get there too early and seem anxious. She wanted Derrick to wonder if she would show and wait to find out. She had stood him up a few times before, so he could never be sure about her. She didn't want to start being predictable. Being unpredictable was a lot more fun.

The Club was actually the local VFW but no one referred to it by its name. At one point it was the only nightclub in town, so people just asked, "You goin' to the club tonight?" There were now other places to go out in Ferguson, but all of the other clubs were just lumped together because they never lasted longer than a year or two, but the VFW had stood the test of time.

119

Christi and Vanessa always looked fly when they went out, but they decided they would look extra super fly this night. Everybody already knew that Vanessa had come home to put Vickie in rehab, and they expected her to be ashamed and stay in the house. Not. Obviously they had forgotten the type of person Vanessa was. She didn't care one way or another what they said or thought about her or her family. "Ain't none of 'em feedin' me, dressin' me or puttin' money in my pocket, so forget what they say" is how Vanessa responded when she heard the latest reports on what people said about her.

When she and Christi arrived at *The Club* that night, they looked good and felt great. "Yeah, we in the house!" was written all over their faces and signed with big smiles. When they entered the dimly lit club, the gold, long, sleeveless dress Vanessa wore and the bright red mini dress Christi wore demanded attention. Their outfits were like the moon on a starless night; they shone brightly in the midst of darkness. The smoke-filled room was crowded with men, women, and a few obviously under-age teens. Everyone was engulfed in conversations, some shallow, others deep. Body movements revealed the inner thoughts that many of the faces hid behind smiles.

Vanessa had not been to a club in two years. The last time she had gone, she felt totally out of place. There had been a time in her life when she planned her schedule around going out, but clubs just didn't excite her any more, especially those in Atlanta. They were filled with pretentious people who were only interested in material possessions and physical features. It wasn't that these things didn't matter to Vanessa, but they were not *all* that mattered. She hated to see the women putting their bodies on display, just to get a drink and a dance from somebody whose name they barely knew. Besides, she didn't want to meet a man in a club any way. Nine times out of ten, if she met him in a club, clubbin' was probably a regular part of his social life, and since it wasn't a part of hers, there would be conflict from the beginning. So, she declared that her clubbin' days were over. She had decided to go out with Christi and Derrick for old times sake, but she promised herself not to make it a habit while she was home, even though going to the club was about the only thing to do in Ferguson. She *had* to find a church, somewhere her spirit could be fed. She had come home to *do* God's will, not to step out of it and back into her old ways.

Because *The Club* was small and she had been there too many times to count, Christi was able to take in the entire scenery, or lack of, with one swift glance. "Three o'clock," Christi whispered without moving her lips. This was her way to inform Vanessa of Derrick's location in the building without being obvious.

Just as Christi figured, Vanessa headed in the other direction, past the cramped dance floor and small tables to the long curved bar. They chose two empty stools at the end of the bar, so they could see everything and everybody could see them. Suspecting that Derrick was watching, Vanessa slid smoothly onto the black leather seat, cracked from years of wear and tear, while Christi adjusted her snug fitting dress to show off her long smooth legs. When Christi finished maneuvering her legs into a perfectly crossed position, she ordered them two shots of Courvosier and two Cokes.

"Girl, I can't do that hard stuff anymore," Vanessa told Christi. I ain't as young as I used to be. "Wine is about as much as I can handle. My body is not used to drinking anymore."

"Ooh girl," Christi responded, "you *are* getting old." She remembered how she and Vanessa would drink until they passed out. She knew that getting old was probably only part of the reason Vanessa didn't drink. The other part probably had something to do with her being saved.

"He needs to make his way over here before these drinks get ready," Vanessa said as she spun around on her stool to see who was there. Almost everybody turned their heads when she looked them in their faces. Most of them had just finished discussing her and her family's business. She averted her eyes from the crowd when she felt someone touch her on the back. It was the kind of touch that could only have come from a man. When she looked back, she saw Derrick. He's too smooth, she thought admiringly. He made his way over without us noticing,

121

and we don't miss a move. That's one thing that can count in his favor. "How are you doing tonight?" she asked and then flashed a smile.

"I'm doing fine. You're looking fine, as usual," Derrick said returning the smile. He had been attracted to Vanessa since junior high school. The feeling was actually mutual, but they could never seem to get anything going. Maybe this time he could convince her that nothing mattered except how they felt about each other.

"Thank you," she said.

"And you Christi?" he asked. "Are you doing O.k. tonight?"

"I sure am," she responded. "I'd be doing even better if this wacked weave-wearin' waitress would hurry with these drinks and stop trying to rap to every man that comes to the bar."

"Girl you still crazy," Derrick laughed. "You must keep all that inside until Vanessa comes to town, because that's the only time I see you out."

"Yeah, basically. I don't have time to deal with these people around here," she said, waving her hand in the direction of the tables. "Almost all of them are up to no good. I can't trust them, so I don't fake with them."

The waitress finally brought their drinks. Vanessa reached in her purse, but when she pulled her money out, Derrick had already paid for the drinks and left a tip. Vanessa said "thank you" as if she were surprised, but she wasn't. She had no intentions of paying for a drink, when a man who claimed to love her was standing by.

"Thanks for the drink, Derrick," Christi said as she lifted her glass of cognac from the bar.

"No problem," her responded. "I got you all night."

"I hope you know what you're saying 'cause I can hang with the best of 'em, she bragged.

"Girl, if I say I got you, then I got you."

"Alright then, get this seat for me while I go dance," Christi said as she slid off the barstool. "I'll be back, Vanessa," she said with a sly smile.

Recognizing that she had just been set up, Vanessa flashed Christi the meanest face she could make. Without Christi around to serve as a buffer, Vanessa would have to deal with Derrick one on one, and she had not yet decided how to handle him. Based on the information she acquired at the beauty salon, there were new variables to be factored into the equation. After a few minutes of cordial conversation and a little laughter about their everyday lives, Derrick went in for the kill.

"Well, Beautiful," he said smoothly, "since you're going to be here for a while, maybe we can finally work things out and have that wonderful love affair that we've both fantasized about for as long as I can remember, at least more than half of our lives.

"I never knew you had fantasies about me," Vanessa blushed.

"Fantasies of hugging you, kissing you, and loving you all night long...I could see myself..."

"I get the picture," Vanessa interjected. She smiled sheepishly, glad she interrupted him before his description became more graphic.

"But I want to describe every detail of it to you," he said, finding humor in her embarrassment.

"I'm sure you can show me better than you can tell me," Vanessa slurred. Astonished by her own lustful boldness, she immediately brought her glass of wine to her glossed lips in an effort to prevent any more such words from flowing out.

"You're right, I can show you better than I can tell, so when will I bet my chance?" Derrick asked with anticipation in his voice and eyes.

"It's not that simple, Mr. Davis."

"Why not?"

"Because you've got a woman AND a baby fool!" she wanted to scream, but instead she said, "Because life and love are complicated. There's no easy way in and no easy way out."

"I'll take that for now," Derrick said as he watched Christi approaching, "but I've waited too long to let this pass me by. We'll talk more about it later, O.k., Beautiful?

"O.k.," Vanessa conceded, staring in his eyes as he brushed against her to give Christi her seat.

"I'll be right back," Derrick said, squeezing her hand softly and walking away.

"It's getting hot in here!" Christi laughed. " I decided to come back over because you looked like you were in a tight fix."

"I was and I didn't do a good job of getting out," Vanessa admitted.

"What happened, girl?"

"Well we were talking and flirting a little bit and then he started talking about us not letting this chance to get together pass us by. But instead of me confronting him about not mentioning his baby and his babymama, I just played right along with it."

"That's cool. If he didn't mention her, she must not be that important."

"I beg to differ. She must be *real* important or he wouldn't be living with her," Vanessa retorted.

"Girl, get over it! You're the only woman I know who will send a man home before he even gets a chance to play," Christi said in disbelief.

"Well if more of us would send more of them back home, they wouldn't be walking around thinking they can love two, or three, or four of us. It's just like trying to love God and the world...you end up loving one and hating the other," Vanessa insisted.

"Oh goodness, it must be getting close to midnight, cause you preaching your Sunday sermon already. Are you going to church tomorrow? Oops...tomorrow's not even Sunday; it's Saturday. Girl you're starting earlier and earlier," Christi teased.

"Yeah, but I am going to church Sunday, but I don't know where, yet. It's not too many churches around here that can come close to my church in Atlanta. Nevertheless, I've got to find one that at least believes in the Holy Spirit. I've watched every video and listened to every tape I brought with me. Now I need a fresh word and some fellowship with the saints," Vanessa said, more to herself than to her friend.

"It's one down there on Magnolia Street. People say they shout and everything. That's a bit much for me, though. I went once and I didn't like it, but different strokes for different folks. I've graduated from St. James, but I'm not ready for the big leagues yet."

"Well you couldn't pay me to go to St. James again. Last time I was home, I went with Vickie and it was worse than when we were growing up. No growth has taken place at all; the same people are in the same seats doing the same thing--nothing. I'll have to check out the one on Magnolia," Vanessa said. "I need to be getting home though," she continued. "I've had enough of this scene."

"Girl, it's still early," Chirsti beamed.

"I know. I'll hang around a little longer, then I'm out."

"Cool," Christi said, spinning around on her stool and directing Vanessa's attention to the dance floor.

The floor was filled with people who swayed and bounced to the beat of the music. Vanessa and Christi were impressed by some moves and insulted by others. Some things, they felt, should be done in private, not on the dance floor in a room filled with other people. Derrick rejoined them and they spent the remainder of their time there talking, laughing, and enjoying each other's company.

When Vanessa returned home and settled in, she had an eagerness to talk to God about her day.

Lord, I want to thank You for snatching me out from the world and bringing me into the Kingdom. Since I've been home, I've had constant reminders of the state my life could be in and I don't ever want to go back to that state again. Lord, strengthen me so that I will not fall into sin because of the lust of my flesh. Help me God to stand on Your promises and to keep the vows that I have made to you. I ask that You draw Derrick and Christi closer to you so that they will learn to know you as Father, Savior, and Lord. God, I thank You for peace and joy in the midst of this great storm, and I will continue to give You praise. Amen.

125

Chapter 8

Vickie had a high like she had never had before. This is better than rocks, she thought. I should've come here a long time ago. I stay high all day...I don't have to be bothered with nobody...and I don't have to pay for my drugs...I got it made. That doctor was talkin' like I wasn't going to like it here. This is live. He can detox me anytime!

In her zombie-like state, Vickie sat Indian-style in a small white room scarcely furnished with only a bed and nightstand. She thought that she was thinking to herself, but she was actually talking out loud. Her words were so slurred that only she could understand them. Her hands were situated mid-air as if she were holding a pipe. She dropped an imaginary rock in, and flicked the invisible lighter. During pauses in her conversation with herself, she took long slow drags from the pipe. She sucked in desperately like a drowning woman who was finally getting oxygen into her collapsing lungs. She even thought that she tasted the drug in her dry mouth and felt it flow through her numb body, but she didn't. It was merely hallucinations. Since she had been in detox, the only drug to enter her body was methadone.

Lie found Vickie's enactments entertaining.

Dr. Winters gave her methadone to make her feel like she was high on crack, even though she wasn't. Once her body became familiar with the methadone, he began to reduce her dosage. He wanted to gradually bring her down from a major high. The process took about two weeks. When she came down, it was nothing nice.

Dr. Winters stopped by Vickie's room every day to check on her and to change her methadone dosage. Normally when he came by, Vickie just looked at him because she was so high that she didn't know who he was, nor did she care. When she started to come down from her high, she was furious because she wasn't high enough, and she slowly began to realize just where she was.

"Hey," Vickie said when Dr. Winters entered her room on the tenth morning, "you know where I can get me a piece like this?" She held her hand out to show him her imaginary rock.

"A piece of what?" he asked, knowing full well what she meant.

"Stop trippin', man. You a brotha. I know you can go get me a little somethin' and bring it back to me. What they giving me ain't hittin' it."

"No, baby, I can't do that. I thought you came here to leave that alone."

"I did, and I will after I get this one last hit. Come on, man. Do a sistah a favor before my doctor comes in!"

"Darling, your doctor is already here."

"Where is he?" she asked searching the room with her eyes. "See, I knew they was spying on me up in here. All right, you can come out now! I already got the scoop, and I know you in here. Show your ugly face!" she yelled.

"I've been showing my face all the time."

"What?!" Vickie exclaimed with a perplexed look on her face.

"I'm your doctor, baby," he said firmly. "And I'm not going to get you a piece, nor is anybody else in here, so you may as well stop asking."

"You my doctor?!" she exclaimed, still confused. She had forgotten about the man she thought she would never forget. "Well, if you were giving me my medicine like you're supposed to, I wouldn't have to ask nobody. You started out doing' good, but I don't know what happened. Must've been trying to save some for yourself. Be stingy though. I don't have to ask nobody for it. I can go get my own!" she screamed, leaping from the bed and heading for the door.

Vickie didn't realize she wore only a gown and slippers. Neither did she realize that she had no idea where she was going.

"Vickie," the doctor said calmly, as she passed him and reached for the door, "get back over to that bed and sit down. I'm not one of those rooty-poot youngsters you're used to dealing with. I know the game because I've played it too many times. It's only fair that I let you know that I always win. You can throw in your hand now, because I definitely have an ace in the hole."

"You can't stop me from leavin' here. I go when I want to!" she yelled. "Don't you know that this is America, Mr. Doctor Man?"

"Miss Patient, you won't get too far, and you will be back. Believe me when I tell you that if you walk out that door, you'll wish you never knew me when you get back. I won't give you a drop of any kind of medicine. You'll go cold turkey from Jump Street."

The look in Dr. Winters' eyes was so intense and his tone so threatening that Vickie just stood there trying to decide what to do. *Lie* urged her to walk out, but she saw a slight glimpse of concern in Dr. Winter's eyes, and she released the door. She walked slowly over to the bed with her head lowered. She felt like a fool.

"Thank you," the doctor said. "Now you have a good day." He walked out of the room and closed the door.

When he came by the next day, he asked Vickie if she was ready to talk. She told him to get out and he did. When she

128

saw him again, it was ten days later, and she was more than willing to talk to him. Talking to herself had gotten to be a bit boring.

Since the drugs were out of Vickie's system, Dr. Winters had a chance to deal with some factors that contributed to the route Vickie had taken to get where she was. Before getting into that, he wanted to explain her addiction to her, discuss the Twelve Step Program that the hospital used, and show her what part she needed to play in her recovery.

Vickie's major role was to believe that her addiction could be overcome with the help of a supreme being. For her, that was God, the father of Jesus Christ who died and rose again, sending His Holy Spirit to dwell on the earth. She honestly believed that God could save her, but she knew that she had to do her part as well. She had to turn her problems over to Him and believe that He would deliver her. Turning over her problems was easy, but not going back and getting them before God finished with them was not.

Dr. Winters wanted to find out what thoughts, feelings, and desires had caused Vickie to turn to drugs. In his sessions with Vickie, he realized that she had unresolved issues from her relationships with most of her family members.

"Nothing I did was ever good enough for my parents," she confided in the doctor. "Vanessa always did everything better. She brought home better grades; she followed directions better; she cleaned up the house better; and she even made better chocolate chip cookies. I didn't have a chance in *that* house.

"Did that make you angry?" the doctor asked.

"Yeah, all the time."

"What did you do about it?"

"I just kept trying to do things right, like Vanessa did."

"Did you blame Vanessa for the way your parents treated you?"

"Sometimes, but it wasn't her fault. She didn't try to be perfect on purpose; she was just born that way. She tried to make me feel important, but I wanted my parents to make me feel important."

"Did they give you the attention you wanted?"

129

"No, but Andre' did?"

"Who is Andre?"

"My ex-husband and the father of my child. He made me feel important-so important that I ended up pregnant and married him. My parents told me that I wasn't obligated to get married, but I chose to marry any way. I knew that my pregnancy was a disappointment, so for once I decided to do what I thought right. After I had Vonshay, I felt even less important to Andre, my parents, and Vanessa. All the attention that I wished for was directed towards the baby. And before I could get a handle on being a wife and mother, my parents died in that wreck." Vickie paused. "I'm glad they had a chance to spend some time with their only grandchild."

"How did you feel when your parents died?" Dr. Winters asked as he flipped the page on his notepad.

"Like a failure, " Vickie said with tears in her eyes. " I never got a chance to show them that I could do something right."

"Was it really your parents you wanted to convince, or yourself?"

Vickie pondered before answering. "Both," she said softly. "They weren't around long enough to see it, and I haven't been around long enough to do it," she said chuckling. "But I'll get it right one day; one day I'll get it right."

"That's enough for today," the doctor said closing his pad. "It was really good talking to you," Vickie. "I'll see you at group tonight."

"O.k., Vickie said, heading for the door. When the doctor closed the door behind her, she leaned back breathed a long sigh of relief. She had been honest with herself about some of her feelings for the first time in years and that was her first step towards recovery.

Truth smiled.

She didn't feel that any of them loved her enough, and she went out of her way to try and please them all, in an effort to win more of their love. Whenever she thought that she had failed to live up to their expectations, she felt even lonelier. As a part of her therapy, Dr. Winters instructed Vickie to write letters to Vonshay, Vanessa, and Andre, which expressed to them how she felt about her relationships with each of them.

The doctor assessed that loneliness led her into her bouts with depression, which gradually became deeper and deeper. By taking drugs, she was able to ignore the depression for a while, but when the high was gone, depression stared her in the face. It was at these critical times that she wanted to take her own life.

Dr. Winters knew that Vickie's dependence on drugs was severe. Her body was so accustomed to having the drugs present in its system, that it had begun to need them for survival. That's why he had no other option, but to place her in the Detox Unit. It took three weeks to cleanse her body, and there was no way that he could treat her with only one week of therapy. Her stay would definitely be longer than thirty days. How long it would be, he couldn't say. He had to deal with her one session at a time.

With each visit, Vickie began to open up more and more to the doctor. She told him incidents that had happened to her that no one else ever knew about. She told him about the times she pawned all of her jewelry, spent Vonshay's child support checks, lied about her whereabouts, and even begged and stole to get money for drugs.

Since the drugs were out of her system, she was able to sit down and think of all the things she had done. Her conscience gave her no rest. Before, what she did didn't matter, but now she felt a tremendous amount of guilt. This was the biggest failure of her life, and it depressed her deeply. She realized that she had failed her daughter and her sister in what she thought was an irreparable way, but most importantly, she realized that she had failed God. She vowed to spend the rest of her life trying to make it up to her daughter, her sister, and her Savior.

The doctor agreed that she had made mistakes, but he did not agree with her lifetime dedication to making amends. He told her that she would have to forgive herself first. Then she could ask for others' forgiveness and move on from there. She could not spend the rest of her life trying to make things up to them. If she did, she would be right back where she started and end up repeating the same cycle she was trying to break. The

131

doctor told Vickie how to love herself first and how to move away from pain and mistakes. "Life goes on," he told her. "You have to take control of it and not let it take control of you."

Vickie listened intently to everything the doctor told her. She really wanted to get herself straight. She could feel the changes coming over her; therefore she knew that the Lord had answered her prayers. She felt much stronger than she did when she first checked in. She actually felt strong enough to go home for a visit. She had heard about weekend passes, and she wanted one. She couldn't miss taking her only daughter to college for the first time. She had been a model patient for almost four weeks so she felt that the doctor just *had* to let her go. She asked him during her next session.

"Dr. Winters, my baby is going to college next weekend, and I really want to be there. This is a special point in her life, and I want share it with her. Is there any way possible that I can get a weekend pass?" she asked pleadingly. There is no way he can turn me down, she thought.

"Vickie, do you really think you're ready? You're going to be around all those people that contributed to your addiction. Are you strong enough to say, 'no'?" he inquired.

"I can say 'no'. My baby is all that's important to me right now. I can't let her go to college without me being there."

"I'll think about it Vickie and let you know something in a few   days."

"That's fine, but please say 'yes'! Today is Wednesday, and I'll have to make arrangements to be picked up."

"We'll see, darling. We'll see."

Later that afternoon, Dr. Winters called Vanessa. He told her that Vickie wanted to come home and asked her opinion.

"I think it's a good idea," she said excitedly. "Vonshay really misses her, and I think it would make all the difference in the world for her mama to be able to take her to school."

"If you're O.k. with it, I'll let her come. You need to keep a close watch on her and call me at the first sign of trouble. Try to make her as comfortable as possible, and please do not make her feel guilty about anything she has done. She does enough of that on her own. I'm not going to tell her I've agreed to this yet.

Be here to pick her up Friday morning and bring her back after you take your niece to school on Sunday. She needs to be back by six o'clock," he warned.

"O.k., doctor. I can handle that. Thanks a lot," Vanessa said. Placing the receiver down, she whispered, "Thank YOU Jesus!" and broke out into a few steps of her holy dance.

Chapter 9

Vanessa had already planned a trip to Jackson that Saturday for her and Vonshay to visit with Vickie at the hospital, spend the night at a hotel, and go to Tougaloo for Freshman Orientation on Sunday. Now that Vickie could get a weekend pass, she would be able to spend the night at the hotel with them. It didn't make sense, but Vanessa was willing to drive to Jackson on Friday, pick up Vickie, drive back to Ferguson, and return to Jackson the very next day. She believed that the less time they spent in Ferguson, the less likely it would be for Vickie to slip. She knew that Vickie had drug contacts in Ferguson, but she didn't know of any she had in Jackson.

Vanessa didn't tell Vonshay that Vickie was coming home because she wanted to surprise her. She slipped out of bed early Friday morning, showered and dressed. Telling Vonshay not to expect her back until late in the afternoon, she left for Jackson to pick up her sister. She couldn't wait to see Vickie, and the fact that her visit would be a surprise to Vonshay made the trip even more exciting.

"I'm going to college!" Vonshay sang over and over again to a tune she composed while floating around her room choosing which items she would carry to school and which ones she would leave behind. Each time she sang the words, her anticipation increased.

Vonshay had been packing for two weeks. She wanted everything to be perfect. Her TeeTee had bought her new clothes, shoes, toiletries, sheets, and towels, and her daddy had

134

bought her a refrigerator, a microwave, and sent her money to get anything else she needed. He had plans to meet her in Jackson on Saturday to attend Freshmen Orientation for new students and their families. She had almost everything she wanted, but the one thing that was missing could not be bought--her mama.

Although Vonshay was mad with Vickie, she missed her a lot. Her mama had always talked about taking her to college, and now she wouldn't even be around for the occasion. Well, it's her own fault, Vonshay thought. I'm not going to let her mess this up like she did everything else. I'm going to school with TeeTee and Daddy and have just as much fun. I'll call her or maybe stop by to see her, but I'm not going to cry no more. I'm a big girl going to college-- I'll make it if she's not there.

Vonshay wanted badly to believe the lies she told herself, but she knew it was all a facade. Still, she *had* to pretend that everything was all right; it was the only way she could get through it all. Some people would break down in her situation or give up on school, but not her. The misfortunes that had taken place in her life only made her desire to succeed that much stronger. Whatever she had to do to deal with it, she did. Holding back tears, cursing out the walls, ignoring nosey neighbors, and striving to keep her sanity were battles she fought daily. She won a few and lost a few, but she was determined to win the war. She had not yet learned to be still and let God fight her battles.

Sitting on the floor thinking, as she arranged her new belongings for the umpteenth time, Vonshay heard Vanessa come in. "I'm back here, TeeTee," she yelled from her room, not realizing how much time had lapsed since her aunt left that morning.

"O.k., I'm on my way back there. I brought you something, too." She walked down the hall, pulling Vickie behind her.

"I already have everything I need. What else did you get?" Without pausing for a response to her question, Vonshay continued talking. "Ooowee. I wish Mama could see all this stuff. I'll take some pictures and show it to her. We got any film?"

"Unh-unh. We don't need any pictures. She'll see it soon enough," Vanessa said as she stood in the doorway.

"When? I want her to see it while it's still new."

Vickie walked past Vanessa and into her daughter's bedroom. "Mama sees it all, baby," Vickie said with tears in her eyes.

"Mama!" Vonshay yelled when she heard the familiar voice. She jumped up and ran to Vickie with outreached arms. Tears streamed down her face as she held her mama tightly. She had longed for her arms. The arms that had rocked her gently on many sleepless nights. The arms that had reached for her as she struggled to take her first steps. The arms that had picked her up when she hurt herself playing. The arms had that steadied her in her seat when cars came to abrupt stops. These were the arms that she thought of every day since her mama became addicted. Not the arms that pushed her away. Not the arms that no longer reached out for her. Not the arms that held the pipe. Not the arms that swung at her in frustration. But these arms-- her mama's arms. These were the ones that she had missed. These were the ones that she wanted around her always. It felt so good to be back in her mama's embrace that she wanted to stay in that moment forever.

Vanessa looked on silently with tears trickling down her cheeks. After they all finished crying, Vonshay began to show Vickie all of her new acquisitions one-by-one, explaining where they came from, how much they cost, and why she needed them. Vickie was happy for her child and pleased that Vonshay did not suffer because of her mistakes. She wished she could share in her daughter's excitement, but she couldn't. She was glad that Vonshay would go to college, but Vickie wanted to be the one who gave her all of the things she needed to make her life away from home enjoyable. She wanted the joy in her daughter's eyes to be because of what she had done, not what Vanessa and Andre' had done. She forced an exterior smile to hide the interior rage she felt each time Vonshay unintentionally bragged to her about another item. She was glad when it was over and everything was put in the car.

They spent the remainder of the evening just as Vanessa planned it. She wanted to keep Vickie busy so she wouldn't have time to think about drugs, so she ordered Chinese food and rented some videos. They ate popcorn and watched movies until they fell asleep in front of the TV.

Vickie was accustomed to getting up early in the hospital, so she was the first one out of the bed the next morning. She went to the kitchen to fix herself a cup of coffee and smoke a cigarette. On her way, she passed the den and stopped to look at the empty room. She pictured the room full of all of Vonshay's belongings that were now packed in the car and ready to go. I need to get something for my child, she thought. I don't have a thin dime. If I ask Vanessa, it'll be just like she bought it, and I've got to get something on my own.

She went back to her room and started rummaging through the closet. Here it is, she said to herself as she held up a checkbook. I'll get her as much as they did and get me a little something to celebrate with. "It's not every day your only child goes to college," she smirked.

Lie burst into a robust laughter.

She quietly showered and dressed. Heading down the hall towards the door, Vickie heard Vanessa shift sleeping positions. She stood motionless as she waited for her sister to settle back into her sleep. When the movement stopped, Vickie continued towards the door.

After getting in the car, Vickie gently pulled the door closed. She carefully turned the key in the ignition as if she could keep the car engine from making its normal cranking sound. Slowly and cautiously she pulled out of the driveway. Her first impulse was to go the mall, but she knew that no one there would accept a check from her. The foreigners didn't know her, so they wouldn't be as smart. As she steered the car downtown, thoughts of all the things she would buy floated through her mind. She envisioned Vonshay strutting across the campus in one of the many outfits she planned to buy for her. She even planned to pick up something for Vanessa, feeling that it was the least she could do, since her sister always bought her nice things, and Vickie knew that Vanessa would even give her some of her personal belongings if she really wanted them. Besides, she had been looking out for her child while she was away, and had done a pretty good job of it, too, though she hated to admit it.

The entire time Vickie devised her strategy, not once did she consider the fact that she planned to buy all of these items with checks that were from a closed account. Neither did she consider the real reactions that Vonshay and Vanessa would have. Vickie thought they would be appreciative of the gifts, but she didn't foresee the anger that would leap from their mouths, nor the disappointments that would burst from their hearts. She only saw what she wanted to see, not what was actually there.

Truth struggled to escape the trap that Lie had set for him.

When Vickie arrived downtown, she entered every store she passed and bought everything she thought her baby might want or need. She bought Vanessa a few things, too. She didn't buy anything for herself though, because her treat would come later. Just as she left out of the last store, she ran into Christi.

"Hey, girl," Christi said with a smile. She knew something wasn't right because she noticed Vickie trying to avoid her.

"Hey," Vickie responded with a guilty look. "I'm out trying to get some last minute items for Vonshay. You know she's going to college tomorrow," she said proudly.

"Vanessa told me. I'm glad for you. She's a pretty little thing and smart, too."

"Yeah, well I better run. See you later," she said getting into the car. She sped off as if the devil himself were after her. She drove to an empty parking lot nearby to figure out where to go from there.

I know Christi is going straight to Vanessa and tell her she saw me, she told herself. Do I go home now or do I go later? Either way, I'll be in hot water. I can't deal with her trippin' right about now. Ain't nothin' wrong with me trying to get some stuff for my baby to take to school. Hmph, I'm her mama--that's what

I'm *supposed* to do. I'm not thinking about Vanessa or Christi. I'm going to finish taking care of my business. I'll see her when I see her. If I'm gon' get in trouble for something, I may as well make it worth my while, she mused as she cranked the car.

Vickie had been so distracted with her thoughts that she didn't realize that she was exactly where she needed to be. Having decided where she wanted to go, she drove out of the church parking lot without ever looking up.

Christi knew something was wrong. Vickie didn't have any money, and she knew Vanessa was too afraid to send her out alone. She got in her car and went straight to the Morgan house. She knew that Vanessa must have been asleep because it took her longer than usual to get to the door. Finally, she peeked out and let Christi in.

"Girl, what are you doing here at ten in the morning?" Vanessa asked, still wiping sleep from her eyes.

"I just ran into Vickie, and I figured that I needed to tell you.

"What?!" Vanessa said confusedly, letting the information seep in. She looked out of the window and saw that the car was gone. Then, she opened Vickie's bedroom door to an empty bed. "I can't believe this girl! Christi, will you take me to find her? I'll be ready in one hot second."

Christi waited for her in the car. They rode over Ferguson for an hour and a half looking for Vickie. They went to the mall, downtown, and by the local crack houses. No one admitted to having seen Vickie. They couldn't find her anywhere, so Vanessa decided to go home and call Dr. Winters. She had a feeling deep inside that Vickie was somewhere getting high. She needed him to tell her how to handle the situation, because she was about to lose control.

When she arrived at home, she went directly to the telephone to call Dr. Winters. After she reached him, she explained to him what had happened. He was obviously very upset. He told her to bring Vickie back to him as soon as she found her. "When I finish with her this time, she'll never want to get high again," he said.

Before Vanessa had a chance to respond, the door opened and Vickie appeared. "Where in the hell have you been?" she screamed. Realizing she had cursed, she added, "You're going to make me lose my religion, and I ain't planning on going to Hell for nobody! Lord, please forgive me," she pleaded as Vickie just stood gazing at her with glossy eyes. Her sister was as high as a kite.

"Put her on the phone," Dr. Winters yelled, trying to get Vanessa's attention again. She heard him and handed her sister the phone.

"Hello," Vickie said wondering who was on the other end. She had no idea it would be *him*.

"Well, well, well," the doctor hummed. "You couldn't handle it after all, could you? You probably didn't intend to. You just had to get you a hit, huh?" Vanessa hadn't told him that Vickie was high, but he was her doctor, and he knew where she had been.

"You checkin' up on me?" Vickie blurted. "Well, for your information, I ain't high." She was lying through her teeth. She knew that her lie would turn to truth soon because all of the commotion had almost blown her high. She wished she hadn't come back so soon. She was not ready for all the drama.

Lie laughed at her state of internal confusion.

"Well, you'll wish you were when I see you again."

"You won't be seeing me again, because I'm not coming back!"

"That's bull!" Vanessa shouted. "You're on your way right now!"

Vonshay woke up to the sound of loud voices. She stayed in her room listening, and when she could bear it no more, she got up and went to the kitchen. She saw the look on her mama's face and heard the tone in her voice that she had wished away so many times before. It was back. Not again, she thought. "Mama!" she yelled.

Vickie was so startled that she dropped the phone to the floor. The doctor was still on the line. She spun around and looked into her daughter's face. It was as pitiful as a puppy's. Vickie couldn't take it. At that moment, she realized that she had

140

messed up once again.   She began crying and screaming, "Mama's sorry, baby. I don't mean to keep hurting you over and over. Please forgive me!"

Vonshay just stared at her mother with contempt in her eyes. Vanessa picked up the phone to speak with the doctor. He instructed her to bring Vickie back to the hospital immediately, and promised that he would be there waiting. Vickie was crying and trying to explain herself to Vonshay. Vanessa and Christi left them alone and went to finish packing the car. Vanessa struggled to restrain the curse words on the tip of her tongue from rolling off. (She had been convicted about cursing after understanding the double mindedness in using the same tongue, which she praised God with, to speak curses to man.) In between Vanessa's outbursts of anger, Christi managed to tell her friend that she would return all of the merchandise to the stores and pick up the checks that Vickie had written that morning. Vanessa was glad because she had not thought that far ahead, yet. Her main focus was getting Vickie back to Jackson, so she was thankful to have a friend like Christi, one who was there to help out in the good times and the bad.

The two- hour drive to Jackson seemed like it would never come to an end. Neither the miles nor the minutes passed fast enough. Words were as absent as many of our children's fathers.   Their existence is known, but they can't be found. Vonshay was blessed that she had a father whose participation in her life was both definite and definitive. Each time she thought of him and how he was always there for her, she smiled. Having his love at this point was very important to her. She thought about him all the way to Jackson to keep from thinking about her mama. Vickie was only an arm's length away, yet Vonshay felt that she couldn't be reached.

Once they arrived in Jackson, Vanessa headed straight for the hospital. Vickie tried to prolong her return by saying that she was hungry. She really wasn't because the drugs had totally removed her appetite. Vanessa acted as if Vickie wasn't even sitting there talking to her. She proceeded to the hospital and escorted Vickie in. Dr. Winters was waiting at the front. He timed their trip and made it his business to be at the door when they arrived. Vickie dropped her head when her eyes met his. He politely nodded to Vanessa and thanked her for bringing Vickie back.

Vanessa returned to the car to find Vonshay sitting in the front seat crying. She didn't say anything to her niece because she wanted her to release as much of the hurt as she could. If crying was her relief, so be it. Vanessa used crying as a release, too, now that she had given up cursing. She figured Vonshay cursed for relief as well, having grown up around it, but she knew that her niece wouldn't dare use profanity in front of her. Vanessa pictured the child sitting in the car cursing the entire time she waited for her to return. That picture was worth the thousand curse words that Vonshay cut short when she saw Vanessa approaching the car.

When Vanessa got in the car, she reached over and held Vonshay's hand. "What you sow in tears, you will reap in joy, baby," she assured her. "I know it seems bad now, but its gonna get better…just keep praying." Vonshay nodded and released Vanessa's hand. They left the hospital and went downtown to the Marriott Suites where they were scheduled to meet Andre'.

Vonshay searched the parking lot for her daddy's car, and when she spotted it a smile spread across her face. While Vanessa checked in, she ran up to her daddy's room. When Andre' opened the door, he could tell his baby had been crying. He hugged her tightly and asked what was wrong. She explained to him what had happened.

"That's O.k., baby," he told her. "Your mama will be all right." Andre' hoped that he was saying the right thing. He didn't really know how to handle this situation or what to tell his child to help her through it. Although he really wanted to, he could not talk negatively about Vickie to Vonshay. No matter how mad Vonshay was, that was still her mama, and he knew that she would defend her. What he didn't know was that his daughter defended him as well when the shoe was on the other foot.

"I know. I'm all right," she said wiping her eyes.

"TeeTee's checking in, and she'll be up in a minute. How was your drive?"

"It was pretty good. You hungry? I thought we might go out for dinner."

"Yeah. So much has been going on that I haven't even thought about eating. I know TeeTee hasn't either," she replied.

When Vanessa came up, Vonshay went to their adjoining suite to dress for dinner. This gave Vanessa a chance to talk privately with Andre' about Vickie. She hadn't discussed the situation with him before because she didn't want to betray her sister. After talking it over with Christi, she decided that he had a right to know exactly what was going on. He was Vonshay's daddy and what affected her, affected him. And this was definitely affecting Vonshay, no matter how she tried to hide it.

Andre' was surprisingly sensitive toward Vickie's situation. His main concern was his daughter's welfare, but he knew that this was entangled into Vickie's welfare. Therefore, his only choice was to do whatever he could to make the situation as tolerable as possible for everybody involved. This was still his family, and they needed him to help hold them together, not pull them further apart. He offered Vanessa his support and thanked her for taking care of Vonshay.

They decided to have dinner at the waterfront. Andre' had heard about a new seafood place that served excellent food and drinks and had a beautiful view of Lake Picard. More than anything, he needed a drink. He figured Vonshay and Vanessa did, too. Although Vonshay wasn't of legal drinking age, he didn't mind her drinking. As a matter of fact, he had been giving her beer and wine since she was a toddler. When wine coolers first appeared on the market, he brought some home and encouraged her to drink them. Vickie had accused him of turning their child into an alcoholic like him. He didn't take her seriously because he didn't think that he was an alcoholic.

Sitting on the patio of the restaurant watching the evening sun set on the still water gave them all a sense of peace. They wished that their lives were as calm as the lake instead of impetuous like the mighty Mississippi River. They took advantage of the temporary peacefulness by discussing the positive things in their lives while they enjoyed the variety of seafood offered on the all-you-can-eat buffet.

After dinner, they returned to the hotel. Vonshay spent the night in Andre's room sharing her excitement about college with him. He was really tired, but he could not go to sleep on his baby girl. He was glad that she wasn't showing any signs of depression from the day's events. They stayed up to almost three o'clock, but neither of them noticed the time. They were enjoying each other just that much.

Vanessa went to her room to get some sleep. She made it to her room, but sleep was nowhere to be found. All she could think about was Vickie. She wondered what Dr. Winters was doing to her. He sounded furious on the phone and promised to make Vickie pay. She wondered how he would do it.

After hours of thinking and wondering, she was exhausted. Still, she could not fall asleep. She closed her eyes and said a silent prayer.

Lord, please clear my mind of all that is troubling me. Take control of my sister and her life because she has no control of it. I am turning her over to You, Lord, and leaving her in Your hands. Please watch my sister's child as she goes off to school. Keep her mind focused on her reason for being there. Don't let her get bogged down with anger and depression concerning her mama. Lord, give us all strength and hold us together. Thank You for Andre' and his willingness to help and his love for this family. Thank You, Lord, for all You have done, for being there for me and for just being You. I give You all the glory, honor, and praise, forever, Amen.

With all of the things going on, her intimate time with God had decreased and she missed it greatly. Nevertheless, she knew that He was still with her, although sometimes she felt as if He was far away and she was alone.

Even though no one slept well, everyone was up the next morning by eight o'clock. Vonshay was scheduled to be at her dormitory by ten and at orientation by twelve. She didn't want to be late, so they dressed quickly and went to the hotel cafe' for breakfast. When they were finished eating, they headed to Tougaloo College.

Vonshay had never been on the school's campus before, and she couldn't wait to see her new home. Whenever she was in Jackson with either her parents or her auntie, they always asked her if she wanted to go by and look at the campus. She always said "no". She didn't tell them at the time, but initially she had no intention of attending Tougaloo. She had heard how raggedy the Black college campuses were, so she wanted to go to one of the white state-supported universities. She had visited the campus of one on a field trip and was impressed by the big buildings, the large dormitory rooms, the private rest rooms, the personal phone lines, and the school's overall appearance. She had also heard that you got a better education at white schools, an old white lie that they just won't turn loose. When the time came to fill out applications, she filled out one for all of the major white institutions in Mississippi.

While she was sending applications all over the state, Andre' was sending just one, the one for Tougaloo College. He knew that his daughter would get a better education there than she would at any of those white schools she applied to. He admitted that the school was old and a little worn down, but he knew that her education was not based on the physical deficiencies of the school, like the cracked walls, rotting steps, unpaved roads, and the buildings which lacked air conditioning. Her education would come from the richness of the school's history, the depths of the professors' knowledge, the genuineness of their concern, and the diligence of their efforts to educate young Black minds in the ways of the two worlds in which they would live, the Black one and the White one. No experience at any white school would offer, let alone give her that. His daughter couldn't see this at her age, so he decided to help her out. It was his duty as a father, and he knew that one day she would thank him.

When the acceptance letters came back from the various schools, they all sat down and looked over them. The white schools had accepted Vonshay, but had offered no financial support, although she had above average grades and test scores. The fact that Tougaloo offered her a full scholarship made Andre's task of winning her over much less difficult. She decided on her own to attend Tougaloo College.

As they drove onto the narrow roads of the small campus, Vonshay's eyes widened as her smile faded. It was worse than she ever imagined. Tears began to well in her eyes when she saw the ancient buildings, the gravel roads, and the grass infested tennis court. No way! They'll have to tie me down before I stay here, she thought.

When Andre' pulled up to the door of Judson Cross Hall, the freshman dormitory known to the campus simply as JC, and announced that it was where Vonshay would be residing, she just sat dumbfounded. It looked like a huge Antebellum home (columns and all). Look at this place, she told herself. I can't believe they think I'm going to actually live here. They must be out of their everlasting minds. Daddy may as well leave my stuff in the car. This place is a HOT mess! Oh, God, its ridiculous.

"Let's go get the key to your room," Vanessa said excitedly, as she opened the car door. Vanessa got out, but Vonshay sat motionless. Vanessa opened Vonshay's door and saw the tears flowing down her face. "What's wrong with TeeTee's baby?" she asked while trying to keep a straight face. She didn't want to laugh, but it was funny to her because she knew exactly what was wrong with her niece. She and Vickie had both acted the same way when they first came to Tougaloo. Judson Cross was the same dorm they had lived in as freshmen.

"I can't stay here, TeeTee," she sobbed with all sincerity. "Look at this place. I bet it looks even worse on the inside. I bet it's a hundred years old!"

"Oh, girl, don't act like that. You'll get used to it and you'll love it. It's just freshman shock, that's all. Everybody goes through it. In no time, you'll feel right at home.

"At home? This place can never feel like home to me. I wouldn't even want to visit this place, let alone live here!"

"I'm telling you from experience that it'll be all right. Everybody acts like this when they first see the campus. Just give

146

it a chance. The school has even more now that it did when I was here. At least, you'll have a phone in your room. When I was a freshman, everyone had to use the one phone in the hallway. By my senior year we were able to have phones in our rooms, but we had to set up our own accounts and pay for it through Bell South. After a little time here, we'll have to beg you to come home," she teased.

"O.k., but I already know it will not and cannot work. Look at it! The paint is peeling from the walls and the floors aren't even flat—they're lopsided and it's HOT. This place isn't capable of growing on me."

"We'll see," Vanessa said as she led Vonshay through the main entrance and into the lobby to pick up the keys to her room. A feeling of nostalgia came over her as she remembered the days that she hung out in the lobby watching TV, playing cards, and attending popcorn bashes.

As she led Vonshay to her room, Vanessa continued to give her a list of improvements that the school had undergone since she had been a student there.

"Girl, there's the Social Science Complex and the new Health and Wellness Center on campus. The Woodworth Chapel has been renovated, and oh, you *must* go to chapel services on Wednesdays at 10 o'clock. There are no classes or offices open during that time so there's no reason to miss it. It's not a church service; it's educational enrichment. It may sound boring, but you'll enjoy it and learn a lot from the programs and the speakers. O.k. back to the campus-soon, Judson Cross will be a part of a renovation project, as well. The Eagle Queen is on the move! I feel proud every time I come back because Tougaloo is where history meets the future, honey. The most successful African Americans in Mississippi graduated from this school, and the school not only selected you, but it offered you the highest scholarship. You should be honored to be here," Vanessa said firmly. She did not want her niece to base her perception about people and places on mere appearance--she wanted her to realize their essence.

After following what seemed like an obstacle course to The Annex, the name given to the back area of the building,

Vonshay wanted to scream when she opened the door to the room she had been assigned. It was small, hot, old, and stuffy, with a small window that had a torn screen. There was a set of twin beds made from iron with the thinnest mattresses she had ever seen. At the foot of each bed next to the closet-which was only an open space in the wall-stood leaning rusted iron chests of drawers which had more knobs missing than present. In the middle of the room between the two beds stood a large table, with storage shelves on each side. None of the tan and brown furniture matched the baby blue paint on the walls. Vonshay could not see any potential for the place. She envisioned day after day of misery. Vanessa assured her that with a little work, the room would be transformed in to a comfortable and inviting place. Vonshay seriously doubted that that was possible.

By lunch, Vonshay and Vanessa had put all of her things away neatly, and Andre' had hung her pictures of her family and friends and posters of her favorite singers and actors. Even all of the extras didn't make the room look or feel like home to Vonshay. It was still small, hot, old, and stuffy. The only difference was that it had added color. She couldn't believe that she would have to share the small space with someone she didn't even know. It was barely enough space for one person. Two would really be pushing it.

At the orientation meeting, Andre' and Vanessa saw some of their classmates from Tougaloo College who were bringing their children and loved ones to school as well. That is one of the great aspects of historically Black Colleges like Tougaloo; they are traditions. One day many of the students who were brought to the campus that day would return to bring their own children. The parents reminisced about their days at Tougaloo and introduced their children to their friends' children. They were all excited, but the new students just watched in bewilderment.

At the end of the orientation, it was time for family and friends to leave. Both Vanessa and Andre' gave Vonshay private departure lectures. They told her what to do, what not to do, when to do, when not to do, where to go, where not to go, how to act, and how not to act. If she did or didn't do everything they

148

said, college would be the worst time of her life, not the best.

When the time for them to leave was at hand, Andre' and Vanessa didn't want to go any more than Vonshay wanted them to, but they all knew it was inevitable. They hugged, kissed, and cried. Then, Vanessa and Andre' left.

Vonshay sat on her bed motionless and speechless. She had always dreamed of going off to college, but now she felt alone. She cried and cried and cried, but no one was there to wipe the tears away or to tell her that everything would be all right. When she reached for a Kleenex from the shelf on her side of the desk, she noticed that Vanessa had placed a small Bible next to the tissues. She picked it up and noticed that it was a pocket-sized Bible with a snap, which had her name engraved in gold lettering on the outside cover. She held the Bible in her hands and did what she had seen her aunt do on many occasions-she began to pray and ask God to lead her to the scripture that would speak life into her present situation. When she opened the Bible, it separated itself at the pages containing Psalms 126, and in verse 5 she found the word from the Lord for that moment in her life. It read, "They that sow in tears shall reap in joy."

Chapter 10

Vickie felt extremely guilty about what she had done, and she began apologizing to Dr. Winters as soon as Vanessa walked out of the door, but to no avail. Dr. Winters was not interested in her story.

"It's too late to be sorry now," he told her as they walked down the hospital corridor."

"But you don't understand," she tried to explain. "I just don't know what happened. It was like I couldn't control myself. It kept calling my name."

"I know, darling, and you just had to answer, didn't you?" Not waiting for a response, he continued. "Well, I'm about to teach you how to ignore that little voice that just won't leave you alone."

"Where are we going?" Vickie asked, as the doctor walked right past her room.

"I'm taking you to a private room. For the next few weeks, it'll just be me and you," he promised.

And he kept his word. It was just the two of them. During the next few weeks, Dr. Winters was the only person Vickie saw. She was not allowed to leave the room, so he brought her food to her room three times a day. The methadone was now obsolete. He promised to make her go cold turkey, and he did.

He attempted to counsel Vickie on his visits. Some days she responded, and others she did not. Her mood swings were like a metronome in sixteenth time. They went swiftly from one extreme to the next. He never knew what to expect when he walked in the room, but he was capable of dealing with the unexpected.

After four weeks of what Vickie saw as solitary confinement, she decided that the doctor was crazy enough to keep her in that room alone until she responded to him. Knowing that she hated being alone and realizing that it didn't bother the doctor one way or the other, she came to the conclusion that she would be a good patient and talk to him every time he entered the room.

Lie tried to convince her not to be truthful, but for the first time in a long while, she chose not to follow his advice.

The doctor was pleased when he noticed the change in Vickie's attitude. For the next week, they had wonderful sessions. He learned a lot more about Vickie as she learned a lot more about her addiction. She planned on using talking to him only as a way of staying out of "solitary," but she soon realized that it was something she needed. Dr. Winters was looking out for her best interest.

Because the sessions were going so well and Vickie's behavior was no longer calculated, but natural, Dr. Winters decided to resume her group sessions with other patients and to allow her to go back to her room. At this point in her treatment, she needed support from people who had gone through similar experiences.

When Vickie walked into her room, Carol was sitting on the bed reading a magazine. Although Carol was white, Vickie was glad to see a face other than that of Dr. Winters.

"Hi," Carol said. "Long time no see."

"Too long," Vickie replied. "I've been cooped up in "solitary" with the good doctor. I thought I'd never get out."

"I'm surprised he kept you up there so long. A week is usually his max," Carol stated.

"Well, I didn't start out as a cooperative patient. Maybe if I had adjusted sooner, I would have been out sooner, but I guess it worked out," Vickie said in an unsure tone. She was still contemplating that issue.

"Can I see your new schedule?" Carol asked. "Maybe we're still in some of the same groups."

Vickie showed the schedule to her, and when Carol compared it to her own, they realized that they were identical. Their first session together would begin in fifteen minutes, so they prepared to go.

When Vickie walked in, she thought that they were early. There were only six people in attendance, including Dr. Winters. This frightened Vickie because she knew that this meant she could not just fade into the crowd as she had done at the first sessions she had attended. There was no crowd this time. She would be up close, but she refused to be personal.

Waiting for the session to begin, Vickie looked at each of the people and wondered why they were there. I know that they've got some kind of addiction, but what kind? They look normal to me, but that doesn't mean anything because I looked normal to me, when all my friends and family thought I was half dead. I'll stop trying to figure them all out and just ask Carol when we go back to the room. She's been here a while and probably knows the 411 on everybody. I'm trying to find out from Carol why everybody else is here, and I don't even know why she's here. As she focused her attention to Carol, she heard Dr. Winters' voice.

When she tuned in, he was asking them all to think of the worst thing that their addiction had caused to happen. Vickie stared as she watched the various expressions of deep thought appear on the people's faces. She journeyed deeper in her mind as well. I wonder if anybody is going to really tell their personal business to strangers. I'm definitely not going to tell mine, especially to a room full of white people. They already have in their minds that almost all Black women are drug addicts who do nothing but get high and have babies. There is no way I'll give them a personal testimony to support the notion. I only have one child, but they'd probably assume that the only reason is because I'm incapable of having another.

Vickie heard a voice. She followed the sound and realized that it was Carol. She listened intently.

"The worst time for me," Carol began slowly, "was the day I got caught getting high on the job. I'm an anesthesiologist. This particular day, I was in the operating room preparing the anesthesia for a patient. For the last two years, every time I made my preparations, I would take a hit of the anesthesia. Well, that particular day, I just couldn't get enough. It was almost time for the surgery, and I was standing over in the corner with the mask up to my face trying to take in as much as I could. I didn't stop when the doctor saw me. I couldn't stop. I felt like I had to have it right then, no matter what. I knew that my career was over when the doctor caught me, so I tried to get even more. When he approached me, I cursed him out and left the room. When I reached the front door of the hospital, security officers were waiting, and as they say, the rest is history," Carol said regrettably.

"What makes you feel that was the worst day?" Dr. Winters asked.

"Because that's the day I lost total control. At the onset, I could stop in ample time for surgery. Then, I started pushing it to three or four minutes before time. Soon, I only had seconds to spare. This day, I couldn't let go of the drug. I let my job and all of my hard years in school go because I couldn't let go of the drug."

Everyone sat quietly for a few minutes. Another voice broke the silence. It was the voice of a man named Randy.

"The day I lost my family was the worst. I committed an unspeakable crime." He paused for a moment, then slowly with tears in his eyes, he continued. "I attempted to rape my daughter, my own child, when she came home from school one day. I had been getting high since the night before. She looked so beautiful to me, just like her mama. She walked in and came over to kiss me on the cheek, like she always did. I was aroused. I grabbed her and began passionately kissing her in the mouth. When she pulled away, I grabbed her again and started ripping off her clothes. I can still hear her screaming, 'No, Daddy! Stop! Don't do this to me!' I didn't stop though. By the time I had pinned her

153

to the floor and was pulling down my pants, my wife, her mama, who I hadn't even heard come in, was yelling, 'Get away from my child before I kill you, you old dirty dog!' The sound of her voice snapped me back to reality, but it was too late. She shot me. The bullet went through my back and came out of my chest, missing my heart by only a half of an inch. To this day, I wish she had killed me. I really wish she had," he sobbed.

Before the doctor had a chance to reply, another member of the group, Nikki, began to tell her story. He didn't want to interrupt her because he preferred to let the patients speak whenever they felt the urge. If he had chosen to put them off, they may not have been willing to share later.

"I sold my body and tried to take my life all in the same day," she shared. "Suicide is an unforgivable sin, and I considered it. At the time, I thought my problem was too big for God. I knew it was too big for me. Now, I know He can handle anything. I wanted to take my life because my only desire was to get high—by any means necessary, and I had started doing whatever it took. I used to turn tricks and make two and three hundred dollars. The more drugs I did, the faster the money went, and the harder it was to come by. One day I gave a man a blowjob for just two dollars. That's when I knew I was gone. Can you believe that--two dollars? I sold my body for two measly dollars!"

"Yeah! I can believe it!" another lady named Cynthia blurted out. "It's whores like you that give other whores a bad name. I been hookin' for a long time, and I always made good money 'til you desperate ho's started coming on the street giving it away. Nobody wanted to pay anymore. Said we cost too much and they could get whatever they wanted from a junkie for little o' nothin'. It put me out of business."

"Well," Nikki, responded, "you're a junkie, too. That's why you're here, remember?"

"Honey, I know that," Cynthia retorted. "But, I ain't no two-dollar-whore. When I give it up, I get paid a lot more than a coupla dollars. That's the difference between you and me. I'll keep it to myself before I let it go cheap. Some of us junkie whores do have standards," she said sarcastically.

"That's enough ladies," Dr. Winters intruded before either had a chance to continue. "The session is almost over and I have some things to say before we dismiss. Those of you who did not share today should write down your feelings about your worst day and share them at the next session. Being able to identify your worst day shows you how much progress you've made and how much you need to make to be at your best.
Let's recite the creed."

Vickie had learned the creed and she joined with the others in the recitation. When they finished, Dr. Winters dismissed them by saying, "Remember, keep it simple and take one day at a time."

Vickie watched as everyone began to leave the room. Nikki and Cynthia are walking out together-- after all that! she thought. They're talking like nothing happened. I don't believe it. I would be too mad to say anything to her, much less leave with her.

"They're not mad at each other," Carol said, reading the expression on Vickie's face. "Nothing in Group should be taken personally. We just share our thoughts and feelings. Nobody's opinions are the same and nobody concentrates on the differences because we are all at a common place, addiction. We just took different routes to get here."

"Oh" Vickie said.

As Dr. Winters gathered his belongings, he noticed Vickie heading for the door. He called her to him. "Vickie, I hope that next time you will be ready to share with the group," he said. "You'd be surprised to know how good it makes you feel afterwards. Releasing what you're keeping inside is always healthier than holding it in."

"I can't tell these people my business. *I* don't even want to know *my* business," she said. "I wish I didn't have any to tell nobody."

"Vickie, you have to face what you have or have not done. Ignoring it is just like ignoring your problem. Once you face everything, you have to learn to forgive yourself for it. It's

155

over; we all make mistakes. The God that created us is a forgiving God. If He forgives you, why can't you forgive yourself?" he asked.

"I feel so guilty, like I'm not even worthy of forgiveness. I've hurt too many people. People who were supposed to be important in my life."

"Like I said, if God can forgive you, who are we not to? Think about it, and each day work on forgiving yourself for something you've done."

"All right," Vickie answered, "but I'm not making any promises."

"Whenever it's right for you. Only *you* are in control of it," he said as he walked out of the room.

Vickie returned to her room. She was glad Carol wasn't there because she needed some time alone. She sat on the bed and thought about all of the things she had heard in Group. She couldn't believe some of the things people had done for drugs. Then she thought of the things she had done and it seemed more real. She kneeled down and prayed. As she asked the Lord for forgiveness, tears filled her eyes. Her words turned into mumblings and then to moans. She could no longer articulate what she wanted to say, but God understood the pleas of her heart because the Spirit made intercession for her. Her healing process had begun. She lifted her body up, but tears continued to stream down. Each tear that fell washed away stains that had penetrated her being and revealed the true creation of God that was hidden beneath.

As Vickie sat on the side of her bed, all she could think about was Vonshay. She wondered if her daughter would ever be able to forgive her. When Vonshay was younger, the two of them were very close. Vickie had always spent quality time with her daughter, and they had developed a very special mama/daughter/friend relationship. Once, Vonshay could talk to Vickie about anything, but things had changed. Vickie's drug use damaged the relationship. The more drugs Vickie took into her body, the less time she spent with Vonshay. Vickie had noticed the difference, but she had not been able to do anything about it. It had gotten to the point where she'd rather see the dope than her daughter.

Vickie knew that Vonshay was angry with her, and she certainly had every right to be. The person who had filled her life with the comforts of middle-class living and the joys of a loving mama had reneged on her. She was now lower class, at best, and her mama had been less than loving towards her. After having fed her with a silver spoon all of her life, she suddenly snatched it away from her lips without a warning. Vickie realized that she was at fault for the drastic changes taking place in her daughter's life, and she wanted more than anything to make it up to her. Unfortunately, she just didn't know how, she continually tried to think of ways she could make amends for all that she had done.

It's so hard for me to talk to Vonshay now, she thought. Whenever I say anything to her, her response is short and dry. She only answers specific questions, and she doesn't say anything else; I've got to work on our relationship because I can't stand the idea of losing my daughter. Although others may not have known, Vonshay has always been my strength. I would have given up on life a long time ago had it not been for that little girl. Now, I am beginning to wonder why I didn't. It probably would've been easier for both of us because I've made such a mess of my life and hers. The child's life has to be miserable, and I don't know how I can salvage what's left, but I have to try. I know that she loves me. I just hope that love is strong enough for her to forgive me.

Vickie tried to go to sleep but couldn't. She felt the need to communicate with Vonshay immediately. She wanted to call, but she was afraid. She didn't know what to say or how to say it. The last time she had seen Vonshay was the day that they brought her back to the rehab center. That was the day before Vonshay was to go to school. Umph, Vickie thought. I botched that up, too! I had a chance to take my only child to school, and I messed it up. I couldn't wait a few more hours until she was safe in her new environment. No, I had to run out and get high. I wasn't even there to share the excitement of going to college with her. How can I expect her to forgive me over and over again?

I've told that child 'I'm sorry' so many times in the last year that she probably doesn't even believe it any more. I bet she thinks more of the little boy who cried wolf than me. "The Lord knows every time I said I was sorry I meant it, and I mean it now," she said softly, as if she were actually talking to Vonshay.

She reached for the phone and dialed the switchboard at Tougaloo. It was a shame she didn't even know how to call her daughter directly. While the operator had her on hold, Vickie hung up the phone; she wasn't ready for this. She didn't know what to say and had no idea how Vonshay would react to her call. She sat on the bed and wondered if Vonshay would be glad to hear from her or be mad because she called. She imagined dialogues between the two of them and anticipated what each one would say, but it still did not make her comfortable.

Vickie decided to take the easy way out and write a letter. When she was younger, Vonshay had always written her letters to apologize for something she had done wrong. If Vickie wrote a letter, she wouldn't have to see or hear Vonshay's reaction. Neither one of them would be put on the spot. She could say exactly what she wanted to say without being interrupted. This was the best she could do for now because she didn't feel strong enough to do it any other way.

Truth stood guard as the words flowed from her and found rest on the beautifully designed stationery.

Vickie wrote Vonshay an eight- page letter in which she tried to explain to her child that a lot of her negative behaviors were because of the drugs. She told Vonshay that it was not her desire to push her away or to neglect her, but that it was the drugs that were controlling her. She attempted to explain how she had gotten hooked on the drugs and how she planned to overcome the addiction.

It took Vickie a while to write the letter because she had to choose her words very carefully. She couldn't afford to say the wrong thing. When she finished Vonshay's letter she decided to write Vanessa. She needed her forgiveness as well.

By the time she finished the letter to her sister, she was tired. She looked over at the clock, and it was only ten o'clock, but her body was drained. She took a shower and slipped into the emerald nightgown from Victoria's Secret that Vanessa had bought her. The silk felt so soft against her skin. She slid under the covers and was sleep within minutes. She rested peacefully the entire night.

The next morning, Carol woke Vickie up at eight o'clock so that they could have breakfast before their ten o'clock session. While Carol was in the shower, Vickie kneeled down beside her bed and prayed. She thanked God for watching over her and allowing her to wake up to see another drug-free day. She also praised Him for being so good to her and asked that He bless her entire family and keep them covered by His angels.

Vickie felt rejuvenated after she said her prayers. She actually felt good about herself for the first time in a long while, and she wanted to look as good as she felt. She went to the closet and pulled out a caramel colored linen dress that matched her complexion perfectly. After her shower, she slid into the dress and admired herself in the full-length mirror. She resembled her old self again. She looked good. She had the feeling that it would be a special day.

The morning sessions went exceptionally well that day. On her way back to her room, Vickie was called to the rec room. When she arrived at the desk to inquire about the call, Andre' was standing there smiling. "Andre' what are you doing here? Is Vonshay all right?" she asked.

"Yeah, she's fine," he answered, thankful for her renewed concern for their daughter. "I just left her. I had a meeting in town today, so I dropped by the school and I was going to bring Vonshay to see you, but she has classes all day. I just came by to see how things are going and if you need anything."

"Things are going good. Come over here and sit down." Andre' followed her to two empty chairs. "I'm learning a whole lot and I'm getting better," she said when they were seated. "I don't think about or crave drugs like I used to. I'm depending on me and the Lord--what I should've been doing all the time."

"That's good." He paused. "I want to ask you something, but please don't take it the wrong way," Andre' said cautiously.

"O.k. What is it?"

"How did you get hooked up with crack? We always did weed and 'caine, but when folks started talking about smoking 'caine, I told you that we shouldn't try it. It sounded too dangerous."

"I know, but the coke wasn't getting me high anymore. Then, we split and I figured I didn't have nothing to lose by trying it."

"What do you mean?"

"It seemed like everything was falling apart. You didn't want me anymore, and Vonshay didn't seem to need me anymore. The two of you were my life, but it became obvious that I wasn't either of yours. I was looking for a way out. I didn't know I'd end up this far out," Vickie said with a smile, trying not to show how painful it was to answer his question.

"Well, I'm sorry you felt that way. It's not that I didn't want you. I still loved you when I left, and I always will. It's just that we had grown so far apart, and neither of us wanted to come back, or even meet each other half way. We couldn't go on like that."

"I know, and I'm glad that we still talk. In the beginning I was mad and hurt. I said a lot of things about you that I didn't mean, but I accepted that you would always be a part of my life because of Vonshay. I didn't want you to be out of her life just because you were out of mine."

"You know me better than that. I'll always be there for her, and you too, if you need me. You brought my only child in the world, and I have to love you, if only for that reason alone.

"Well, I hope it was more than just that when you married me," Vickie laughed.

"It was. I just said that to make a point."

"I got the message. I was just teasing," she said, looking at her watch.

"You got somewhere to go?"

"I have a session in a few minutes. The topic is "Accepting Addiction". It's a general session, so you can go with me if you want. It might help you to understand what I'm going through a little better."

160

"Well, I'm not in a hurry, and I planned to spend a little more time with you, so I think I will go."

Vickie and Andre' were the first to arrive in the meeting room. They chose their seats and continued their conversation while the others filed in. When Carol entered, Vickie introduced her to Andre'. While they were exchanging pleasantries, Dr. Winters came in.

"Good afternoon," he said, as he closed the door and proceeded to the front of the room. "Today's topic is 'Accepting Addiction'. I want to take a different approach today and let you all facilitate, while I sit and watch. I see we have some new faces and I'd like to welcome each of you and encourage you to participate. Who'd like to begin?" he asked, as he took his seat.

"I will," Randy said, walking to the front. " I want to begin by thanking Dr. Winters for teaching me so much about addiction. When I first came here, I had just acknowledged that I had a problem, but I hadn't really accepted it. When he began to explain addiction to me, and I could see what he was saying in some of my actions, I began to accept my problem. When my family started attending and expressing their feelings about my addiction, I truly realized and accepted it. Hearing people close to you explain how they feel and what they've gone through because of your addiction really makes you think. Once you accept that you've messed up, and you try to straighten things out, they can start to forgive you. My wife forgave me in this very room, and that was something I never thought would happen, so I know that anything is possible and these sessions have a lot to do with it. They help you heal."

Vickie glimpsed at Andre' to see if she could tell what he was thinking. She hoped that he would be able to forgive her for what she had done. His face gave no clue as to what was on his mind.

"That's true, Randy," Nikki said, exchanging places with him. "My family hated me for the things I did, but Group helped them to understand that drugs were controlling me. They learned to hate the things I did and not me. Now they see that I'm really trying and that I'm getting better, and they are helping me to do it. My mom brought my baby to see me, and I could see the love

161

in her eyes. Being away from her has made me hunger to be clean. I know that it's hard for them to love us when we're out there and even harder to understand and forgive us, but if you come back in and believe in yourself, your family will believe in you again."

Vickie glanced at Andre' again, and he was getting out of his seat and going to the front of the room. She had no idea what he would say.

"I didn't know what to do when I found out that my ex-wife had a drug problem, he began. "We had done drugs together throughout our marriage, but we were always able to handle them well--if there is any such thing. Not knowing what else to do, I condemned her. I realized while sitting here listening to you, that I'm no better than she is because I'm an alcoholic and a drug addict. I haven't received any treatment, but I know that's what I am.

"I can't go through one day without a drink. I thought it was O.k. since I only drank beer and I went to work everyday and church on Sunday. I've been drinking beer all my life and I can't do without it. I started out having one or two after work and a few more on the weekend. I started to realize something was wrong when I got to the point where I was oversleeping; I couldn't make it past ten in the morning without a beer, and then I added wine, and occasionally liquor to my list of preferred drinks. I stopped going to church because worship services began after the time for my first beer. Since I wasn't at church, I didn't pay my tithes. That coupled with the fact that I was gradually increasing my drinking budget caused my money to get short. I got behind on rent and I owed friends and family money. I started gambling to make ends meet and at the same time, my need for drugs increased. I still smoke a joint after work everyday. I used to snort 'caine once or twice a month, but now it's every weekend and sometimes during the week. I see now that I have no right to judge Vickie. I'm no better than she-- I just went about things differently. I want her to know that I'm sorry and that I understand that she doesn't want to be like this. I don't either. I don't like the man that I've become. I want to be the man that my daughter would be proud of."

Andre' paused and a persistent tear fell from his eye. "I need some help," he said as he walked toward his seat. Emotionally overwhelmed, Vickie stood up and hugged him.

Truth shouted with joy!

When the session was over, group members gathered their belongings and began to exit, some hugging and shaking hands with others on their way out. Dr. Winters made his way over to Vickie and Andre' and offered Andre' his assistance. Andre' accepted and took down the name and number of one of the doctor's colleagues in Memphis. He told Andre' that his acceptance of his addiction would be vital to his and Vickie's recoveries.

"I never knew you felt that way," Vickie said when they were alone.

"I guess I should have told you," he responded. "We've both made mistakes. I can't throw any stones at you when I'm living in a glass house. I guess all we can do is just work on building some new houses, stone proof, that is."

"Do you forgive me," she asked hopefully.

" I forgive you. Do you think you can do the same for me?"

"It's already done," she answered.

Vickie walked Andre' to the exit and thanked him for a wonderful day. When she got back to her room, she thought about their afternoon together. Her feeling that morning was right; the day turned out to be truly special.

Chapter 11

Vanessa's first two months back home were really hectic. Between registering her sister for the rehab program, enrolling her niece in college, starting a new job, and taking care of business in both Atlanta and Ferguson, she didn't know if she was coming or going. She hadn't had time to attend to personal matters such as pampering herself and bonding with Christi because she was worn out. It was the first of October now, and she wanted to do something for herself---- have some fun.

Vanessa called Christi to see if she had any plans. Hanging out and spending money were no fun if you were alone. "Expecting a call?" Vanessa asked jokingly, when Christi answered on the first ring.

"Yep. Been waiting on one from you for a few weeks now," Christi answered.

"Well, I guess I left myself wide open for that one, huh?" Vanessa said.

"You sure did, girlfriend. So what's up?"

"I think I'm finally settled in, and I want to go out and celebrate. It's a nice autumn day, probably our last weekend of warm weather and I want to get out and enjoy it. A few weeks from now we'll be begging for days like today!" Vanessa said enthusiastically.

"Don't you think it's a bit early; it's not even noon yet."

"Girl, this is an all day process. I want us to get our hair done, our nails manicured, our feet pedicured, and buying a new outfit wouldn't hurt either. Then, we can relax for a while and maybe finish the celebration later tonight at *The Club*."

"You go girl! If you want to do all this in one day, I wouldn't miss it for the world. Let's call and make our appointments. My baby's gone for the weekend, so I'm footloose and fancy free!"

Without warning, Christi clicked over and put her three-way calling into motion. There had been two cancellations at the beauty salon, so they both were able to get an appointment, which was a hard task on any day, especially Saturday. When Christi clicked back over, she and Vanessa said their goodbyes and began to prepare for a day of beauty and a night of fun.

Christi and Vanessa arrived at the salon simultaneously. Their beautician was a little behind schedule. It was probably because she had stopped to run to the store or take a break. They realized that she needed a break, but they couldn't figure out why she wouldn't just set aside time for breaks in her appointment book, instead of setting appointments back to back. Although waiting was really unnerving, they waited and she knew that they would. Changing beauticians wouldn't solve the problem, because the majority of them had the same habits. The ones that didn't were those whose chairs that women who cared about their hair wouldn't be caught dead in.

As they waited for LaShun, they thumbed through Essence and Black Hair Care magazines to decide how they would get their hair styled. Vanessa decided that she would get hers cut. She had been letting it grow out, but she hated those in-between stages like the one she was experiencing now; besides, a fresh cut always did something for her spirit. It made her feel more alive and confident. The fact that her styles drew a lot of attention was a bonus as well. Women who didn't even like her were forced to comment on how "laid" her hair was, and men who didn't even know her had to admit that "the girl's got it going on".

When LaShun sent for Christi, she knew that Vanessa would appear, too. Since Christi hadn't decided on a style and Vanessa gave LaShun creative freedom, Vanessa went first. The snap of the scissors and the clinging of the clippers were music to her ears. She already felt like a new person. She encouraged Christi, who usually wore her hair a moderate length, to get hers cut as well. She did. When the two of them left the shop four hours later, they were convinced of why they wait hours for LaShun to do their hair; God had blessed her with the gift to enhance the beauty He had already given them.

Vanessa and Christi decided to leave Christi's car at the salon and go to the nail shop together. Vanessa was appalled at the prices. They were almost twice as much as what she paid in Atlanta. After Christi reminded her that she was in Ferguson, Mississippi, where there were only two nail salons whose owners were Korean cousins, she resolved herself to the fact that she would have to pay elevated prices if she wanted the services. After an hour and a half of drilling and filing, they left with brightly colored nails and toes.

The Ferguson Mall did not excite Vanessa much because it only had about twenty stores where everybody in town shopped. It wouldn't be unlikely to meet two or more people wearing exactly the same outfit as yours--each time you wore it. Since she never wanted to be a twin, let alone a triplet or quadruplet, she was forced to shop at one of the two local boutiques that were patronized mostly by Whites. The prices were more expensive; but to her, being an individual made it worth the additional money. Neither Vanessa or Christi were die-hard shoppers, so it didn't take them long to select the clothing that fit their individual styles, complemented their hair do's, and matched their freshly done nails.

The goals of the afternoon were accomplished, so they decided to get something to eat and have a drink. Their choices of locations were limited. The only places in town that they could sit down to eat *and* have a drink were Pizza Hut and Golden Hunan, the Chinese restaurant. Neither wanted pizza and beer, and they were not in the mood for stir-fry. It was on these days that Vanessa missed Atlanta even more. Finding somewhere to eat and drink there would not have been a problem. On such a beautiful day, she would go the Cajun Crab House, Houston's, or the Cheesecake Factory (depending on her

166

taste buds) to sit out on the patio and enjoy the food and drinks while she bonded with her girlfriend and experienced the beauty of the outdoors. Out of all the ways she wanted to spend the rest of the evening, the only accommodation Ferguson could offer was nature, so they decided to have steamed shrimp and spumante to enjoy on the patio at Vanessa's house.

"It's gonna be *on* tonight," Christi said as she poured their drinks and took a seat in the patio chair. "We'll look so good it'll be like Salt and Peppa; 'I'll take your man.'"

"Honey, I don't want nobody else's man. I want my own. If he'll leave the one he's with for me, he'll leave me for the next one," Vanessa replied as she leaned back and took a small sip out of her glass.

"I don't mean take him forever, just for the night. He can go home tomorrow," Christi laughed. She took a drink and continued. "You're out here in this nice house by yourself all the time, and I know you've got to get lonely sometimes. All you would have to do is call Derrick, and I'm sure he'd come running as long as he's been after you."

"For your information, Missy, I have called Derrick a few times, and he has come running. It's just that by the time he gets here, I realize that I've made a terrible mistake."

"How?" Christi asked with wonder, looking directly into Vanessa's eyes.

"Because I'm not a one-night stand kinda woman. The thought of him being with me and then going home to someone else won't get it," Vanessa insisted. You reap what you sow, and I'm not messing around with another woman's man-married or not-because I don't want anybody messing with mine when he comes. Besides, I can't see myself married to him, so there is no need wasting my time or his. I just haven't figured out how to tell him what I've decided."

"Girl, sometimes being the other woman is best. You can just enjoy him, but she has to put up with him 24-7; cook for him, clean up behind him, wash his clothes, and all of that. Is that what you wanna do?" Christi asked, enjoying the cool crisp breeze.

167

"Well that depends. If he's my man and the right kind of man, doing those things won't be a burden-- they'll be a pleasure," Vanessa responded, as she contemplated what that would be like.

"Tell me, girlfriend, what is the right kind of man?" Christi questioned, as if she'd been waiting for an answer to that forever and someone had finally figured it out.

"The right kind of man," Vanessa began, "is one who will take the time to know me, who I am and what I'm about. He'll respect me as a woman with goals and dreams. He'll support and encourage me as I strive to reach these goals, and he'll believe that I can. He will listen to what I feel and have to say, and he will share what he feels with me. He will accept me for me and not try to make me someone else. If he feels the need to change me, then he has not accepted me. He will love me at my worst and understand me at my best. I won't have to ask him to do things for me. He will do them because he knows they need to be done, and he wants to be the one to do them. He will enjoy my company even when I am silent. He will realize that my silence is not ignoring him, but enjoying him. But most importantly, he will be a man who loves the Lord with all his heart and walks according to God's will for his life. He will be led by the Spirit of God, and he will help me reach my divine destiny in God as I help him reach his..." Vanessa's voice drifted as her mind became inundated with thoughts of the manifestation of her God given mate.

"Wait a minute," Christi interrupted. "Where on God's green Earth do you ever think you will find this man?"

Vanessa snapped out of her vision and answered, "Wherever on the Earth God put him." Seeing the dumbfounded look on Christi's face, she attempted to explain herself. "When God made the world, He made someone for me. When the time comes, He will put us together. My man will be ready for me and I will be ready for him," Vanessa responded adamantly.

"O.k. I'll go for that, but check this out. I know anything is possible, but I really don't believe that he's going to show up at the door one day and say 'God sent me to you'. You've got to get out there and be approachable," Christi explained.

"I know, but I really don't believe he's here in Ferguson. Not too many new people relocate here, and I know I don't want the ones who are already here." Vanessa said.

"We'll see, girlfriend, we'll see," Christi said, reaching for bottle and filling their glasses.

They sat quietly for a while, enjoying the cool breeze and admiring the amazing arrangement of fluffy white clouds drifting through the golden evening sky. They felt as if God had painted the scene especially for their personal viewing. They both prayed silent prayers. Each one prayed for the other's happiness.

Christi broke the silence. "While you're waiting on the right man, you may as well enjoy another man," she laughed. "Like Derrick. Why don't you call and tell him to meet us at *The Club*?"

"You don't give up, do you? Is that man paying you for props? If he's not, you need to talk to him about it because you sure are campaigning for him," Vanessa said jokingly.

"He pays according to the number of appointments I can set up. Do me a favor and make one for tonight," Christi pleaded.

"Be for real," Vanessa said.

"I am. Do it. You'll have a dance partner and a drink buyer. What more could you want? He's not a stranger, since you say you don't do *them*."

"I thought this was Girls Night Out," Vanessa said trying to come up with an excuse.

"It is, but boys make it more fun! Just call him girl, so you won't be sitting all by yourself while I'm dancing with strangers. You need a little male companionship and at least you *will* talk to Derrick, which is more than you do with other men," Christi smiled.

Vanessa thought for a minute and once again Christi had read her right. For some reason, she was really shy around men who were interested in her. She would smile at them but hardly say two words. She was trying to get over it, but it was hard. She had been hurt before, and she didn't want to be hurt again.

She felt that opening her mouth was like opening her heart, so she had decided not to take any chances by keeping them both closed. She remembered hearing once that the best way to overcome fear was to face it head on, and she knew that God had not given her the spirit of fear. With Christi and the Spumante boosting her up to do it, she decided to call.

"All right, I'll call then," she said with slight hesitation. As she reached for the cordless phone, it rang. She answered.

"Hello. Fine. How are you?" she asked with a bewildered look.

"Who is it?" Christi asked in the background.

"Hold on for a minute," Vanessa said. She pressed the mute button on the phone and said to Christi, "It's him. Can you believe it?"

"Must be telepathy!" she replied. "My man. Perfect timing."

"What should I say?" Vanessa questioned.

"Girl, just talk!" Christi yelled. "And hurry up before he hangs up!"

"I'm back," Vanessa said. "Just talking to Christi. We're thinking about going to *The Club* later."

"We're not thinking," blurted Christi, "we're going. Now tell him to meet us there."

"Around eight," Vanessa continued. "Why don't you stop by and have a drink with us. O.k., I'll see you then. Bye."

Before Vanessa could hang up the phone good, Christi was asking questions. "Is he coming? What time? Now, was that so hard?"

"Yes, eight, and no," Vanessa replied. "Now it's already six and you know it takes you forever to get ready so you'd better go home and start now."

"Honey, I don't need to go home. I brought everything with me to get ready here, so I've got plenty of time."

"Well, I'm going to take a nap so I'll be rested. What about you?"

"I guess I will too," Christi said as they cleared the table and went inside.

170

After their naps were over, Vanessa and Christi opened another bottle of spumante and prepared for their evening. Getting ready that night reminded them both of when they were in high school getting ready to go to the Friday night social in the school gymnasium. They would go from room to room asking each other's opinions on how they looked. They already knew that they looked great, but a confirmation from a fellow diva is good for a girl's ego.

The Club was jumping! It was blue lights in the basement night and the DJ played most of the major old school funk jams. Vanessa didn't normally dance, but the music moved her. The sound of the grooves from back in the day got a hold of her and she danced with Derrick until she was down-right tired. Not wanting to start anything that she knew she wouldn't finish, she took extra care not to rub him the wrong way.

It was approaching time to go, and Vanessa dreaded it. It was not that she wasn't ready to go home, but she didn't know what to do about Derrick. He had hinted around all night to the two of them spending time together after they left *The Club*, but she had constantly ignored him. When Christi finally returned to the table after an hour's worth of dancing, Vanessa whispered to her, "Meeting in the ladies room."

"He's talking about coming by the house after we leave," Vanessa said, behind the closed doors of the cramped ladies room.

"*And*?" Christi said, gazing in the mirror. "I don't understand the problem. So what? Let the man come by, girl!"

"I don't know what to do," Vanessa responded.

"Girl, you still got them training wheels on," Christi laughed. "I thought I taught you how to ride a *real* bike."

"I'm not playing, Christi. I'm serious. What should I do?"

"What on earth do you want to do, my dear friend?"
"I want him to come over, but I'm scared."
"Of what might I ask?"
"Of what might happen."

"You can't worry about what might happen. You've got to take a chance and see what will happen. Please, honey, do it for me. Put them training wheels in the closet when you get home and leave 'em! At least for tonight," Christi said as she walked out.

Vanessa looked at herself in the mirror and asked her reflection, "Can we really do this?" A thousand thoughts of loneliness flashed through her head. Then she answered, "We can do it, girl. Come on, let's go get our groove on."

Early the next morning Vanessa woke up in Derrick's arms. She maneuvered out of bed without waking him, put on a pot of coffee, and settled into a hot tub of water filled with bubbles. She spent the first few minutes of her bath enjoying the peacefulness and reflecting on the past days' events. She smiled as she thought about the fun she and Christi had pampering themselves and hanging out. She even smiled as she thought about Derrick. She knew how badly he wanted to make love to her, but that just wasn't how she operated. She had every intention of keeping her vow of celibacy; the next man to make love to her would be the one God sent to make love to her the rest of her life--her husband.

Derrick had known how she felt without her even saying it. Aside from a few passionate kisses, they spent the night holding one another. Now, for most women that would have been boring, but for Vanessa, it was soul stirring. Still, she wondered if she should feel guilty. After all, a man had spent the night in her bed. Was that acceptable since she had no intention of anything happening between them, and nothing did?

After she finished her bath, she emerged from the water and slipped into her robe. Then she went to the door to get the paper and realized that she had not checked the mail the day before because she expected it to be more of Vickie's bills, and she didn't want anything to spoil her day. Today it didn't matter, so she reached in and got the mail. When she turned around in the doorway, she was startled by Derrick's presence. Before she could gain her composure, he engaged her in one of those long, passionate kisses that she enjoyed so much the night before. The

172

kiss was so powerful that she dropped both the mail and the newspaper on the floor. Neither one wanted the kiss to end, but they had to come up for air.

Vanessa picked up the paper, and the mail before they headed toward the kitchen. She noticed that the first letter was from Vickie. She was anxious to read it, but she wanted to be alone when she did. She hoped that Derrick would not accept her invitation to join her for coffee, but he did. After about three cups of coffee, it was evident that he had no intentions of leaving any time soon, so Vanessa had to encourage him to do so in a nice way.

"I'm about to get dressed," she told him, clearing their cups from the table.

"But you look wonderful in that," Derrick responded, more with his eyes than his words.

"Thank you," she said, "but I'm going to church this morning and I have some student papers I need to grade before I go back to work on Monday. I should've done it yesterday, but I was hanging out with Christi, and it slipped my mind."

"You want me to help you?" he asked, still in his seat.

"Don't you have to get home?" she questioned remembering that this was *another* woman's man and hoping that reminding him of that would speed up his departure.

"No," he said. "We're not together right now. She knows that you're back in town, and she's heard that I've been stopping by and spending time with you. We had a big argument about it and I just left."

"So, is that why you spent the night here--because you're homeless?"

"Girl, don't even go there. You know that this not the first time I've stayed out all night with you. Remember when you were here last time, and the time before?" he asked, smiling.

"Yeah, I remember," she conceded, feeling a little guilty because each of those times he had been out with her most--if not all--of the night, trying to explain to her why they should be together. Even then she knew that he was not the one, but sometimes it's a struggle to release the familiar to prepare for the unknown.

"Well, I'll give you some time to go to church and take care of your business," Derrick said reluctantly, rising to leave. "Is it O.k. if I call you later? I would really like to talk to you."

"I'll be here," Vanessa responded. She walked him to the door where he kissed her once more before leaving. She knew it was the last kiss they would ever share because she knew that if she wanted God to send the husband she desired, she had to prepare herself to receive him. That meant releasing Derrick and breaking the soul ties that bound her to him.

Back in the kitchen, Vanessa picked up Vickie's letter and went to the table to read it . She lit a cigarette first to keep her calm, because she knew that reading the letter would be emotional. After one puff, she extinguished it. "I AM DELIVERED!" she said loudly and emphatically. "I don't need nicotine to help me through this; my strength comes from God who is my source of everything! Please give me strength Lord, " she asked as she opened the letter and began to read.

Dear Vanessa,

I'm writing you this letter to share with you my feelings. I wish I could tell you what I need to say face to face, but I think the letter is best for right now. First of all, I want to apologize to you. I am truly sorry for all of the lies that I have told you, all of the money I have caused you to spend to bail me out of trouble, all of the mistakes that I have made, and all of the pain that I have caused you. I know that it will be hard to do, but will you please try and find a way to forgive me?

Secondly, I want to thank you. I want to thank you for being a wonderful   sister, for listening to me, for helping me, for loving me, and for taking care of me and my child when I didn't. I have made some very bad choices lately, but you have been there through them all, and I thank you from the bottom of my heart.

Now, I want to tell you about what's going on here. I am learning so much about me, what I think and how I feel. Before, I never gave much attention to a big part of what makes me who I

174

am, but I know now that I have to learn to love myself for who God made me and allow Him to finish the work that He started. Still, it's hard because I have done so many things that I hate myself for doing. I have totally jacked up my life, but I am really trying to make it right. I know that I should be doing it for me, but I'm really doing this for you and for Vonshay. I want you both to know that I'm not really the person that you've been dealing with these last few months. The drugs were influencing that person. The real me should be influenced by God, and I know that He can deliver me. I've been praying for deliverance, and I hope that it comes. I know that I will never be able to repay you for all that you have done for me. I don't just mean monetary things. You have given me things that money can't buy, and I just pray that one day I can be a blessing to you like you've been to me. Whatever I can do for you, I will. I owe you my life!

Love, Vickie

P. S. Please keep me in your prayers. I know that you pray for me all the time, but I've never asked you myself to pray for me, so now I'm asking that you say a special prayer for me.

Vanessa didn't know what to expect in the letter, and she was pleasantly surprised after she read it. She stared at the words that her sister wrote to her and saw the smears in the ink that were made by her Vickie's teardrops. She folded the pages neatly and carefully and placed them in the envelope as delicately as she could. After all, she was handling a piece of her sister's   heart.

Vanessa took the letter to a safe place—the ballerina jewelry box she used to keep special items in when she was young. After locking the jewelry box and returning it to the dresser, Vanessa lifted her hands to heaven, looked up with a smile, and said, "Thank You, Lord!" over and over again. As she thanked God for His goodness, a praise welled up in her spirit and she released it by falling to her knees with her hands still raised, and crying out, 'Hallelujah to Your name O Lord. I give you the highest praise—for You alone are worthy!" As tears of joy rolled down her cheeks, she said a heartfelt prayer unto God.

Lord, I thank You for this day, for You have shown Yourself to be faithful. You promised me that my sister would be delivered and set free from drugs and I am seeing the manifestation of Your words this very day. I ask right now Lord, that You will continue to protect her as she strives to overcome. Lord show her Your mighty power and your faithfulness so that she will know You to be her Father, Savior, and Lord. I declare peace over her life and call her body, soul, and spirit to come under the authority of Your divine rule. She IS delivered! She WILL walk in divine favor, and she WILL be who You declared her to be before the foundations of the earth! Lord, You are my strength and I am forever grateful to You for saving me and teaching me Your ways. I shall depend on You, oh God for You are my source. I release my fears and my loneliness unto You, and I accept the power and comfort that You promised me in Your word. Oh God I thank You. I thank You for understanding when no one else did and standing with me when no one else would. I am forever grateful, God. Therefore, I will bless Your holy name forever and ever, Amen.

That morning Vanessa attended church at Joy Temple, and her experience was truly a joyful one. She was elated that a church in Ferguson had finally allowed the anointing of God to enter into His own house. She decided that this would be her temporary church home until she returned to Atlanta. She was moved by the fact that other churches in town bashed it; they were traditional and blind to the things of the Spirit. Her prayer was that one day they would allow themselves to be led out of religious darkness and into the spiritual light.

Chapter 12

Although Vonshay hated to admit it, her aunt had been right: Tougaloo College was really not that bad. As a matter of fact, she found it to be like a haven. She had tried early on to make her stay there miserable, but that had been tiresome. Eventually, she decided to just go with the flow. After her self-imposed misery had been put behind her, she adapted well to her environment. Her life would have been picture-perfect had it not been for her mama's absence.

Vonshay sat on her bed thinking about her mama. She wondered if she was O.k. and if the rehab center was doing her any good. A lot of days she wished that she could just take her mama away from that place because she didn't think that she could be happy there. She knew that she held her mama's happiness, and she wanted so badly to be with her.

She was about to spend the evening sulking in despair when her roommate, Daquita burst into the room and shouted, "The Ques are having a party! Get dressed! I've already got us a ride."

Vonshay smiled at her excited roommate. She really liked Daquita. They connected the first day they met. They didn't have to go through the trouble most freshmen girls went through, like walking on tiptoes trying to figure out what kind of person they were living with. They immediately felt that they would get along fine. As each day passed, not only did they feel they would be good roommates, they knew it.

Daquita was an only child from Chicago. The majority of the students at Tougaloo were Southerners who believed that people from "up North" were wild. Vonshay didn't accept the generalization because she knew for a fact that her roommate was not wild; she was just citified. Growing up in a big city had exposed Daquita to a much wider array of social activities than those offered in the South. Her festive and jovial moods at events stemmed from her lack of opportunities to attend them on a regular basis, rather than an innate wildness as her classmates had erroneously presumed.

Vonshay sprang up from the bed and searched for something to wear while Daquita combed through her shoulder length hair. They moved quickly to avoid missing their ride and being late. Everybody knew that the Que's had the best parties, and that if you missed one minute-- you missed some *real* action. After attending the first one, Vonshay and Daquita vowed to make them all, and so far they had.

The party was as live as they expected it to be. There were people from everywhere and enough Q-punch to go around. Everybody had a good time! No one would have thought that it was a Tuesday night, and that they all had classes the next day. Vonshay didn't get back to campus until four o'clock the next morning. She had an eight o'clock class, but she wasn't worried because she had already mastered juggling her academics and her extra-curricular activities.

Vonshay went to her literature class the next morning and then went back to bed. She figured that she could get a two-hour nap before her next class. As soon as she drifted off to sleep, the phone rang.

"Hello," she grumbled.

"Hey, honey chile," Andre' said enthusiastically.

"Hey, Daddy," Vonshay responded with much less enthusiasm.

"What are you doing asleep this time of day? Shouldn't you be in class?"

"My next class isn't until later. I have to take a nap first, so that I can be alert. You know, so I won't miss anything."

"Yeah, right," Andre' said, knowing his daughter was teasing. So are you doing all right? I haven't heard from you?"

"I'm fine--just busy with the books," she laughed. "What about you?"

"Oh, I'm cool. I talked to Vanessa and your mama yesterday. They are both doing good."

"Why didn't anybody call me? I haven't talked to Mama in   weeks."

"They did call you, baby, but you weren't there. It was about ten last night."

"I knew I shouldn't have gone anywhere," Vonshay said softly. "Mama needed me, and I was out having fun."

"Baby, you'll get a chance to talk to her. Nothing's wrong with you going places. You can't stay cooped up in that room waiting for the phone to ring. Having fun is part of the college experience. If you don't take advantage of it now, you'll regret it later because you won't have another chance."

"I know, Daddy, but I miss Mama and I want to talk to her."

"I know. You'll get your chance. Don't sit around that room moping all day. Get up and go outside and hang out with your friends. Everything will be fine; I promise you. Go back to sleep and I'll call you later and check on you, all right?"

"All right, Daddy. Bye."

"Love you."

"Love you, too."

Vonshay sat on the side of the bed feeling guilty. To add to her guilt, she reached in her drawer and pulled out the letter that Vickie had written her. Vonshay never wrote her mama back. She didn't know what to say. Vickie's letter was so emotional that Vonshay cried for days after reading it, and trying to respond to the letter was even more emotional for her. She attempted to write her mama on three occasions, but none of her responses seemed appropriate.

How could she respond to her mama's declaration that she would give up her own life to make Vonshay happy without

179

saying, "I would die for you, too"? What words would embrace her mama's heart-wrenched pleas for forgiveness other than "I accept your apology"? In what way could she attest to her reciprocated love for her mama aside from a mere "I love you, too"? She didn't know the answers to these questions that plagued her for weeks after she received the letter. The words she attempted to write did not and could not express the depths of her feelings.

Vonshay's phone rang and interrupted her thoughts. "Hello," she answered in a dismal tone.

"How's college life treating you?" Vanessa asked.

"It's good," she replied.

"I told you it would get better, didn't I?"

"O.k., you were right. How's Mama? Daddy told me that you all talked yesterday."

"She's doing fine," Vanessa proudly reported. "She sounds good, and she's talking like her old self. We called you last night, but you weren't there."

"I know. Daddy told me. I wish I had been here. I wanted to talk to her."

"Well, next time I talk to her, we'll call you. She can't wait for you to tell her about school. I was calling to see if you wanted to go visit her Saturday for Family Day. I talked to Dr. Winters, and he thinks she's ready."

Vonshay thought about it. I really want to talk to mama, she told herself, but I don't know if I want to see her. It would be hard leaving her behind when the day was over.

"You *do* want to go, don't you?" Vanessa asked, interrupting Vonshay's thoughts.

"Yeah," Vonshay said, still confused.

"If you don't, it's all right. I didn't tell her we were coming, so she won't know the difference…but I think it would be good for all of us."

"O.k., when are you coming?"

"I'm leaving Friday after work. You can spend the night with me at the hotel, and we'll go first thing Saturday morning."

"O.k., TeeTee. I'll be here, but next time, we stay in my room."

180

"All right, see you then. Bye."

"Bye."

Vonshay was jittery all week. She had no idea what she should do or say around her mama. She felt like she was going to visit a stranger. Even though she was apprehensive about going, she still felt that the weekend was not coming fast enough. She knew that the sooner it came, the sooner it would all be over. She wished that it would hurry up and get there.

That Friday, an hour before Vanessa was scheduled to pick her up, Vonshay sat on the side of her bed staring into her closet. She couldn't figure out what clothes to wear to go see her mama.

"What's wrong with you?" Daquita asked as she walked in and put her books on the desk. "I thought your aunt was picking you up?"

"She is."

"Well, why you look so pitiful? You're getting a chance to eat some real food and sleep in a real bed for a change. I wish I had somebody to pick me up for the weekend."

"Girl, who's going to drive all the way from Chicago to Mississippi, just for the weekend?"

"Nobody. That's why I'm wishing and not going."

"Well, why did you come so far away to school?"

"I had to get away."

"From what?"

"It's more like from who?"

"Well, who?"

"My mama."

Vonshay had never heard of such. "Why would anybody not want to be around her mama?" she asked. Once the words were out, she thought of several times she wanted to be away from her own mama.

"My Mama has changed from the person that I grew up with. She hasn't been the same since my daddy died. She almost gave up on life and me too. All she lives for now is drugs. I

181

couldn't stand watching her throw her life away, so I came down South."

"And left her all alone?"

"I have some aunts and cousins up there who watch out for her. I still talk to her on a regular basis."

"That doesn't sound like the lady that calls here for you all the time. She sounds like she misses you."

"She does, and I miss her too, but she's got a problem and won't admit it."

"For real," Vonshay said. "I thought it was just me." She finally realized what her aunt meant when she told her to "be thankful for all things because there is always someone else with circumstances worse than yours."

"What do you mean?" Daquita asked her.

"My mama does drugs, too. She's in a rehab center right now, and that's where me and my aunt are going tomorrow. I'm scared, though. That's why I'm just sitting here. I thought I was trying to find something to wear, but I'm really looking for the right attitude.

"Just wear the one that fits best tomorrow. She's got to realize that you've got feelings too. If she's anything like my mama, she'll want you to feel sorry for her, but she's got to realize that she made the choice to do drugs; you didn't."

"How do you deal with your mama's situation?"

"I used to get mad, worry, and cry a lot, but now I just pray because I realized that I can't change her; only God can."

"You sound like TeeTee," Vonshay teased.

"Well, how do you deal with it?" Daquita inquired.

"I pray and read the Bible, but I still get mad and cry, too."

"Well, after a while it won't bother you as much."

Vonshay was about to respond when she heard a knock at the door. She unlocked the door for Vanessa and scurried around getting her overnight bag ready. Vanessa chatted with Daquita while she waited. When they were leaving, Vanessa invited Daquita to have dinner with them and stay overnight at the hotel. She accepted and Vonshay was glad. Her roommate was a long way from home and an even longer way from her mama. She was eager to embrace her as the sister she never had but always wanted.

During dinner, Vonshay and Daquita filled Vanessa in on all of the activities that were taking place at Tougaloo. Their descriptions were a lot more colorful and detailed than the ones in the alumni newsletter that she received quarterly. When they had finished eating, they went to the hotel.

Vanessa got bored with the eighteen year olds' conversations. She wanted some adult company, so she decided to go down to the hotel lounge to have a glass of spumante. She hoped she would meet some new people, since the hotel was popular and it usually hosted most of the conventions in town. She had noticed quite a few people hanging around in the lobby when she checked in, and she anticipated them being downstairs when she went to the lounge.

The dimly lit lounge was almost empty when she arrived, aside from the few individuals seated at the bar. Vanessa chose a seat at a table next to the window so that she would have a view of the happenings both inside and outside of the hotel. When the waiter came to serve her, she ordered a glass of cranberry juice, having decided to forego the glass of spumante because the taste of alcohol was no longer as appealing to her as it once was. God was working the desire for it out of her life, and the more time she spent with Him, the less time she spent thinking about other things, like drinking.

While waiting on her juice, Vanessa glanced around the room and noticed several muscular Black men in jeans and T-shirts setting up musical equipment on the tiny round stage. She expected the crowd to pick up when the band began to their first set. By the time she finished her juice, the band was tuning up. She swirled around in the swivel chair seat to see if the members of the band were Black, White, or Other, because their race would determine the type of crowd they would draw. Fortunately for her, they were Black because she hated it when White artists played Black music and received more credit and attention than the original artists.

While she enjoyed the mellow sounds of the live jazz music, she noticed the crowd growing larger. She decided to watch the entrance because she noticed that there was a constant flow of newcomers. She wasn't looking for anyone in particular; she just liked to know the type of people in her midst. It was easier to look them over at the door than at the dimly lit tables. Her attention was fixed on the door when she felt a hand brush her shoulder. She quickly turned to whom she thought would be someone apologizing for accidentally touching her.

The face of the man she was now facing caught her off guard. She hadn't seen him enter the bar, and she would have definitely remembered him if she had because he was handsome. His features had to have been painted onto his face by a master artist. Each stroke was obviously equally as important as the others. Had either stroke been altered, even minutely, the perfection of his face would have been lost. She yearned to frame the face and place it on her wall. She needed proof that such a face existed. A mental picture and a verbal description would not suffice. His face was something you had to see to believe.

"Hi," Vanessa said after realizing that she had not responded verbally to his touch.

"Is anyone sitting here?" the man asked pointing to the empty chair across from Vanessa. He smiled broadly.

"No. Help yourself," she responded trying not to stare.

"Thanks," he said as he slid into the seat.

Unsure whether or not the man's interest was in her or the vacant seat, Vanessa turned towards the band and pretended that she was into their performance, but she was really into the man sitting across from her. She hoped that he would attempt to hold a conversation with her. She wanted to be able to look at him without staring. She was relieved when he asked her what she was drinking.

For the next several hours, the two of them laughed, talked, and enjoyed the music. Vanessa could not believe that she was having so much fun with a man she had just met. She felt like they were long time friends, even though all she knew about him was that his name was Titus Richmond and that he was a banker from Houston who was in town on business, and in the process of relocating to Atlanta.

Vanessa and Titus were still at the bar when the band stopped playing music and the bartender stopped serving drinks. Vanessa was so into their conversation that she didn't notice the change. It was not until the lights came on in the room that she noticed the time-- it was after two a.m. When she saw Titus' face in the light, she thought that she had died and gone to heaven. His face lit up like an angel's.

"I'd better be going," she said fighting off her desire to remain in his presence as long as possible.

"Do you have to? We could find somewhere to finish our conversation or go to breakfast or something," he said anxiously.

"I wish I could, but my niece and her friend are in my room and there is no telling what they haven't done by now. Maybe some other time," she said eagerly hoping he would ask her out.

"What about lunch tomorrow?" he asked.

"I'll be out with my niece until tomorrow evening. I won't be able to do anything until after then."

"O.k., let's have dinner around eight. We can meet here."

"That's fine," Vanessa agreed. "I'll see you then." She turned to leave.

"Can I at least walk you to the elevator?" he asked.

Impressed by his gentlemanly manners, she said "yes," and they entered the elevator in silence. Once they pressed the buttons for their respective floors and the elevator began to rise, they stared at each other without speaking. Their delectable evening was swiftly drawing to an end. The silence spoke loudly what neither tongue uttered; they desired to live in that moment forever.

When the elevator stopped at Vanessa's floor, she responded to Titus' goodbye with a whispered "good night," and walked slowly to her room with a smile on her face. She was glad that the girls were sleeping because she wasn't ready to answer the thousand questions they would ask about her lengthy absence. She prepared for bed, but could not sleep. Her mind flashed through the photographic images of Titus that it stored over the course of the evening. She hoped that her visit with her sister would be as pleasant as her evening with him. Before she drifted of to sleep, she said a prayer, thanking God for placing Titus in her path and allowing her to have such a wonderful evening. Then she asked Him to be with them on their visit with Vickie and to allow healing and restoration to occur in all of them.

The next morning, Vanessa dropped Daquita at the campus, and she and Vonshay went to Charter. When they arrived, they checked in at the front desk and were directed to the cafeteria where the patients were having breakfast. They didn't see Vickie there, so they asked for directions to her room.

On their way to her room, they ran into Carol, her roommate. She told them that Vickie was getting dressed for breakfast. She offered them her key to the room in case Vickie was in the shower when they knocked at the door. They accepted it and decided to enter without knocking so that they could surprise her.

When they walked in Vickie was looking for something in a drawer and her back was turned to the door. "Did you forget something?" she asked, thinking it was Carol. After she didn't get a response, she turned around. When she looked into Vonshay's and Vanessa's faces, tears immediately began to flow down her cheeks.

"What are you two doing here?" she asked excitedly, reaching out to embrace them.

"Well it is Family Day, isn't it?" Vanessa responded.

"We're your family and we came to see you." Vonshay added.

"Why didn't you tell me you were coming?" she asked.

"We wanted to surprise you!" they responded simultaneously.

"Well you definitely did that," she laughed. "I was looking for my earrings, so I can go to breakfast. Have you eaten yet?" she asked, while fastening her earrings.

"No," Vonshay said, "we came right after we got up. Can we go to breakfast with you?"

"Of course you can! Let's go."

Vickie was elated that Vonshay and Vanessa were there. She introduced them to everyone she saw. There had been several Family Days that she sat and watched with envy as mothers, fathers, children and siblings laughed, talked and bonded with one another. Not today, she thought proudly. My family is here today, and we're going to have more fun than the rest of 'em know how to have.

After breakfast they went to a special group session, "Addicts and The People Who Love Them." The doctor in charge of the session first explained chemical dependency and the effects that it has on the body and mind. He explained that a lot of things that chemically dependent people do and say are not a part of their normal behavior and personalities, but the result of the drugs' possession of the brain. Next, he talked about how an addict's addiction affects the family and the importance of how the family reacts to it.

He said, "In most families the addict has an enabler, a family member who usually unknowingly assists the addicts in their quests for drugs by giving them money, overlooking their behavior, correcting their mistakes, and defending their actions. As long as family members enable the addicts, they do not have to accept the responsibility for their actions--the family does it for them. Another type of family member, whom he described as the hero, does as much right as the addicts do wrong in an effort to keep the attention away from the addicts, hoping that no one will notice the problem. It is difficult to accept that a loved one is an addict and even more difficult to allow that person to fall, but the family must learn to practice "tough love." You must not give in to the addicts' pleas, but force them to stand on their own and deal with whatever situations they get themselves into. It's the only way they will accept the results of their behavior."

After a brief pause, he continued. "I would like the family members and friends of addicts to identify the roles that you have played in an addict's life, based on the descriptions I gave earlier and to explain why you feel that you fit into those particular roles."

Vonshay immediately looked at Vanessa when she heard the doctor's request. "Do I have to?" she whispered pleadingly.

"You don't have to, but it will be good for you and your mama," she responded, patting her niece's hand. Vonshay turned around and listened to the family members share their stories.

Vickie saw the discomfort on her daughter's face and wished that she hadn't done the things that had brought them to that moment. She touched Vonshay and whispered, "You don't have to if you don't want to."

Vonshay said "O.k." with a sigh of relief.

When her turn came Vanessa stood up and said, "I was an enabler for my sister...I gave her money. I accepted her excuses and I bailed her out of unpleasant situations."

It shocked both her and Vickie when Vonshay stood up and said, "I played the role of the hero. I always tried to do things to get attention, like make good grades and get involved in extra-curricular activities. I thought that if people concentrated on me, they would not pay a lot of attention to my mama or not see what was going on."

When Vonshay sat down, Vickie kissed her on the cheek. Vonshay felt the moisture on her mama's lips and knew that she was crying. Vanessa reached for Vonshay's hand. The firm but tender grip let her know that her auntie was proud.

When the session ended, they went to the recreation room. Vickie wanted to introduce them to more people and Vonshay wanted to play some games. After all the introductions were over, they played a game of Boggle. About an hour later, Vonshay announced that she was going to the session for children of addicts and that she would see them later.

Vickie and Vanessa were glad she was taking advantage of the sessions. They had seen a lot of people try to handle difficult situations alone instead of seeking support from friends, family members and other people dealing with the same thing. Most of them ended up having nervous break-downs or being depressed and stressed. Some even took their own lives, and they didn't want Vonshay to be in that type of predicament. They had always told her to talk about whatever bothered her, and if not with them, then with someone. They instilled in her that no matter how devastating the situation appeared, she was too blessed to be stressed.

Vonshay was pleased to see a room full of people who were dealing with the same issues as she. She felt a lot more comfortable in this session because neither her mama nor her aunt was there and that a Black man led the session.

She learned that she should not feel guilty about her mama's situation. It was not her fault, nor was it her responsibility to try and correct it. She learned, also, that she had a right to be angry and that she needed to share those feelings with her mama. The man explained that the healing could not take place until the wounds were exposed.

At the end of the session, the man stood at the door thanking those in attendance. When he thanked Vonshay, she thanked him for all of the information she learned from the session.

"I'm glad I was able to help," he responded. "What's your name?"

"Vonshay."

"You're Vickie's daughter," he said jovially. "I've heard a lot about you. I'm your mother's doctor."

"Really? How's she doing?" she asked.

"She's coming along just fine, except maybe she is becoming forgetful because she didn't tell me you were coming."

"Oh, it was a surprise. She didn't know," she laughed.

"Well, I'm sure it was a good surprise. Did your aunt come too," he asked.

"Yes. They're in the rec room. I'm going to go get them so we can have lunch."

"Well, I'll go down with you," he said as he noticed the last person leaving.

On the way to the rec room he talked more with Vonshay about some of the things he said in the session. She felt even more enlightened because he was her mama's doctor and he knew not only what, but *who* she was dealing with. She wondered what her mama had told him about her.

Vanessa and Vickie were sitting right where she left them when she returned. The doctor spoke to them and teased Vickie about not telling him that they were coming. He also complimented her on what an intelligent daughter she had. They carried on a conversation for about five minutes, and then the doctor dismissed himself.

The remainder of the day went by quickly. They spent their time laughing and talking about everything from men to Mars. Before they knew it, time had slipped away from them, and it was time for Vanessa and Vonshay to leave. They all cried when they said their goodbyes. The tears were a mixture of joy and sadness. They were happy that they had such a wonderful day together and sad that it had to end. Before they departed, Vanessa prayed for sister's strength. There was a time when these impromptu prayers irritated Vickie, but now she welcomed them.

On the way back to the hotel, Vonshay asked Vanessa if Daquita could spend the night again. Vanessa was quick to agree because she didn't like the idea of Vonshay being alone at the hotel while she was out with Titus. She picked up Daquita, and they went to the mall.

Vanessa had not planned on going anywhere special while she was in Jackson (especially not on a date) so she needed something to wear. Because she didn't have a lot of time to spare, she went directly to the McRae's department store so she would be able to purchase everything she needed in one store. She didn't want to overdress for her date, but she didn't want to be too casual either. With the help of Vonshay and Daquita, she decided on a two-piece black pants suit and a pair of black leather shoes with a simple, yet definitive heel. They were in and out of the store within thirty minutes, which gave Vanessa a few moments to relax in their hotel room before preparing to meet Titus.

"Who are you going out with TeeTee? The man from last night?" Vonshay asked, watching Vanessa as she was getting dressed. She loved to see her auntie get ready to go out. She had natural beauty and class. She could get ready in fifteen minutes and look as if she'd taken hours.

"What man?" Vanessa asked stunned.

"The one you were talking to in the lounge last night." Vonshay laughed. "After you were gone for a while, I got worried so me and Daquita came down stairs to check on you. We saw you at the table talking to this man. He was cute and you looked like you were enjoying yourself so we came back to the room."

"So you're checking up on *me* now?" Vanessa asked jovially. "I thought it was my job to check up on *you*."

"Not really checking on you, just concerned about you." Vonshay said, hoping she had not offended her auntie.

"Well, I'm glad to know you got my back," Vanessa laughed, as she slipped into a black slacks and jacket, suited for any occasion. She slipped the new shoes onto her feet and admired herself in the mirror. Then she took a few moments to put on make-up, which she wore lightly because she preferred a natural look. After shining her lips with a golden gloss, she slid her signature sterling silver bangles onto her arm and fastened her large silver hoop earrings. Once she ran her fingers through her hair, she decided that everything was in order.

"It's about time for me to go," she told the girls. "Here's some money in case you two need anything. Be good, now," she said, as she sprayed herself with Gio' perfume, her favorite.

"O.k. Bye." Vonshay and Daquita said in unison.

"You look good TeeTee," Daquita assured her, noticing that she was slightly nervous.

"Thanks baby," Vanessa said. She kissed her on the cheek, and said, "Goodnight."

Vanessa smiled at herself in the elevator mirror as she waited to arrive on the first floor. When the elevator reached its destination, she felt her stomach flutter. Oh my God, I'm nervous, she thought to herself. "Give me strength Lord," she whispered, watching the doors part before her.

Titus was sitting in the hotel lobby when Vanessa exited the elevator. He immediately came to greet her. "I was hoping you wouldn't stand me up," he said smiling. "You look beautiful tonight, and you smell wonderful, he said noticing the subtle scent of perfume that she wore.

"Thank you," Vanessa said, trying to prevent the blush she felt rising in her cheeks. "So do you," she added, admiring his body. She had not noticed anything but his perfect face the night before.

"I made reservations for us at the Waterfront. Is that O.k. with you.?"

"That's fine," she said. "It's a nice night for dinner on the lake and I hear that they have a pretty good band, too."

"Good," Titus said. "Let's get a move on."

The two of them had a wonderful evening together. It was even better than the one before. The two of them talked endlessly about their lives and the lives of their people as they sipped Chardonnay with their dinner. They felt so comfortable with each other that they shared many things that they had only shared with the closest of friends. Taking advantage of the musicians' talents, they danced frequently. Their bodies were in tune with each other. The entire evening was enjoyable, but what they enjoyed most of all was each other's company.

At the end of their evening when they reached the floor of Vanessa's hotel room, Titus asked, "May I walk you to your door this time? I want to make sure you get in safely. And to be honest," he added, "I just want to spend every minute I can with you."

"Thank you for being such an honest man," Vanessa said. "You can definitely walk me to my door, because I want to spend these last few minutes with you, too."

When they reached the door, Vanessa turned to tell Titus "good night". He was so close to her that she could feel his breath in her face. They stared deeply into each other's eyes, searching for something only they knew existed. They found what they were searching for simultaneously, and they christened their discovery with a long passionate kiss. Then said, "Good night."

Vanessa had not intended to kiss Titus, nor had he intended to kiss her. Because she was an old-fashioned girl and he was a true gentleman, neither of them believed in kissing on the first date, but whatever they found in each other's eyes, overruled their minds and let their hearts take over.

When Vanessa went inside the room, Vonshay and Daquita were up waiting for a report. She told them all about both of her evenings with Titus, minus a few details. They were almost more excited than she was. After she answered all of their questions, they fell asleep and she kneeled down to pray.

Dear Lord, I thank You for all that You have done. I thank You for the wonderful day that we had with Vickie. I want You to touch her Lord and keep her strong. Lord, help her to learn from her mistakes and let You guide her path for the future. And Lord, touch Vonshay. Help her to deal with her Mama's problem without being ashamed. Give her the spirit of forgiveness so that she can forgive her mama for her mistakes. Let her open up and share her feelings with others and not keep them inside. Protect her, Lord, on a daily basis and keep her safe. And Lord, I ask that you remember me. I've enjoyed the time that I've spent with Titus, and I like him, but Lord I'm afraid of being hurt. If he's not the kind of man that I need in my life, I don't want to go any further. You know better than I do what I need, and I ask that You show it to me Lord. I ask that You forgive me of my sins and once again Father I thank You. I thank You for being so good and for being here for me. I pray this prayer in the name of Your Son, Jesus, Amen.

Chapter 13

After Vanessa returned to Ferguson, she couldn't stop thinking about Titus. She had never been so interested in a man after just one date. She didn't understand what was happening, but she definitely liked it. It seemed like a dream, something too good to be true. She never thought that she would meet an Atlanta man that she liked in Jackson, Mississippi. Only God could have masterminded that one!

Titus called her almost every day after they left Jackson, and she loved the attention. They spent hours on the phone talking about God, their dreams, their goals, their beliefs, their careers, and their feelings about life, love, and each other. They had so much to say to one another that there was never a lapse in the conversation. It felt so good to be stimulated intellectually by a man she was physically attracted and one who knew how to treat a woman. The combination had been rare for her. For the first time in her life, she felt that she had met her soul mate-- the one that she could and should spend the rest of her life with.

The conversations with Titus along with the frequent visits with Christi made Vanessa's stay in Ferguson more bearable. Contrary to Christi's advice, she honored her decision not to see Derrick anymore, and she was glad she did. She had enough drama in her life without dealing with Derrick and his baby's mama. Besides, she honestly believed that when she moved him out her, she made room for Titus to enter in. Time flew by quickly, and before Vanessa realized it, it was almost time for Vonshay to come home for Thanksgiving break and for Vickie to come home from the hospital for good. It didn't seem as though three months had passed.

Vanessa was excited about her family being home for Thanksgiving. Since Andre' was not going to come for Thanksgiving, but waiting until Christmas, Vanessa planned a private holiday for just the three of them. She felt that it would give them time to do some bonding, something they hadn't had a chance to do in a long time. Vanessa cleaned the house thoroughly and filled the cabinets and refrigerator with groceries before she left for Jackson to pick up her sister and niece. She wanted everything to be in order when they arrived home. All of them could use a little order in their lives, and what better place to start than at home.

Vanessa picked up Vickie first so she would have a chance to visit Vonshay's room. She went through discharge planning sessions with Vickie and Dr. Winters. The sessions were designed to help them understand and deal with various situations that could arise during Vickie's readjustment to life outside of the hospital. Dr. Winters explained the fear, shame and depression that Vickie would probably experience, as well as the patience, support, and understanding that would be necessary to help her overcome it. He suggested that Vanessa and Vonshay put forth extra effort to make her feel comfortable and loved. He gave Vickie prescriptions for anti-depressants and explained their dosage and side effects. As he signed the release forms, he told them both that her leaving did not mean he was no longer her doctor. He encouraged them to call him any time they needed his assistance, and they promised that they would. He shook both of their hands and reminded them to "keep it simple and take one day at time."

Vonshay was packed and ready to go when Vanessa and Vickie arrived to pick her up. She and her mama were so glad to see each other, outside of the confines of the hospital, and they seemingly hugged endlessly. Then Vonshay introduced Vickie to Daquita and showed her around their room, explaining the function of everything and when and how they used it all.

"Mama, can Daquita come home with us?" Vonshay asked when she finished her tour. "Her plans to go home fell through, and I don't want her to be here by herself."

Vickie instinctively looked at Vanessa for an answer. Vanessa smiled and nodded. "Of course, she can," said Vickie. Looking to Daquita she asked, "Are you packed?"

"Yes, Ma'am. I had already packed for home when my ride cancelled," she said excitedly.

"Well, let's go!" Vanessa exclaimed, eager to get home.

By the time they made it to Ferguson, it was about seven o'clock. Vanessa decided to pick up something to eat on their way home, because the only cooking she wanted to do was for the next day--Thanksgiving. Once they had eaten and were settled, they divided the tasks that were necessary to prepare the meal. Vonshay and Daquita were in charge of cutting, slicing, dicing, measuring, and cleaning, while Vickie and Vanessa were in charge of everything else.

After the onions, celery, bell peppers, and gizzards were mixed with the homemade cornbread to make the dressing, and the turkey was seasoned and put in the oven to cook, Vickie said that she was tired, so she went to her room. Vanessa noticed that she hadn't been very talkative, so she went to see if she was all right.

"I'm just tired," Vickie told her sister as she changed into her nightgown.

"Yeah, Dr. Winters said the medicine would make you feel tired. Go ahead and get your rest, and I'll finish things in the kitchen with the girls," Vanessa said.

"I'm sorry, "Vickie said. "I wanted to stay up 'til we finished, but I was about to go to sleep just sittin' there. Maybe I'll feel better tomorrow."

"Maybe so. Don't worry about getting up so early. Get your rest, and we'll have dinner whenever you're ready.

"Thanks, sis. Good night"

"Good night," Vanessa said as she closed the door and headed back to the kitchen.

After Vanessa left, Vickie stumbled over to the bed. She wanted to kneel down and pray, but she was afraid that she would fall asleep on her knees. Since she knew that the Lord would hear her wherever she prayed, she said her prayers as she rested on her pillow.

Dear Lord, I thank You, I thank You that I am home. I thank You for watching over me even when I turned from You to drugs. If it had not been for Your protection, I might have been dead today. Forgive me, Lord, for my mistakes, thank You for my deliverance. I know that it's going to be hard being back home. People will be talking about me and laughing at me, but I pray that You keep me strong. Lord, keep the thoughts of drugs from my mind and the taste from my mouth. I want to stay clean. I know that it's a day to day struggle, and I need You to be with me every one of those days. I promise that I will try to keep my life on track, but I need You, Lord, to keep me focused. Lead me in the way that I should go, and help me to be a better mama, sister, and just help me to be a better person....

Vickie had so much more to say, but she fell asleep before she finished praying. An angel said, "Amen" for her.

When Vanessa returned to the kitchen, Vonshay and Daquita were standing at the counter attempting to pick the mustard greens that were soaking in the sink. She smiled at how carefully they examined them to try and figure out which part to keep and which part to throw away. "I didn't know you two knew how to pick greens," she said. "Tougaloo has really exposed you, huh?"

"Tougaloo *has* exposed us," Vonshay agreed, "but *not* to pickin' greens."

"Cause we don't have a clue as to what we're doing," Daquita laughed. "We were just trying to help out."

"You're doing a pretty good job for beginners," Vanessa said. "Keep working with 'em while I put on the ham hocks and the macaroni. When I finish, I'll come over and help you out."

"O.k.," they laughed as they splashed water everywhere.

197

Vanessa put the pots of water on the stove and turned on the fire beneath them. While she waited for them to come to a boil, she grated the sharp cheddar cheese for the macaroni. When the water began to boil, she dumped elbow macaroni in the smaller pot and three huge ham hocks in the larger pot. Then she went over to the sink and gave Vonshay and Daquita a demonstrative lesson on picking and washing greens. When the greens were ready to cook, Vanessa dumped them in the pot with the ham hocks and turned down the fire. She and Daquita cleaned the kitchen while Vonshay prepared the macaroni.

Once everything was in order, they made some hot chocolate and went in the den to rest and enjoy the scents of their labor.

"So ladies," Vanessa said in her reporter voice, as she lifted her legs onto the couch, "you're only a few weeks away from completing your first semester at Tougaloo College. What do you think about it?"

"Well," Vonshay said, setting her cup on the coffee table, "in the beginning I didn't particularly care for the place, but it has grown on me. To sum it up in a few words, I would have to say, it's the bomb!"

"And you," Vanessa said, nodding to Daquita.

"I like it!" Daquita said enthusiastically. "The social life there leaves a lot to be desired, but school is cool. I like all my teachers and they don't mind givin' extra help."

"Well, that's good," said Vanessa, taking a sip from her mug. "Sounds like the same Tougaloo I went to. It's good to know that some things stay the same."

"I hope my final grades are the same as my mid-term grades," Vonshay laughed, thinking about how proud she was to receive three A's and two B's, even though she hadn't done her best.

"If you study hard for your final, they will," Vanessa said encouragingly. "What did you get for mid-term Daquita?"

"Three A's, a B, and a C in Calculus. I just can't get those numbers right."

"You should get Vonshay to help you out," Vanessa suggested. "She's pretty good in math. You two have got to learn to use your resources. If one of you is good in one thing and the other is good in something else, you can help each other out."

"I need help with my writing," Vonshay interjected.

"English is my favorite subject," Daquita boasted. "I got an A."

"See," Vanessa said, "Tougaloo is all about community--everybody helping everybody to succeed. We all have strengths and weaknesses. The key is that we use ours strengths to help others with their weaknesses. If everybody does that, then we all win."

"We never thought about it like that," said Vonshay, after she drank her last sip of hot chocolate.

"That's why you've got me," Vanessa smiled. She loved sharing knowledge with younger sisters. She knew that they had to learn the lessons of life for themselves; but at least, when they learned those lessons, they would know that they were not alone. They could think back to conversations with her and other women, and know that they had to learn some of the same lessons, too.

When they were finished with their hot chocolate, they put the food away and went to bed around 3 a.m. They were all tired long before, but they enjoyed the conversation so much that neither of them wanted to go to bed. They were afraid that they might miss something.

When Vanessa woke up the next morning, the girls were in the family room watching the Thanksgiving Day Parade.

"Good morning,"she said as she passed them on her way to the kitchen.

"You mean good afternoon," Vonshay laughed.

"Good afternoon," Daquita said.

Vanessa looked at the clock, and it reflected one-thirty. She realized that she was not as young as she used to be. There was a time when she could stay up half the night and be up by eight the next morning, however those days were long gone. "I guess it *is* good afternoon," she chuckled. "Where's your Mama?"

"She's still sleep," Vonshay said, joining her aunt in the kitchen. "I checked on her when I got up. She must've really been tired because she didn't even move when I walked in."

"Yeah, that Mellaril and Elavil that Dr. Winters prescribed really drains her. I'll go ahead and get dinner heated, and then I'll check on her. You girls want a snack?" she asked, as she took the food from the refrigerator.

"Been there, done that, and got the T-shirt," they laughed.

After Vanessa put everything on to warm, she told the girls to watch the food while she went to check on Vickie. "Rise and shine!" she said when she entered the room. Vickie didn't move. She was still as an opossum.

"Time to get up!" Vanessa announced, while gently shaking her sister.

Vickie heard her sister's voice, but she didn't have the strength to open her mouth and talk. When she tried, the words came out as inaudible mumblings.

"Huh?" Vanessa asked trying to decipher what Vickie said. "Wake up, girl."

It took everything in Vickie to try and open her eyes. Her lids were so heavy that she felt like there were weights on them. It was a slow process, but she finally got her eyes open. Then, she saw the worry on Vanessa's face that she had detected in her voice.

"I'm O.k.," she slurred. "I'm just tired."

"Girl, you've been sleeping for well over twelve hours. The longer you stay in the bed, the harder it'll be for you to get up. Why don't you take a shower? You'll feel better," Vanessa said going into Vickie's bathroom to get everything ready. When she walked back into the room, Vickie was asleep again.

Vanessa woke her sister up, undressed her, and put her in the shower. She thought that the water would revive her, but it barely kept her eyes open. Vickie was in some kind of daze. After she helped Vickie with the shower, Vanessa slipped a lounging dress on her sister and led her into the family room. She hoped that the activity there would keep her awake;

however, it didn't. Vickie sat down and spoke to Vonshay and Daquita, but by the time Vanessa made it to the kitchen, she was asleep again.

When all of the food was ready, Vanessa and Daquita set the table, while Vonshay went to awaken her mama. Vickie came to the table, but she was still in a daze.

"Let's bow our heads and pray," Vanessa said when they were all seated. "Vickie, why don't you lead the prayer?"

In a soft whisper, she said, "Lord, I thank You for this day and that I am able to share it with my family and friends. I thank You for the love we have for You and each other. Please bless our home and our lives and keep us together, Amen."

Vonshay prayed next, "God, I thank You for Mama, Daddy, TeeTee, and Daquita. They are all special to me, and I ask that You keep each of us out of harm's way. I thank You for all You have done, Amen."

Daquita was hesitant, but she said the next prayer. "Dear God, thank You for this family that invited me into their home to celebrate this day. I ask that You keep them safe and that you bless my family wherever they are. I would like to ask a special blessing for my mama. Please help her with what she's going through, Amen."

Vanessa said the final prayer. "Lord, we thank You for allowing us to come together to give thanks for the many things that You have done. We know that we are not worthy of the blessings, but we thank You for Your grace and mercy. I pray, dear God, that You keep each of us near, and that You protect us from whatever comes against us. We thank You for the food that You have provided for us, and we thank You for each other. These and other blessings we ask in Jesus' name, Amen." After heads were raised she added, "Now let's eat!"

Everyone passed their plates around to get servings of turkey, dressing, cranberry sauce, macaroni and cheese, greens, cornbread, and rolls. Vickie didn't request much because her medication had taken away her appetite, but Daquita and Vonshay made up for it on their plates. Once everyone's plate was ready and their meals were seasoned to taste, they began to eat.

The dinner was nothing like the one that both Vanessa and Vonshay had imagined. Vickie was barely with them. Her mind was far away, and even *she* didn't know where. They all tried to keep a steady conversation flowing, but they were really focused on Vickie. Raising her fork and chewing her food seemed to be more of a task than staying awake. She was operating in slow motion. Finally, her body and mind gave up the fight, and she fell asleep at the dinner table with food in her mouth. Vanessa put her sister to bed and that's where she stayed for the remainder of the weekend. Vonshay was disappointed, but at least her mama was at home.

Chapter 14

Vickie remained in a zombie-like state for weeks. All she did was sleep and eat. Seeing her sister in this state bothered Vanessa, so she called Dr. Winters and asked him how long Vickie would have to take the medication. He told her to bring Vickie in for a visit and that he would decide then.

Vanessa took Vickie to the doctor the day that Vonshay finished her semester exams, so she would only have to make one trip to Jackson. Dr. Winters examined Vickie and counseled her before he decided to take her off the medication. After her visit was over, they picked up Vonshay and went home to get ready for Christmas.

"When are we going to get the Christmas tree?" Vonshay asked on her first morning home. She had been disappointed when they didn't put it up the Saturday after Thanksgiving like they normally did, but she understood that her mama had not been in any shape to do so.

"Why don't we get it today," Vickie responded. She looked at Vanessa for approval because she didn't have the money to buy it.

"That's fine. We should go now so we don't have to deal with a big crowd; maybe just some teachers who are off for the holidays like I am," Vanessa said.

"You don't have to get my approval to make decisions," Vanessa told Vickie when Vonshay left the room. "This is still your house."

"I know, but I don't have the money to do anything and I can't tell you how to spend yours."

"Thank you for being considerate, but you know that I am not going to let either of you do without anything, especially a Christmas tree! Do you need any money for gifts?"

"Thanks, Vanessa, but I took care of that already," Vickie said. She was pleased that she had done something on her own. "Vonshay really looks forward to decorating that tree every year. She still acts like she did the first time we let her help decorate. Do you remember?"

"How can I forget? She was so excited by the lights and all of the people. She's the main reason that we've made it a point every year to have friends over to eat, drink, and be merry while we decorate the tree. I guess after eighteen years, it would be safe to say that it's a tradition. Who do you wanna invite this year?"

"I don't think I'm ready for company yet. A lot of people, who I thought were my friends, turned on me when I really needed them. When things got thick, they thinned out. Instead of trying to help me, they used what they knew about me to put my business in the streets. The only person who never treated me different was Christi, and she's *your* friend."

"Christi's not just my friend, she's yours, too. We'll just invite her and if Vonshay wants, she can invite a friend. Is that good?"

"Sounds good to me."

"What sounds good?" Vonshay asked, as she walked in putting on her brown leather jacket.

"We're going to have a private party to decorate the tree this year," Vickie said.

"We're going to invite Christi and you can invite whoever you want," Vanessa added.

"Well, my friends won't be home from school until later this week, so I guess I'll have to hang with you old ladies," laughed Vonshay.

"Take notes," Vanessa suggested, pulling her and Vickie's coats from the rack near the door.

"You might learn a few things," Vickie added as they were on their way out.

Vickie hoped that Vanessa was right when she said that there wouldn't be too many people out. She really didn't think she was ready to handle people whispering and gossiping about her, and she definitely didn't want to deal with the people who asked questions feigning concern about people, only to use the information they acquire as a gossip tool. She knew that she would have to deal with that eventually, but she was not ready just yet.

Since both Vanessa and Vonshay were cost conscious, they ended up stopping at several stores to get the best prices on trees, ornaments, and lights. When they were at the register in the last store, Vickie felt relief because she had not seen anyone that she knew personally. When they realized that they had forgotten the snow, she volunteered to go get it. A Christmas tree was not a Christmas tree without it.

On her way down an aisle, she recognized one of her "friends" that had betrayed her. She immediately turned and went down another aisle. She listened attentively for footsteps to fade then she returned to the aisle. She was reaching for the can of snow, when someone tapped her on the shoulder. She immediately turned around. The soft hand that had touched her belonged to Ms. Hazel Higgins, an old friend of her mama's.

"Calm down, chile. It's just me," the older lady said soothingly.

"I'm sorry," Vickie said. "I thought you were someone else."

"Who, that lady you was running from? I saw you honey. You made a three sixty in the middle o' the aisle," the woman said, making a circular motion with her finger.

205

"Oh," Vickie said feeling ashamed.

"It's all right, baby. I heard about what's been going on wit you, and I know that you don't wanna be bothered with these fools in Ferguson, but don't be runnin' from 'em. Truth be told, they done had plenty o' stuff happen to them, ten times worse than you."

"Yes Ma'am," Vickie agreed. "Everybody go though hard times. It ain't what you go through, it's how you come out. Long as you done learned yo lesson and you right wit God, you hold that head o' yours up and don't be shame o' nuttin'! You hear?"

"Yes Ma'am, I hear you. Thank you, Ms. Higgins."

"Now gimme a hug and finish yo' shoppin'."

"O.k.," Vickie said as she wrapped her arms around her.

"Awright baby, remember what I said and don't be a stranger now. My number's been the same for thirty years," she laughed, as she released Vickie from her embrace and sent her on her way.

Vickie smiled and headed back to the counter. She noticed her "friend" standing in her path. "Merry Christmas," she said cheerfully as she walked passed her with her head held high.

The woman looked up and by the time she realized who it was, Vickie was at the counter taking care of her business. The woman was on her way to the counter to say something, but Vickie waved and headed for the exit. She could feel her "friend" watching her all the way out of the door. She was glad she ran into Ms. Higgins because she really needed that pep talk.

That night Vanessa, Vickie, Vonshay and Christi had their own private tree trimming party. First, they ate a Chinese meal of hot and sour soup, fried rice, lo mein, Schezuan Beef, Hunan Chicken, and egg rolls. Next, they drank egg nog and listened to Christmas CDs while they planned their strategy for decorating the tree. Then, they put their plan into action. They laughed, talked, sang, danced, drank, and decorated all at the same time. When they were finished, they turned off the lights and admired their work, while listening to "Silent Night" by The Temptations.

The six foot tall Christmas tree stood in the center of the den and lit up the room with its sparkling multi-colored lights. The synchronized blinking lights added an air of mystery. From second to second, the tree offered a different view as musical lights chimed familiar Christmas carols. Silk balls, matching the colors of the lights, were systematically arranged on the tree's limbs. The shiny silver icicles and flakes of snow glistened as the lights reflected upon them. The golden Star of David, which Vonshay ceremoniously affixed to the center branch, made the tree complete.

While enjoying the beauty of the tree and the warmth of the fireplace, the four of them reminisced on Christmases past and shared fond memories of their favorite Christmas season.

Vonshay's favorite Christmas was the Christmas that she was sixteen years old. To her, sixteen was supposed to be a magical age. At thirteen, when she asked her mama if she could get her hair cut in one of the popular short styles, Vickie answered, "When you turn sixteen." At fourteen she wanted to get acrylic fingernails, but Vickie told her, "Not until you're sixteen." At fifteen she asked if her male friends could come and visit. Vickie said, "You can receive company after you turn sixteen!" Nightly, she ended her prayers with, "And God please spare my life at least until I turn sixteen." It seemed to Vonshay that sixteen would never come, but it finally did, and she thanked God for allowing her to live to see *that* day.

For her birthday, Vonshay requested all of the things that she had asked for over the past few years. Vickie told her to wait until after her birthday. She waited for days, weeks, and months, but the "right time" never came. Finally, Vonshay decided that her mama had tricked her because sixteen did not turn out to be as exciting as she had been promised.

Vickie didn't try to trick Vonshay; she just tried to hold on to her little girl as long as possible. When she realized the frustration that she caused her daughter, she made a decision that was difficult for her. She decided to cut the apron strings and let Vonshay be a young lady. It was frightening, but necessary.

That Christmas Eve, almost six months after Vonshay's birthday, Vickie and Vanessa took her to the nail shop to get a set of nails and a pedicure and to LaShun's beauty salon to get her first major haircut. They even took her to get a second piercing in her ear. Vonshay thought it couldn't get any better than that, but it did. Christmas morning she opened over twenty boxes that contained the latest fashions in clothes and shoes. She got several pairs of gold earring studs for her new hole and larger sized hoop earrings for her first hole. Plus, she got five sterling silver bangles like the ones her aunt Vanessa always wore and a gift certificate that gave her permission to receive male company.

Vonshay was no longer upset about the months Vickie had procrastinated because she figured her mama needed the time to plan the best Christmas of her child's life. She smothered Vickie with kisses and comforted her with thank you's and I love you's. The happiness and excitement in her daughter's eyes that stimulated from the gifts she gave her, made that Christmas Vickie's favorite Christmas, too.

Vanessa and Christi's favorite Christmas was an experience that they shared. Both of them had recently ended long relationships with men they were in love with. It was hard for them to do, but they had chosen to be happy by themselves instead of miserable with a man. The Christmas season that they were twenty-five was their first Christmas in a long time without boyfriends. They were sitting around having a pity party when Christi's neighbor stopped by to offer them tickets to the Bobby Bland show at *The Club*. Her neighbor knew that the tickets sold out before Vanessa and Christi had an opportunity to purchase a pair, and since she would not be able to attend, she offered the tickets to them. Neither of them was really in the mood, but they knew better than to turn the tickets down.

They dressed in black for the show as a reminder to themselves that they were in mourning, but the snug fit and sexy style of the dresses reminded the men at *The Club* why they loved Black women so much. The attention, complements, and drinks the men gave them lifted their spirits. They were glad to know that they could still pull the men, even in the midst of personal sorrow.

By the time Bobby Bland mounted the stage, their pity party had turned into a satisfying celebration. They swayed, danced, and shouted as his songs taught them about life and advised them on how to deal with it. When he sang, "If it hurts, drop it. If it's not sincere, you ought to stop it," they felt that it was a confirmation that they had made the right decision when they decided to let go of their relationships. As the words "If you gon' walk on my love, baby, the least you could do is take off your shoes" rolled off Bobby's lips, they agreed that there's a way to do everything. While he sang, "Members only, it's a private party. Don't need no money to qualify. Don't need your checkbook, bring your broken heart," they felt in their hearts that they were in the right place at the right time. Spending that Christmas with the smooth encouraging sounds of Bobby Bland helped them to be content spending other Christmases without a mate. Now with God in her life, Vanessa had learned to be content in any situation.

When the beauty of the tree lulled them closer to sleep, they said their good nights. In their respective rooms, they all said a prayer thanking God for His Son Jesus Christ the Savior.

The next few days, Vanessa made herself scarce. She felt that Vickie and Vonshay needed to have some time alone together to mend their relationship, and she didn't want to be in the way. She knew that she had some things to work out with Vickie, as well, but she would still be there when Vonshay was back at school, and they could work on their relationship then.

Vickie and Vonshay didn't realize that Vanessa's absences were planned, but they took advantage of them, nonetheless. Simplicity was not a word that could be used to describe their lives over the past year, so activities such as cooking, cleaning, eating, watching television, laughing, playing, and talking together were a lot of fun for them.

Most of their conversations centered on everything and everybody except Vickie. One day Vickie decided that they should talk about her. "Vonshay, are you still mad at Mama?"

209

she asked, as they were washed dishes. "It's O.k. if you are, you know?"

"I'm not mad anymore," Vonshay said. "I understand addiction a little better and TeeTee talked to me about forgiveness." She paused then said, "I forgive you."

Tears formed in Vickie's eyes. "Thank you, baby," she whimpered. I needed to hear that."

"Mama, I love you and I always will, no matter what you do. I just pray that nothing like this happens again."

"I am going to try hard not let it happen," Vickie insisted. "But I can only take one day at a time. This is something that I'll have to deal with the rest of my life. I just need to know that you'll be there for me."

"I will," Vonshay assured her as she reached over to wipe away her tears.

"Did somebody on the soaps die today?" Vanessa asked when she walked in and saw Vonshay wiping Vickie's face. "Or did somebody get married?" she laughed. "No, I got it—you just finished watching *The Five Heartbeats* again, didn't you?"

"Not today," Vickie laughed. She knew Vanessa was making fun of her because she really did cry when something happy or sad happened on television, and she could never hold back the tears, when she heard the lines "You sure you wanna hang wit' ol' Eddie Cain?" After what she had been through recently, the words had even more meaning for her life. She was glad that Vanessa and Vonshay were willing to hang with her.

"Just checkin'," Vanessa replied as she answered the phone. When she heard the voice on the other end, she smiled.

"Who is it?" Vickie and Vonshay whispered.

"I'm fine. What about you?" Vanessa said into the receiver, ignoring them.

"I'm already in the Christmas spirit. I've done all of my shopping and now I can relax until the big day." She watched her sister and her niece make faces at her as she listened to Titus talk. "I'd like to see you, too," she told him, "but I won't be back in Atlanta for a while."

Her audience was about to burst in laughter.

"You don't have to do that," she said, signaling to them that he wanted to come to Ferguson to spend Christmas with her.

"Let him come," Vickie whispered.

"Yeah, TeeTee, tell him it's O.k.," Vonshay added.

After Titus finished explaining why he wanted to come and Vickie and Vonshay finished chanting, "do it," Vanessa finally agreed to his visit.

"This is going to be fun!" Vonshay exclaimed when Vanessa hung up.

"You and Titus, Mama and Daddy." Then her voice lowered, "Me and nobody."

"Don't rush it honey," Vanessa said. "You are young and you have your whole life ahead of you. Do the things that Vonshay wants to do first, then start thinking about a man and not just any man, but the one God sends you."

"Yeah, baby," added Vickie. "You have to find yourself before you find the man. If you don't, it won't work 'cause you'll still be looking for you and changing in the process, and he'll be expecting the "you" he met. All you need to do at this point in your life is just date. Find out what you like and what you don't like in a man."

"Well, it'll still be fun," she said. "When is he coming?"

"Christmas Eve," Vanessa answered.

"Well we'd better get busy," Vickie said. "That's just four days away."

When Christi heard that Vanessa was going to let Titus come for Christmas, she was elated. She realized that Vanessa must have known what she was doing when she went against her advice and told Derrick that she didn't want to see him anymore. She was so excited that she even volunteered to help them get everything in order. Vanessa insisted that they would not do anything that they didn't normally do just because he was coming. She didn't believe in faking! She kept it real because she had seen too many relationships destroyed because people tried to be someone that they were not. Nonetheless, she welcomed the extra pair of hands offered to provide.

211

The four days went by quickly. Titus called from the hotel on Christmas Eve morning to tell Vanessa that he was in Ferguson. On her way over, she thought about seeing him again. I can't believe I'm so calm about this, she thought. I am definitely looking forward to seeing him, but I'm not nervous about it in the least. He's here in Ferguson waiting to see me, and I'm acting like this is normal. It's been years since I brought anybody home to meet the family. I guess this all means that he's special. I hope so.

When Titus opened the door to his room and saw her standing there, he reached out to hug her. They lingered in each other's arms and enjoyed the comfort. When Vanessa looked up at him, he leaned down and kissed her softly on the lips. "I'm glad you let me come," he said. "I really wanted to see you."

"I wanted to see you, too" she whispered. Knowing what might happen if she remained in his arms any longer, she stepped away from him and asked, "How was your flight?"

"It was good," he said. "I just thought about you here waiting for me and I floated all the way."

"You should have called me to pick you up from the airport," she scolded.

"Well, I took a red-eye flight, and I didn't want to wake you from your beauty rest."

"Alright," she responded. Then asked, "Do you want something to eat?"

"Yes, I do. Why don't we go down to the restaurant and get something?"

When they got to the lobby, Titus asked her to get the table while he took care of something at the desk. When he returned, he was holding a dozen roses in a crystal vase. He said, "These are just to thank you again for allowing me to spend Christmas with you and your family."

"Thank you for the flowers and for coming," she smiled.

Their conversation at lunch flowed as smoothly as their phone conversations had, and their desire to be in each other's presence was as strong as it was the first night they met. They both knew that there was something special about the other.

Titus decided to rest after lunch and Vanessa agreed to pick him up that evening to spend Christmas Eve with the family. When Vanessa got home, Andre' was there adding gifts to the tree. Vonshay was trying to figure out what was in the boxes, and Vickie was in the kitchen cooking. They wanted to know all about Titus.

"Wait until tonight," she told them.

"You can ask him whatever you want to know then."

Later that evening, when Vanessa arrived home with Titus, they were all pleased, especially Christi. He was intelligent, charismatic and respectable, plus he had a sense of humor. And boy was he fine. The fact that he had bought gifts for everyone earned him even more points.

They spent the early part of the evening sitting in front of the fireplace drinking eggnog, while they talked and listened to music. At midnight, Vonshay announced that it was time to open gifts. Of all the gifts that were exchanged, Vickie's gifts meant the most to everyone. She gave each one of them something that she had made with her own hands in the arts and crafts class at the rehab center. She had not made a gift specifically for Titus, but she had one for him. She gave him a ceramic pen and pencil holder. She gave Andre' a hand-made leather belt and a wooden whatnot box with his name on it. Christi received a set of ceramic canisters and ashtrays, and Vanessa was given a family of three ceramic elephants in varying sizes to add to her collection she started when she pledged Delta Sigma Theta. Her gift to Vonshay was a wooden jewelry box and lapboard with her name painted across them in calligraphy.

Vanessa, Vonshay and Christi cried as they watched everybody open their gifts. They knew what a difficult time Vickie had gone through at the center, and they were touched because in the midst of her trials, she had thought about them. The gifts that she gave them were reminders of her struggle to overcome her addiction as well as tokens of her love for them.

The evening ended just as it had begun, wonderfully. After everyone exchanged pleasantries and said their good nights, Vanessa left to take Titus back to the hotel.

"Your family is really nice," he told her, as they sat across from each other in his hotel room. "You all get along so well. I would've never thought that Vickie and Andre' were divorced."

"Most people don't understand their relationship, but its really simple. Their friendship worked, but their marriage didn't, so they went back to being friends. I think that's the way divorces should be--if it has to come to that--especially when a child is involved."

"You're right. Has Vonshay adjusted well to it?"

"Once she realized that she could still love them both, she was O.k. because she knew all the time that they both loved her."

"Have you ever thought about marriage and children?"

"The older I get, the more I think. What about you?"

"The same. It's just that I want that person and the marriage to be special and I never felt that I had found that special person, until now."

Vanessa blushed. "So what are you trying to say, Titus?"

"I'm trying to say that I love you. That's why I wanted to come here. I needed to tell you this face to face. It was too important for just a phone call."

She stared silently into his eyes.

He continued, "I know that you probably think I haven't known you long enough to love you. I've been thinking the same thing, but my feelings are real. I have never felt like this about anyone before, and I don't believe that it was by chance that our paths crossed. God brought us together to fulfill a purpose."

Vanessa was still silent, still staring.

"Please, say something," Titus pleaded.

After a few more moments of silence, Vanessa said, "Titus I have feelings for you, too. They're strong feelings and they would probably be even stronger if I didn't hold them back."

"Why are you holding back on me?" he asked.

"Because I'm afraid of being hurt. So far, you're been everything that I dreamed of finding in one man: intelligent, compassionate, humorous, generous, handsome, considerate, understanding, and easy to talk to. And to top it off, you're a praying man who loves God and you live according to His word. It seems too good to be true, and though its what I've prayed for, it scares me."

"Vanessa, I don't want to be hurt either. I've taken a chance by just opening up to you and telling you how I feel, but I had to do it. Neither of us deserves to be hurt, but we have to act on our feelings or we'll never know what could have been. All I'm asking is that you give me a chance."

"A chance to do what?" Vanessa asked seriously.

"A chance to love you," he replied. "Will you?"

Silently staring, Vanessa answered, "Yes." She pause and then said, "But you know love is patient…"

"Love is kind," he chimed in. "It does not envy, it does not boast, it is not proud, it is not rude, it is not self-seeking, it is not easily angered, it keeps no record of wrongs. Love does not delight in evil, but rejoices with the truth. It always protects, always trusts, always hopes, always perseveres." As he spoke "Love never fails," the final words of the passage of scripture, Titus lifted her mouth to his and kissed her long and hard. When he released her, he said, "Baby, I know what love is and I thank you with all of my heart for giving me the chance to love *you* because you are truly a blessed woman of God."

"You're welcome and thank you," she said.

"For what?" he asked, puzzled.

"For taking a chance on me," Vanessa smiled.

"Believe me, you're more than welcome, and for the record, I'm not taking a chance; I'm standing on God's promises."

"I'd better be going," Vanessa said after several hours of talking, hugging and kissing. "It's getting late."

"O.k.," Titus conceded reluctantly. He really wanted her to stay, but he didn't want to pressure her.

"What time are you going to pick me up tomorrow? I mean today," he asked.

"Whenever you get ready. Just call me. I'll be up around nine, so I can get dinner started."

"Why don't you pick me up then, and I'll help you," he said trying to spend as much time with her as possible.

"That's fine. I'll call you before I come."

"I can cook, too, you know," he added to assure her he would not be in the way.

"That's what I'm talking about!" she smiled. "We'll see for sure tomorrow though."

Titus walked Vanessa to her car and kissed her goodbye. During the short drive home, Vanessa reflected on the day's events. Everything had gone so well. When she thought about the conversation with Titus, she hoped that she had made the right decision, and in her heart she knew she had.

For the past few years, it had been just she and God. She had actually learned to enjoy being alone without being lonely. Now she would have to create space in her life for Titus without neglecting God and other people and areas in her life. It would be difficult, but she asked God for the wisdom to manage it.

When Vanessa woke up the next morning, she heard Vickie and Vonshay in the kitchen cooking breakfast. Before she went to join them, she kneeled down and said a prayer. She thanked God for sending His son and then she thanked Him for Titus. He had to be a godsend.

"Merry Christmas, TeeTee," Vonshay said when Vanessa walked in.

"Merry Christmas," Vickie echoed.

"Merry Christmas to you," Vanessa replied.

"So, how was the rest of your night?" Vickie asked, turning away from the sink and leaning against the counter.

Vanessa could not keep from smiling.

"That good, huh?" Vickie laughed.

"Not as good as you think!" Vanessa exclaimed, understanding her sisters' hidden meaning.

"Well, tell us what happened," Vonshay urged, as she plopped down on a barstool.

Vanessa poured herself a cup of coffee and told them about her conversation with Titus. The happiness that leaped inside of her heart manifested itself in her voice.

"So does that mean that you go together?" Vonshay asked. Thinking that her aunt may not have understood her terminology, she added, "Is he your boyfriend?"

"I guess you could say that," Vanessa said.

"Well, good for you!" Vickie added.

"Merry Christmas," Andre' said entering the room.

They all responded, "Merry Christmas."

"Now what's so good for Vanessa?" he asked.

"TeeTee and Titus go together." Vonshay announced.

"What do you know about going together?" Andre' asked.

"Come on Daddy, I'm eighteen," she laughed.

Andre' still looked serious.

Coming to Vonshay's defense, Vickie told him, "Andre', we don't have a baby any more. We have a young lady now. She could probably tell us a few things."

"I know, but I just don't want her to grow up too fast," he replied.

"I don't either, but we can't stop time," she said.

"You're right," he admitted. "So Vanessa, do you think Titus is the one?" he asked, changing the subject. It was hard for him to accept that his little girl was not a little girl any more.

"So far, so good," she answered.

"Well, I'm happy for you. You deserve a good man and from what I've seen so far, I think Titus is just that. I checked him out last night and asked all the pertinent questions. And I am a pretty good judge of character, you know."

"I hope so," she said, answering the phone.

"Did you give him some?" Christi asked excitedly.

"Well, merry Christmas to you, too," Vanessa laughed. She walked out of the kitchen and into the den, so she could say what she need to say to Christi.

"I'm sorry, girl. Merry Christmas. Now, did you?"

"No, I didn't. This is only like our third date, and besides, I told you that the next man I give it to will be getting it for life."

"Leave it to you to get technical. If you really want to be technical, we can count every time you talked to him on the phone as a date. If you do that, you've been on more dates than you can count."

"If you say so," Vanessa conceded.

"What are you doing?" Christi asked.

"Getting ready to go pick up Titus."

"Don't wanna hold you, bye," Christi said and hung up the phone.

Vanessa laughed as she put the receiver down.

"Breakfast's ready," Vonshay announced.

After they finished eating, Vanessa called Titus to tell him that she was on her way to pick him up. When she got back to the house with him, everybody was already making preparations to cook dinner. The two of them joined in and Andre' and Vickie went to pick up forgotten staples.

"Have you been going to any AA meetings?" Vickie asked him on the way to the store.

"I've been to a few and they've really helped. I haven't stopped drinking all together, as you probably saw last night, but I am making an effort to cut back. I don't wanna go cold turkey. I need to wean myself off it. What about you? Are you O.k.?"

"Yeah. I'm doing good. I'm so glad to be at home. Drugs haven't even crossed my mind. It's easy with everybody around all the time. The test will come when I'm by myself. I think I'm strong enough to pass, though. Well, I take that back— I can do all things through Christ who strengthens me."

They went in the store to get the items they needed and then rode in silence all the way back home. Each one wondered what their lives might have been like if they had not divorced. If they had known then what they knew at that point, they probably would have given more effort to working it all out.

That evening the family had a beautiful candlelight dinner. Afterwards, Vonshay went out to visit some friends, and the others stayed home. Several of Vanessa, Vickie's and Andre's out-of-town friends who only come home once a year, stopped by to wish them a Merry Christmas. When all of the

218

company had gone, the four of them sat around the fireplace and talked the night away.

The next few days Vanessa spent a lot of time alone with Titus. Andre' was gone back to Memphis and she felt that Vickie and Vonshay still needed time together for bonding. Plus, she wanted to know more about the man she had entrusted her heart to. The more time she spent with him, the more she learned about him, and the more she liked him. She didn't expect it, but she was actually sad when it was time for Titus to leave. Being in his presence for those few days ignited her desire to be in his presence constantly.

The feelings Vanessa experienced with Titus frightened her. Vanessa had been practicing abstinence in an effort to be closer to God and to avoid being hurt by man. Before Titus came along, abstaining from sex had been easy for her because she was not tempted. Now temptation was staring her in the face. She had never felt this way about anyone, not even her first love. This was deeper than anything she had even dreamed of true love being. In the natural she wanted to give herself to him, but in the spirit she knew that she could not. Titus had been sexually active before he met Vanessa, but after hearing her explain sex outside of marriage and its affects on people's minds, bodies and spirits, he decided that he would refrain from sex as well, unless of course Vanessa changed her position on the matter. He knew that was highly unlikely, but he was willing to wait and see what the end would be because he was sure that she would be worth the wait.

That night they were lying in Titus' hotel room holding one another and talking about their dreams and desires. Vanessa had almost forgotten how good it felt to share all of her personal space with a man. It had been a long time since she had been held. She wasn't sure how to behave. A few years ago, she would have known *exactly* what to do, but she was no longer the same person. She was now a born again Christian who was striving to live a new life of holiness. How does it work on this side? Wondered Vanessa. How do I date and still keep my commitment to God? She had heard so many varying opinions about what was "too far" that she decided to allow God to be the judge of that by convicting her spirit when she went to far.

During pauses in the conversation, Titus kissed Vanessa. Sometimes he ended a conversation, even though he had more to say, because he couldn't wait for his lips to touch hers. Their conversations became shorter and shorter-- their kisses longer and longer.

The touch of Titus' soft warm lips on her body aroused Vanessa. She didn't know what to do. Her body wanted to respond, but she remembered her commitment to God. Her spirit was willing, but her flesh was weak. She searched for every scripture she could remember to build up her resistance. The kisses he gave her left the confines of her mouth and moved across her face, down her neck, over her shoulders, underneath her blouse, across the length of her body. Titus had no intention of going any further, but something in the way Vanessa rubbed his head and the way her body relaxed told him to go on. Overwhelmed by the yearning of his body and detecting the same from hers, Titus looked into her eyes for confirmation. He saw her desire and longing in her eyes, but he also saw fear and uncertainty. He eased the tension between them decreasing the length and number of kisses that he planted on her, and then ceasing the strokes he caress across her body.

Titus respected Vanessa's vow of celibacy, and he sensed that she was not ready. He did not want her to do anything she would regret later because he actually found it impressive that she possessed the strength to resist temptation in the midst of a passionately heated moment. It was true indication of the depth of her relationship to God, her commitment to keeping the vows that she made, and her respect for herself.

Vanessa knew that if she ever gave her body to Titus, she would not be able to take it back…a part of her would be gone forever. She was beginning to believe that he was her God sent mate, but what if he wasn't. What if he was a counterfeit, someone to get her off focus so that she missed the arrival of her true mate? She couldn't afford to risk it. She was glad that he understood. He hadn't responded simply to the signals that her body gave off, but he responded to the signals of her heart and soul. She had never felt this way about anyone, not even her first love. This was deeper than anything she had even dreamed of true love being. When God did it, He did it. All she had to do was wait and believe.

They spent the remainder of the evening laughing, talking, and enjoying each other's company. It was refreshing to have so much in common with a man, be attracted to him, and not feel threatened by him, nor he by her. The new day found them resting in each other's arms.

"I really enjoyed my visit," he told her while waiting for his flight to board. "You're the hostess with the most-ess."

"I enjoyed your being here," she said.

"We *must* do this again sometime," he smiled. "I hope it's very soon. Next time we'll do it in Atlanta. I want to be as gracious a host to you as you were to me. Is that a deal?"

"It's a deal," she said, shaking his hand. The warmth of it reminded her of the night before and a tingle shot through her body.

"So when can I expect you?" he asked. He couldn't wait to see her again. He enjoyed giving her pleasure and the pleasure she gave in return.

"Can I check my calendar and get back to you?" she asked, trying to buy some time. She didn't want to answer while she was still on cloud nine.

"Sure. Whenever you decide to come, it's fine with me. My calendar will always be clear for you. Just don't make me wait too long."

"I won't, because I can't wait that long either."

"Well, it's about that time," he said when they made the last boarding call for his flight. He stood up, pulled Vanessa to him and kissed her passionately, knowing that his lips would not touch hers for an indefinite amount of time. He said, "I love you," as he released her.

She said, "I love you, too," before she even realized it.

He smiled brightly and boarded the plane. She cried joyfully and walked away.

If the last week of the outgoing year were any indication of what the incoming one would bring, there would be an abundance of peace, happiness and love.

Chapter 15

After all of the holiday festivities were over, Vonshay went back to school and Vanessa went back to work. This meant that Vickie was home alone often. She had enjoyed being home when Vanessa and Vonshay were there with her, but now that they were gone, she felt lonely and depressed. Going to church on Wednesdays and Sundays was uplifting, but she decided that it was time for her to get out of the house and back into the world of work.

With Ferguson being as small as it was, most people were aware of Vickie's bout with drugs. Even if they didn't know her personally, they knew her name from conversations. The people there were very vindictive and didn't like to see people achieve. Most of them did everything in their power to keep others down. Some loved the company and others didn't want any competition.

Vickie felt that her past would be used against her in her efforts to find employment. Not many people were willing to hire admitted drug addicts, just as they were not willing to hire convicted felons. She knew, however, that she would have to take her chances. She couldn't sit in the house forever, letting Vanessa take care of her. She asked God to touch someone's heart so that she could get another chance to do right.

When Vickie first told Vanessa her plans to get a job, Vanessa was not very enthusiastic. She knew that if Vickie got a job, she would no longer be able to shield her and she felt that she would no longer be needed. "Do you think you're rushing things?" she asked her sister.

"No," Vickie said. "I haven't worked in over six months, and I can't expect you to take care of me and my child forever."

"You know that I don't mind," Vanessa stated. "It's not like we're struggling."

"I know we're not struggling, and that's not the issue. The point is that I can't keep depending on you so much. I've got to get out there and do something for myself. I feel like a little child. I have to ask you for money and permission to do anything."

"You don't have to ask me anything. And I give you money to put in your pocket."

"Yes, you do, but twenty dollars won't pay my bills. I know you're scared to give me money because of what I've done in the past and I don't blame you. That's why I need to get out and get my own. That way if I mess up, it'll be my loss, not yours."

"No Ma'am, it's not that simple. If you mess up, it's everybody's loss, no matter whose money it is. The issue is not money; it's sobriety. What you do affects me and it definitely affects Vonshay."

"O.k., so why don't you let me make a positive step toward a change. When I start working, I can start back paying my own bills and sending my own child money. Is that too much to ask?" Vickie questioned.

Feeling defeated, Vanessa answered, "No." She hoped that Vickie was really ready for this. She wanted to trust her, but trust is so hard to find once it has been lost.

Vickie registered with a local temporary employment agency. After successfully working on several short-term assignments, she was given a long-term position as a temporary office manager. This position had the potential of becoming permanent, so she worked really hard hoping that one day the job would be hers.

When Vickie first began working again, Vanessa was a nervous wreck. Each time she had a break at work, she would call Vickie. She convinced herself and Vickie that she was calling merely to chat, but in her mind, she knew that she was checking up on her sister. She couldn't seem to help it. If Vickie was five minutes later than usual getting home, Vanessa went crazy. She wanted to know where her sister was and what she was doing at all times.

Each week when Vickie got paid, she gave Vanessa her check to cash. Her bank account had been closed because of the excessive number of bad checks she had written. Together they planned a budget for Vickie's money. Vanessa served as her personal banker, and she issued money to Vickie on an as needed basis. She tried to keep an account of all of the money Vickie spent-- down to the very last cent.

Gradually, Vanessa loosened her hold on Vickie because she was proving herself trustworthy. She still worried about her sister, but she was no longer terrified by what might happen if she was not around all of the time. She realized that she could not protect Vickie forever, so she turned her over to someone who could-- the Lord.

"They're ready to hire someone permanently for the job," Vickie told Vanessa one evening after work.

"That's good," Vanessa responded. "It's only been a month and they usually wait about three. Do you think they'll keep you?"

"I don't know," Vickie said. "I just found out today that the job has to be posted and that I have to apply for it just like everybody else."

"Well, just claim it," Vanessa told her calmly. "Tell the Lord that you want the job, and if it's in His will, it's yours. Showing Him that you want it can be helpful, too."

"How do I show Him?" Vickie asked confused. She had never tried to prove anything to God because she felt that He knew everything.

"Make a sacrifice: fast, plant a seed, or whatever. When you want something from God, let Him know that you're willing to give up something for it. The more steps you take to get it, the more He'll take to give it."

"Sounds like a deal to me," Vickie said. "I think I'll fast. Will you do it with me?"

"I sure will," Vanessa smiled.

Vickie and Vanessa fasted and prayed for Vickie to get the job. Each time Vickie thought the office manager was about to make a decision, he added additional requirements to the qualifications. Each time he added something, she and Vanessa added days to their fast. After several weeks of the same routine, the job was finally offered to Vickie and she readily accepted it.

"I told you girl," Vanessa exclaimed when Vickie gave her the news that Friday. "Once God decides something, man can't change it, no matter how he tries to do it his way."

"I'm proof of that," Vickie added. "Can you believe that they offered me the same amount of money I was making at the Ferguson Foundation?"

"Of course I can," Vanessa assured her. "He is able to abundantly above ALL we can ever ask or think. He is rewarding you for trusting in Him to pull you through!"

"Some ladies from work wanna take me out to celebrate after work today, so I won't be straight home. I'll be there later," Vickie said cautiously.

"O.k.," Vanessa said, trying to fight the worry that overtook her. "Have fun!"

"I will," Vickie laughed as she hung up the phone.

On her way home from work that evening, Vanessa stopped by Christi's. After they had dinner and played catch up, discussing what had been going on in each other's lives, Vanessa went home. She took a nap when she got there, although she didn't usually take naps, especially on Friday evenings. However, for some reason she could not explain, she anticipated a long drama-filled night.

Titus' phone call woke her up. He offered to call her back later, but she declined. She wanted to talk to him then. They had been talking on a daily basis since Christmas, and he always had a way of making her day a little brighter. Right then, she needed the kind of comfort and support that only he could provide for her. They talked for about an hour, and he found a way to make her laugh in the midst of her gloom. At the end of the conversation, Titus asked, "So Vanessa when are you going to make that trip to Atlanta? Or do I need to come back to Ferguson?"

"I wanna come Titus, but I don't feel comfortable leaving Vickie here by herself," she explained.

"I understand," he said, "but I really wanna see you. What about Easter?"

"What about it?" Vanessa asked, pretending not to know his meaning.

"Can I come and visit you?"

"Of course," she said. "I'd like that."

"Well, it's as good as done. I'll be there on good Thursday," he laughed.

"I'll be waiting," she said smiling.

When Vanessa hung up the phone, she looked at the clock and it was ten o'clock. Vickie had not called nor come home. Her panic mode set into action. She worried herself sick about what might have gone wrong. She could not sit still longer than five minutes. If she still smoked it would have been a great time for a cigarette, but since she didn't, she walked back and forth throughout the house, hoping that Vickie would show up. She got tired of walking and wanted to sit down, but she couldn't. Not as long as her sister was out doing God-knows-what. When her legs rebelled against her and began cramping, she went to her room and attempted to go back to bed.

Though Vanessa wanted desperately to go to sleep and forget all of the thoughts that were racing through her mind, she could not. She tossed, and she turned, searching for sleep, but all she found was restlessness. Exhausted, she got out of the bed and on her knees. Surely, the Lord could give her rest.

Dear Lord, I come before you asking for protection. "I don't know where my sister is or what she is doing, but I ask you to watch over her. Lord, send her home safe. If she's out doing drugs, knock the pipe from her hand and sense into her head. Show her, Lord, that you can make it better. Whatever it is driving her to use drugs, show her that you can handle it. Give me peace Lord, and give me rest. Clear my mind so that I can

227

sleep without worry. I have given this to you Lord because I know that You can do more than I can. Whatever Your will is, let it be done. Give me the strength and the power to accept whatever it may be, even if it is not what I asked. Help me to control the anger that I am feeling right now. When my sister returns Lord, help me to be whatever she needs me to be at that time. Empty myself of me Lord and fill me with Your Spirit. Let the Spirit guide me in all that I say and do. In Jesus' name, I pray, Amen.

When she finished her prayer, Vanessa got back in the bed and meditated. Soon afterward, she fell asleep to the cold February wind beating against the windows. She had been asleep for almost an hour when she heard Vickie fumbling with the keys to open the door. She didn't get out of bed. She just listened.

Vickie attempt to close the door quietly, but the wind strongly resisted and the door made more noise than usual. Vanessa listened as her sister walked down the hall and into the bathroom, wondering if she should confront her then or wait until morning. When Vickie walked out of the bathroom and into her own room, Vanessa heard a loud thud.

Vanessa could not ignore the noise, so she went immediately to see what caused it. When she walked into Vickie's room and turned on the light, she saw her sister lying on the floor, trying to get up. "What happened?" Vanessa asked as she tried to help her sister to her feet.

"Nothin', I'm all right," Vickie mumbled.

"How'd you end up on the floor?" she asked desperately.

"I was getting my gown and I started feeling dizzy, and the next thing I knew, I was on the floor," she slurred. She didn't want to tell Vanessa that she was so high that she didn't see the wall, so she ran into it.

"You feel better?" Vanessa asked, as she led her to the bed. She could tell that Vickie was high. She was furious with her, but she couldn't deal with that, right then. First, she had to make sure that Vickie wasn't hurt. She'd deal with the rest later.

Vickie just groaned as her eyes floated back in her head.

"Are you high?" Vanessa demanded, knowing the answer already.

"Too high," Vickie grumbled. "I think I'm gon' die," she moaned as her eyelids closed.

"Open your eyes!" Vanessa yelled. "What in the hell have you been doin'?"

"I'm dyin'. I'm dying," Vickie moaned.

"You're not gon' to die on me," Vanessa insisted. "Open you eyes, now!"

"I can't," said Vickie, no longer attempting to try. "Just let me lay down. I'll be O.k."

"You can't lay down!" Vanessa screamed, while trying to lift her sister's limp body. "Come on, you need to walk."

"I smoked too much," Vickie said as she leaned on Vanessa's shoulder.

"Do you need to go to the hospital?" Vanessa asked as she led her to the bathroom to put some cold water on her face. She had no idea what else to do.

"I ain't goin' to no hospital!"

"Well, we've got to do something!" Vanessa replied as she wet a face towel. When she turned around, Vickie had closed her eyes again. Vanessa slapped Vickie's face and her eyes burst opened immediately. "Oh God, help me!" she cried out. "Don't let her die on me!"

"It's O.k. if I die…please let me go to sleep," she pleaded. "That's all I need."

"You're not going to sleep!" Vanessa yelled. "Have you eaten?"

"No," Vickie answered. "I don't wanna eat."

"I don't want this to be happening, but it is. We're going to the kitchen," Vanessa said as she lifted her sister.

When they made it to the kitchen, Vanessa sat Vickie at the table. Immediately, Vickie put her head down and closed her eyes. "Didn't I tell you not to go to sleep?!" Vanessa shouted while opening a can of soup.

"Can't help it," Vickie replied, startled. "Let me die. I don't deserve to live. I'm tired of this."

"Well, if you're tired, you need to stop it!" Vanessa roared, watching the tears form in her sister's eyes. "This makes no sense whatsoever. After all we've been through this last year and as good as God has been to you, this is what you do in return. Talk about ungrateful," she said, shaking her head in disgust.

"I didn't wanna do it," Vickie tried to convince her sister.

Truth was impressed by Vickie's honesty, but doubted that Vanessa would believe her.

"You did it though," Vanessa reminded her.

"But I didn't plan to. I didn't start thinking about drugs 'til I started drinking. I kept drinking to try and forget about 'em, but I started wanting 'em even more."

"Maybe you don't need to drink," Vanessa said. "How much money did you spend?"

"All of it," Vickie cried. "Everything I had."

"What on earth were you thinkin'?" Vanessa asked as she brought the bowl of soup to the table. "This makes no sense; it's insane," she said more to herself than Vickie.

"I wasn't," Vickie responded.

"Well, that's obvious, " Vanessa smirked. "The Lord gave you a job and you go celebrate with the devil. Ain't that somethin'!"

Lie was proud of his apparent success in confusing her once again.

"Don't be mad at me," Vickie pleaded. "I'm sorry."

"You absolutely right you sorry!" Vanessa yelled. When she saw the continuous stream of tears falling from her sister's eyes, Vanessa regretted her last statement.

Vanessa knew she had to be more careful about the way she talked to Vickie, but it was hard to feel one thing and have to say another. What she said to her sister was so very crucial. If she came down too hard on Vickie, she would go into a deeper state of depression. If she wasn't hard enough on her, Vickie would think what she had done was O.k. In either case, the end result would be getting high, and Vanessa was sure that she couldn't take another night like that one. She was so glad that

Vonshay had decided to stay at school and was not there to witness such a sad occasion.

"Eat the soup," she told Vickie, as she lifted the spoon to feed her.

"I don't want it. It'll make me sick."

"You need to eat," Vanessa said as she forced the spoon through Vickie's cracked lips and into her mouth.

Realizing she had no choice, Vickie ate the soup. "Can I go to bed now?" she asked when she finished.

"Yeah," Vanessa said, hesitantly. She led Vickie to her room, changed her clothes and put her to bed. She was so glad her niece had not come home from school that weekend. Such a scene would have scarred her for life.

"Don't leave me by myself," she begged. "Stay in here with me."

"O.k.," Vanessa said, though she had no intentions of leaving anyway.

It hurt her so bad to see Vickie in this condition. Her sister was just lying there moaning and groaning, tossing and turning. Vanessa got in the bed with Vickie as she did when they were younger and began to rock her gently. Soon, she was quiet and still. As Vickie slept, Vanessa prayed constantly over her and rebuked the spirit of death from around her bed. She claimed her sister's total deliverance and declared it to be so that night. Periodically, Vanessa shook her to make sure that she was still alive. Each time Vickie responded, Vanessa said, "Thank You, Lord" and continued to pray until she drifted into sleep at about five o'clock that morning.

When Vanessa woke up the next morning and did not see Vickie in the bed, she panicked, and immediately went to search the house. She found Vickie in the kitchen, sitting at the table and drinking a cup of coffee.

"I'm here," Vickie said, seeing the worried look on her sister's face. "I fixed us a big breakfast. I think we need it, after last night. At least I do."

"Let me go wash up and I'll be back," Vanessa said with a sigh of relief.

Over breakfast they discussed the events of the night before. Vanessa explained her anger and Vickie explained her frustration. By the end of the long conversation, they had totally accepted the fact that they would have to deal with Vickie's addiction for life. Before her relapse, even though they had been told differently, they both believed that Vickie would never do drugs again. Now, they knew that there was no guarantee that she wouldn't. They realized that they had a long road ahead of them and decided to make the journey one day at a time. Vickie's deliverance was done in the spirit—she just had to recognize it and learn to walk it out in the natural.

Chapter 16

After Vickie's near death experience, Vanessa easily slid back into her role as protector. She monitored Vickie's every move, afraid that her sister might slip. She hated having to treat Vickie like a child, but she saw no other alternative. Even though Dr. Winters had told her, "You can't control what your sister does. If she wants to do drugs she'll do them, no matter how tight you hold the reins," Vanessa held on anyway. She felt that the restraints she put on Vickie would keep her away from drugs. She didn't realize that they could not keep the desire for drugs away from her.

Vickie had not done drugs nor had the desire to do them since the night she almost overdosed. After that night, she began going to Narcotic Anonymous meetings on a regular basis. Talking about her fears and desires with other addicts was good for her. She no longer felt that she was alone and that no one understood her. The people in her sessions were familiar with what she was going through and were able to provide the guidance and support that she needed. She wished her sister understood as much as they did, but she realized that some lessons could only be learned through experience.

Vanessa worked really hard to understand Vickie's addiction and to be there for her when she needed her, but there was only so much she could do. She could never fully understand the difficulties of being an addict unless she was one herself. What she did understand, though, was the difficulty of loving an addict. Through it all, she loved her sister, and she only wanted what was best for her.

The first week after her relapse, Vickie was very hard on herself. She felt really stupid for turning back to drugs, and her self-esteem was extremely low. She felt like a total failure, and she believed that she had failed herself, her child, her sister, and her God. She was glad that Vanessa was there to control her life because she felt incapable of doing it herself. Vanessa's presence was a comfort zone that Vickie wished she could stay in forever, but she knew that was not possible. She had to get up, get herself together, and try again!

Once Vickie asked God to forgive her and forgave herself, she felt much better. She started working towards regaining control of her life, but Vanessa was not willing to relinquish it. Her hold on Vickie was even tighter than it was when she initially returned home.

"What do I have to do to prove to you that I'm O.k?!" Vickie yelled. She was frustrated that Vanessa still didn't trust her.

"To be honest," Vanessa said, "I really don't know. Every time you walk out the door, I'm afraid of how you might come back, or if you'll come back."

"I know I've messed up a lot, but I know better now," Vickie said. "That was over a month ago, and I've gotten it together since then. I wouldn't dare put you and Vonshay through all of that again, not if I can help it."

"Well, that's what bothers me," Vanessa confessed. "I don't know if you can help it."

"Don't you think I've learned anything?" Vickie asked. I would be a certified fool to hit that pipe again. It almost killed me!"

Vanessa looked at her sister with pity. She wanted to remind her that her declaration was similar to the one she'd made after she returned home from rehab, before she almost overdosed. She wanted to ask her why she should believe the words carried any more meaning now than they had then, especially since their credibility had been utterly destroyed the night she went out and got high. Instead, she said, "I know that I'm overprotective. I just don't want anything to go wrong. I feel like if I'm with you, you won't mess up."

"I definitely won't mess up when I'm with you, but you won't be here forever. I've got to get used to doing things on my own. I've got to learn how to trust me with me, not just with you."

"O.k.," Vanessa said, "I'll leave you alone and let you do things your way."

"I'm not saying leave me alone," Vickie said, realizing that Vanessa was about to disconnect herself from her and force her to be independent. "I just want you to trust me a little more and give me a chance to make some decisions for myself. I don't know everything and I may make some mistakes, but I've got to try. Just be there for me, however things go."

"All right," Vanessa said. She felt as if one of her purposes in life was being snatched from her. She had accepted long ago that one of the reasons God put her on earth was to protect Vickie. Now that Vickie wanted to take charge of her own life, Vanessa's job was over. She had no idea what she would do with all the time and energy she no longer had to devote to her sister. She felt like a worker being forced into early retirement.

"Thank you," Vickie said, reaching for her sister.

"You're welcome," Vanessa said, holding Vickie tightly. She hoped that Vickie's desires for freedom weren't bigger than her capabilities of handling it. As she held her sister in her arms, she prayed for God's protection over her.

Fortunately, Vickie handled her freedom well, mainly because she embraced a new lifestyle and a new attitude. She paid all of her bills on time. She sent Vonshay money, and she even saved some money. She learned how to go out with her co-workers and have fun without drinking alcohol. She had discovered that alcohol triggered her desire for drugs, so she only drank if Vanessa was with her to make sure that nothing went wrong. The most important thing she learned was how to like and love herself unconditionally. She began each day with a

235

prayer and read from *Daily Mediations for People with Addictive Behaviors.* Then she declared that she walked in divine deliverance by the power of God.

Vickie's new positive approach to life forced Vanessa to take a new approach to dealing with her sister. She no longer treated Vickie like a child, but as a responsible adult. She enjoyed seeing her sister take charge of her own life because she had never seen it before. Instead of asking Vanessa what to do about certain situations, Vickie discussed with her the alternatives that she had come up with to deal with them. Vanessa gave her opinions, but Vickie made her own decisions, and Vanessa was proud of her big sister.

Vickie and Vanessa became closer than they had ever been. They spent most of their spare time together doing sister/girlfriend activities like getting their hair and nails done, going shopping, and hanging out. They spent a lot of time talking honestly about the thoughts, feelings, and experiences that made them who they are. God used their conversations as a balm to heal the wounds that had strained their relationship. Both of them learned a lot from and about the other. Vanessa was even able to minister to Vickie about developing a stronger relationship with God, without Vickie becoming defensive and thinking Vanessa was putting her down. The richness of their relationship filled their hearts with so much joy that they wanted to share it with others they knew and loved.

Truth was proud that everything between them was out in the open.

Vanessa and Vickie waited anxiously for Easter. They looked forward to spending time with their family and friends. Vonshay, Daquita, Andre' and Titus were all coming to Ferguson for the holiday weekend. They decided to give the house its spring-cleaning a few days before everyone was scheduled to arrive to make sure that everything would be in order for their guests.

"Do you think we should plan something special for the weekend?" Vickie asked, while washing down the walls in the kitchen.

"I don't know," Vanessa answered. "It's not like there's *that* much to do in Ferguson. What'd you have in mind?"

"Well, I figure everybody'll be tired by the time they get here Thursday, so we can just stay around the house and talk, maybe cook or have some drinks. Friday, I'll take the girls shopping and you can spend some time with Titus," she said, dipping her towel back into the bucket of cleaning solution.

"That's cool," Vanessa said, as she pulled the back off a piece of contact paper and placed it on the surface of a cabinet shelf. "I *would* like to spend some quality time with him. Friday night me, you, Titus, Andre', and Christi can go over to the casino for dinner and listen to the jazz band."

"O.k.," Vickie said. "What about Saturday? You wanna put some meat on the grill?"

"Yeah, it hasn't been fired up in a while. We'll do some ribs, chicken, and smoked sausages with baked beans and potato salad. That's enough to keep us busy all day," Vanessa said, admiring her work.

"That's it then," Vickie said, going to the sink to empty the pail of water she used to clean the walls. We know we're going to church Sunday, so we can cook Easter dinner while we're grillin'. What do you want to have?"

"I'm tired of turkey and dressing," Vanessa said, stepping down from a chair. "Why don't we fix some chitlins! This is probably our last chance 'cause it'll be too hot for 'em soon."

"You wanna be bothered with the smell?" Vickie asked. She turned her nose up just thinking about the scent.

"We can put a potato on the pot to kill the smell," Vanessa said. The smell is a small price to pay for the taste, you know."

"I guess you'll be cleanin' 'em, " Vickie said, turning up her nose.

"They have pre-cleaned ones, now," Vanessa said. "They cost more, but it's less work. You still have to clean 'em some, but not nearly as much as you do the ones in those buckets. But in answer to your question, yes, I'll clean 'em."

"Well, chitlins it is," Vickie laughed, glad she didn't have to deal with them. "I'm going to go clean out my closet. When you finish the cabinets, you can come help."

"O.k.," Vanessa said, putting all of the items from the cabinets back in place.

Vickie stood at the door of her walk-in closet about five minutes before she figured out what to do first. She decided to start with the shoes, so she sat on the floor and went through the boxes. She had lots of shoes that she hardly ever wore, but she had not been able to bring herself to part with them. She always felt that one day she would wear them, though it was obvious that she probably wouldn't. As she checked each box, she took the shoes that she didn't wear from their boxes and piled them in a large box. She was relieved when she finally reached for the last box. What she found in it startled her. The box didn't hold any shoes--it held a crack pipe. This had been one of her hiding places for her paraphernalia.

Bored from having been left out of recent activities and conversations that Vickie was involved in, Lie raised his head, hoping for a chance to play.

Vickie lifted the pipe from the box and examined it. It held a half-smoked rock of crack cocaine in its bowl. She emptied the rock into the palm of her hand and stared at it. She took her right index finger and rolled the rock around in her hand. "Forget you—I'm DELIVERED!" she yelled, jumping up and running into her bathroom. "You won't trick me again!" she declared as she watched the rock spin around in the water and disappear down the drain.

Vickie ran past Vanessa, without noticing her, to the closet and picked up the pipe. She took it and threw it in the garbage can in the kitchen. "Unh-unh, too close," she said, as she snatched the bag out of the garbage can and took it to the dumpster outside. "I don't want you nowhere near me!" she screamed, and then she threw the box inside of it and slammed down the lid. Exhausted, she ran back to the house and into the comfort of Vanessa's out-reached arms, crying "I'm free...I'm finally free!"

"I'm proud of you," Vanessa said, while rubbing Vickie's back. Tears of joy streamed down her cheeks.

"Thank you," Vickie said, as tears of relief dropped on her sister's shoulder. She had always wanted to make her sister proud. Now, not only was her sister proud of her, but she was proud of herself, as well. It had taken every ounce of strength she had to get rid of what she had once considered her best friend.

Lie turned away in defeat, knowing that he had finally lost the war, while Truth marched in victory, waving the blood-stained banner of Jesus Christ in whose name the battle was won.

That night changed the course of the rest of Vickie's life forever.

All of their guests arrived on Thursday as planned. They spent the evening talking about all of the events that had happened in their lives since their last meeting. The adults discussed their careers, and the young adults discussed their lives as college students. Friday everyone did take care of personal plans during the day. Vanessa spent time with Titus, enjoying his presence. Andre' visited with friends, reminiscing about the old days, and Vickie and the girls bonded, going on mama and daughter excursions. That evening, the adults came together for dinner, and Vonshay and Daquita went to the movie theatre.

Vanessa, Titus, Vickie, and Andre' met Christi at King's Court Casino. The casino was a large ship docked at the bank of the lake. It was beautifully decorated with ruby-red carpeting, crystal-like chandeliers, and soft-cushioned stools and chairs in varying colors. The floor plan included three levels, each filled with slot machines, blackjack, poker, crap, and roulette tables, bars, and concession stands. The third level also housed the restaurant that rightfully boasted the best seafood buffet in the Mississippi Delta. They enjoyed the satisfying meal of both standard and exotic seafood delicacies, as they watched the gamblers scurry from table to table and slot machine to slot machine.

After Vanessa dropped Vickie and Andre' at the house, she and Titus went to his hotel room.

"I have a surprise for you," Titus said, as he slipped the key into the lock. It was the same suite he had stayed in on his previous visit to Ferguson.

"What is it?" Vanessa asked, excitedly. She didn't normally like surprises, but she knew that if it came from Titus, it would be pleasant.

"If I tell you it won't be a surprise," he said smiling. He opened the door and extended his hand as an invitation for her to enter.

Vanessa walked in and took a seat at the table. When she noticed the purple flower petals sprawled across the bed, she was offended. Surely he didn't think that she was going to break her vow. She decided not to say anything, but wait to see what his intentions were. Titus went to the tiny refrigerator beside the dresser and pulled out two chilled crystal champagne flutes and a bottle of Martini and Rossi Asti Spumante. He joined Vanessa at the table and filled their glasses. "A toast," he said, lifting his glass, "to me and you."

"Cheers!" Vanessa said, as she lifted her glass to meet his.

"Cheers!" he repeated. "Now let me get your surprise." He walked to the closet and returned with a big beautiful basket. "Happy Easter," he said, placing it in front of her. "Open it and see what's inside."

"It's too pretty to open," she said, admiring the work. "Who made it? It's obvious you didn't get it from a store 'cause it's not a typical Easter basket."

"My friend's wife, Robin, made it. She makes them for all kinds of occasions and fills them with whatever the buyer wants. Go ahead and open it."

"All right," she said, as she untied the ribbon and lifted the basket from its cellophane cover. She reached in and pulled out a jellybean filled black coffee mug that read, "Teachers mold tomorrow's minds!" in gold lettering.

"That represents the gift of knowledge that you give your students," Titus said.

Vanessa smiled at him as she reached for the Gio' perfume and body lotion. She sprayed the perfume into the air and leaned her nose in to smell it.

"The perfume represents your sweetness and the lotion represents your softness," Titus said, rubbing his hand across hers.

Vanessa felt special. Not only did Titus have a basket made especially for her, but he actually put thought into what was to be placed in the basket and its meaning. He was truly a romantic. Whereas most men would have told Robin to choose, since they assume that women know what other women like, he did not; he chose everything himself. She couldn't wait to find out what everything else represented. She pulled out the two porcelain elephants and placed them on the table. She looked to Titus for their meaning.

"Those represent me and you," he said, turning the elephants to face each other and then placing their trunks together as if they were kissing. Then he gave Vanessa a short soft kiss on her lips.

"And this," Vanessa said, licking her lips to savor the flavor and pointing to the huge heart-shaped bank in the center of the basket.

"That, my dear, represents where our love is stored. I've already made the first deposit. Open it up and see what it is."

Vanessa pulled the stopper from the back of the bank and looked inside. "Nothing," she said with disappointment, after she didn't see or hear anything.

Titus didn't say a word. He just looked at her and smiled. He picked up the stopper that she set on the table and removed the ring that was taped to it. He lowered himself on one knee and reached for Vanessa's hand. When he looked into her eyes, he could see tears fighting their way through.

"Vanessa," he said, slowly, I know that we've only known each other for six months and that most of the time we were apart, but I also know that you are special to me. The last time I

241

was in this room I asked you to give me a chance to love you, and now I want to ask for the chance to spend the rest of my life with you, loving you until death do us part." He paused and watched the tears flow freely down her face. "What I want to know," he continued, "is will you marry me? I don't want to rush you and I don't mean immediately, but whenever you're ready. I promise that I will love you as God loves the church, even laying down my life for *you*."

He gently slid the custom designed two-carat platinum princess cut diamond engagement ring onto her finger, while reciting again the biblical definition of love found in I Corinthians 13:

"Love is kind, It does not envy, it does not boast, it is not proud, it is not rude, it is not self-seeking, it is not easily angered, it keeps no record of wrongs. Love does not delight in evil, but rejoices with the truth. It always protects, always trusts, always hopes, always perseveres. Love never fails."

Vanessa sat motionless as the tears gushed from her eyes. She couldn't believe that the man who possessed all of the qualities she dreamed of having in a husband had asked her to be his wife. She was shocked speechless as she stared at the beautiful ring and the wonderful man who gave it to her. She felt a "yes" leaping in her spirit.

Titus shifted positions on his knees and rubbed her hand gently. Her silence made him more nervous. He knew that she was truly surprised and needed to grasp what he had said, but he needed her to say *something*. Even though her eyes said "yes," he wanted to hear the sound of the word flowing from her mouth. "Well..." he said, seeking a response.

"Yes," she bellowed, wiping away her tears. She stood up and pulled Titus into her arms. "I would be honored to be Mrs. Titus Richmond...for you are as dependable, diligent, and have as great of a capacity for human affection as the man of God for which you were named...and *you*, my dear, are the man that I've been dreaming of all of my life!

"Whew!" he said, laughing, " For a minute, I thought you were going to turn me down."

"How could I?" she asked, kissing him after each word.

He never had the chance to answer because her kisses kept coming—all night long. They spent the night in sheer wonderment and excitement about the plans that God had for them as husband and wife.

Saturday afternoon, when Vanessa and Titus arrived at the house, everyone was busy preparing for the barbeque. Andre was lighting the grill, Vickie and Christi were at the kitchen counter seasoning the meat, and Vonshay and Daquita were at the table cutting up the ingredients for potato salad and coleslaw. Titus went out back with Andre' and Vanessa went to the kitchen.

"What's up?" Vanessa said. "I see you started without us." I'll have to get used to the word "us" she thought.

"We didn't know if you would make it," Christi said, smiling. She was glad that her friend had a man in her life.

"I knew you were coming," Vonshay said, expressing her faith in her auntie.

"Yeah," Vickie added, "I knew you were coming, too. I just didn't know when. I went ahead and put the chitins on, though, in case you didn't make it. Christi was hoping you didn't show. She said you had better things to do than hang out with us."

"You know I wouldn't let a man come between me and my girls," Vanessa said. She stood next to Vonshay and played in her hair. She wanted to acknowledge the comment Vonshay made and assure her that she could always count on her.

"I don't know," Christi said. "The way you're glowing, you might put us down any minute. Last night must've been all that!"

"All that, then some," Vanessa replied.

"You act like the he asked you to marry him or somethin'!" Christi said.

"He did," Vanessa said calmly, extending her left hand to Vonshay and Daquita and signaling them not to say anything.

"What!" Vickie and Christi yelled, as they turned toward her.

"You heard me the first time," Vanessa giggled, waving her hand just enough for them to get a glimpse of her ring.

"Oooooh!" Christi said, as she wiped her hands and ran to Vanessa. "That brotha's fa real. Look at this ring. You go boy!"

"You go girl," Vickie said, admiring her sister's ring.

"For real, TeeTee," Vonshay said. "This ring is blinging."

"Congratulations!" Daquita beamed.

"Don't just stand there, looking crazy," Christi said. "Tell us about it. How'd he do it? What did he say? What did you say?"

"They all sat down and listened as Vanessa told them all about how Titus had proposed to her. When Vonshay and Daquita took the meat outside, she told Vickie and Christi about the depth of her feelings for Derrick. They were both was excited for her because if anybody deserved a little peace and happiness, she did.

The barbeque turned into an engagement party. The topic of most of the conversations was Vanessa and Titus. Everyone gave advice, tips, and suggestions for their courtship, wedding, and marriage. It was an evening filled with joy.

Vanessa woke up early Sunday morning so that she would have a chance to pick up Titus and still have time to cook breakfast for everyone before getting ready for church. She liked to arrive at church early on Easter because it was usually crowded with EMCs--people who only attended church three Sundays out of the year—Easter, Mother's Day, and Christmas.

When everyone awakened, Vanessa and Titus were sitting at the table having coffee and listening the CD, *Changes*, by Elder William Murphy III, the worship leader at New Birth Missionary Baptist Church where Titus was now a member. Knowing that he would propose, Titus began early attempting to acclimate Vanessa to the church by sending her tapes of the pastor, Bishop Eddie L. Long. He wanted to assure her that the transition from her church to his would be smooth. Vanessa didn't take issue with having to join New Birth because she knew that the "The Bishop" was an anointed man of God who walked in excellence and integrity. She attended special services and conferences that the church hosted and sowed many seeds into the ministry to help support the great work that the church was doing for the kingdom. She had even been referring to Bishop Long as her "local bishop" ever since she began watching his *Taking Authority* broadcast. However, she had never imagined being a member of such a large congregation, nor had she ever considered leaving Mt. Moriah, the place where she was introduced to the power of God and the works of His Holy Spirit. Though feeling nostalgic, she recognized that if God was moving her, it meant that her season and her assignment at Mt. Moriah were completed. The title song to the CD, *Changes*, seemed appropriate for their conversation and the process they would soon undergo as they prepared for marriage.

"Good morning," they said to one another as each person entered the kitchen.

"Breakfast is ready," Vanessa said pointing to the buffet on the counter with scrambled eggs, grits, and toast. They all prepared their plates and sat down to eat.

Andre' was the first to finish, and he hurried from the table to get ready for church. He did not want to be in the way when the women started getting dressed. He wanted to give them all of the space they needed to go from room to room asking everyone's opinions on shoes, earrings, make up, etc. When he finished, the ladies went to get dressed and they did exactly what he expected them to do.

Everyone was in a wonderful mood that day. There was so much joy in their hearts that they could have given everyone in Ferguson some, and they still would have had plenty left. They all went to church with thankful hearts. They were thankful for each other, but even more than that, they were thankful to God for allowing His Son Jesus to die for their sins and be resurrected with ALL power!

After the church services, they returned home for dinner. When they finished stuffing themselves with chitlins, rice, and slaw, it was almost time for everyone to go back to their different destinations. They spent the last few minutes of their time thanking one another for the wonderful weekend they had together. Vanessa and Titus told everyone "bye" and left for the airport. Andre' put his things in the car and waited for Vonshay and Daquita.

Vickie tried to hold back the tears as she watched Vonshay gather her belongings together to return to school. She hated saying good-bye to her loved ones. It didn't matter if they were going to be gone a few days or a few weeks. Whenever someone was leaving, she cried because there was a chance she might never see them again. "Mama's gonna miss you," she said, as Vonshay put the last piece of clothing in her bag.

"I'm gonna miss you, too," Vonshay said, closing her duffel bag. "But school will be out in a few weeks and I'll be back home for the summer."

"I know," Vickie said. "Give me a hug and then we'll go outside before your daddy calls you again."

"O.k.," Vonshay said, walking into her mama's outreached arms.

When they broke their embrace, Vickie held Vonshay's shoulders and looked into her eyes. She knew that they would tell the story. When she saw her daughter's eyes dancing, a broad smile spread across her face. "I'm proud of you, baby," she said. She hugged her daughter again. When she released her, they picked up Vonshay's bags and took them to the car. Vickie waved good-bye and cried as she watched Andre's car disappear.

At the airport, Vanessa cried softly as Titus boarded the plane. She hated to see him leave, but she looked forward to being with him soon. Vickie was able to stand on her on and the school year was almost over, so there was no reason for her to stay in Ferguson much longer. She looked forward to returning to Atlanta, her home, her job and her fiance'.

Driving home from the airport, Vanessa said a prayer,

O Lord, I thank You for this Easter Sunday. I thank You for allowing Your son, Jesus, to come down and die for my sins. I thank You for raising him for the dead, so I can have eternal life. God, thank You for untangling the web that trapped my family. Sometimes I didn't know which way to go or what to do,

246

but You made the path bright. Thank You, Lord, for Titus. I pray that You keep our relationship strong and that You bless our marriage. I promise to always keep You first in our lives. These and other blessings I ask in Your son, Jesus' name. Amen.

When Vanessa arrived at home, Vickie was sitting in the den staring into space.

She didn't notice that Vanessa was watching her. "Penny for your thoughts!" Vanessa said, breaking her sister's train of thought.

"Do you remember the story the preacher told today?" Vickie asked. "It really touched me."

Vanessa smiled as she thought about the story the preacher told…

There was once a lovely flower garden that reached from the edge of the street to the steps of a beautiful building. When the area became more populated, they laid a sidewalk and it covered part of the garden. One day, I was walking by and I noticed a crack in the sidewalk. A few weeks later, I saw a flower growing through that crack, and I stopped to ask the flower what it was doing growing in a crack. The flower said, 'Well, I'll tell you like this. God created me to glorify Him. Man in his infinite wisdom covered me up, and I couldn't get the things that I needed to survive. But one day God cracked the sidewalk and let the rain and the sun come through. Then He looked down from heaven and called out to me and said, 'Flower, man impeded your progress for a while by bogging you down with things you were not created to deal with, but I've moved that to the side and made a way for you. Now that you're free, I want you to get up and be what I made you to be and do what I purposed you to do.' So, here am I.'"

The preacher ended the story by asking the question, "If a little bitty flower can stand trials and tribulations and *still* do what God planned for it to do, then why can't we?"

"I remember," Vanessa answered.

"Well," Vickie said with tears in her eyes, "I'm not going to let a flower, something that doesn't even have a brain, out do me. I am who God says I am, and now I know how to be happy with me. The Lord delivered me from my addiction and called me forth into destiny, now I'm coming *THROUGH THE CRACK*!!"

The author would be delighted to hear your response to her work. To contact the author or to schedule book readings, signings, and discussions of her work, please write or call

Dr. Charrita D. Danley
P.O. Box 960726
Riverdale, Georgia 30296
cdanley@danleywriting.com
770-991-4575 (office)
770-991-4550 (fax)

or visit

www.danleywriting.com

Other Materials Include:

Writing for the Kingdom

The
"WRITE"
Way